A tireless researcher, SARAH-KATE LYNCH trailed the byways of Ireland sampling dairy products for her first novel, *Blessed Are the Cheesemakers*, and perfected French sourdough bread for her second, *By Bread Alone*. In the interests of maintaining her artistic integrity regarding *House of Daughters*, she considers it her duty to drink as much champagne as she can possibly manage. As a result, her website is not always up-to-date, but you can find it at www.sarah-katelynch.com.

House of Daughters

A NOVEL

Sarah-Kate Lynch

A PLUME BOOK

PLUME
Published by the Penguin Group
Penguin Group (USA) Inc., 375 Hudson Street, New York, New York 10014, U.S.A.
Penguin Group (Canada), 90 Eglinton Avenue East, Suite 700, Toronto, Ontario, Canada M4P
2Y3 (a division of Pearson Penguin Canada Inc.)
Penguin Books Ltd., 80 Strand, London WC2R 0RL, England
Penguin Ireland, 25 St. Stephen's Green, Dublin 2, Ireland (a division of Penguin Books Ltd.)
Penguin Group (Australia), 250 Camberwell Road, Camberwell, Victoria 3124, Australia
(a division of Pearson Australia Group Pty. Ltd.)
Penguin Books India Pvt. Ltd., 11 Community Centre, Panchsheel Park, New Delhi – 110 017, India
Penguin Books (NZ), 67 Apollo Drive, Rosedale, North Shore 0632, New Zealand (a division
of Pearson New Zealand Ltd.)
Penguin Books (South Africa) (Pty.) Ltd., 24 Sturdee Avenue, Rosebank, Johannesburg 2196,
South Africa

Penguin Books Ltd., Registered Offices: 80 Strand, London WC2R 0RL, England

Published by Plume, a member of Penguin Group (USA) Inc. Originally published in
New Zealand as *The House of Peine* by Random House New Zealand.

First American Printing, July 2008
1 3 5 7 9 10 8 6 4 2

Ⓟ REGISTERED TRADEMARK—MARCA REGISTRADA

LIBRARY OF CONGRESS CATALOGING-IN-PUBLICATION DATA

Lynch, Sarah-Kate.
(House of Peine)
House of daughters : a novel / Sarah-Kate Lynch.
p. cm.
ISBN: 978-0-452-28938-3
1. Sisters—Fiction. 2. Vineyards—Fiction. 3. France—Fiction. I. Title.
PR9639.4.L96H68 2008
823'.92—dc22 2007037866

Printed in the United States of America
Set in Sabon with display set in P22 Cezanne & MATRIX script
Designed by Leonard Telesca

*For my honorary sister Nicki Robins
and anyone else who knows how and what to celebrate.
A votre santé*

House of
Daughters

Printemps

Clementine

By afternoon teatime on the third Wednesday of spring, Clementine knew there would be a frost.

It was her hair. Her badly cut, madly curly, faded long red hair. When the weather gods sucked the warmth out of the air to prepare it for scooting below zero, her hair was always the first to know.

She had been directing a thick slice of *pain au levain* slathered with pickled pear and a wedge of ripe Meaux brie toward her mouth when she first heard a sharp crackle very near her left ear. It was the sound of a single kink further crinkling in the cold dry conditions. And it was a loud crinkle, too, giving her such a fright that she jumped, almost knocking over the glass of new release Peine champagne that she had been teetering on the brink of enjoying.

In the seconds that followed, as she scrabbled to steady that wobbling flute lest a single drop be wasted, the rest of her hair crackled and snapped, one wiry curl after the other, until her whole head was abuzz and her hair was at least two inches shorter.

It was not unlike being electrocuted and was an extremely rude awakening to the fact that the day, which as it was had started with snapped panty elastic and a stale croissant, appeared about to go steadily downhill, quite possibly taking the whole year with it.

Clementine's hair, to which she paid almost no attention in the first place, in that instant officially became the very least of her problems.

A bad frost in Saint-Vincent-sur-Marne on the third Wednesday of spring would spell disaster for the House of Peine, and the House of Peine had enough disasters as it was.

"Papa," called out Clementine, her follicles tingling on her scalp as she hastily licked a splodge of brie from her finger. "Papa!"

Her father, arguably one such disaster, would be angry with her for being the bearer of bad tidings, but then she only half-expected him to answer. She gave a hefty sigh as she stood up. It seemed he had gone from bad to worse in recent times. He had always been something of a foul-mouthed, cantankerous old bossy-boots, but where he had once at least put in a full day's work before sloping down to Le Bois, the local *tabac* and café, he was now vanishing earlier and earlier, leaving Clementine to shoulder the bulk of the winery work as well as look after their precious vines.

"Papa!" Clementine called once more, this time up the light-speckled stairs of the rambling Peine château. "Papa!" But the house felt bereft of Olivier, as it often did. As it had for some time. She would have to fight the frost without him.

A little hiccup of fear (and pickled pear) emerged from her throat as she trudged out of the house: this was one of the many crucial times in the vineyard, after all. The sap was rising in the canes after the dormancy of winter; the dead were about to spring from the grave. The last thing the Peines needed now was for that emerging lifeblood of the future to freeze in the veins of the vines.

Who could forget the terrible spring frost of two years before? It had taken out a third of their crop. There had been no vintage wine made that year, not a drop. In fact, it was all they could manage to produce their normal tongue-tingling traditional house *brut,* and that was only because of Olivier's skill at the famous *Champenoise* art of blending.

Blending? The very thought triggered an agitated humming as Clementine scurried across the courtyard. Her miniature horse, Cochon, bucked delightedly at this, his tiny unshod feet falling to the cobblestones with a muffled scuff. Humming, in his experience, was quite often followed by a trip to the kitchen for pastries, and he loved pastries. But Clementine did not have time for pastries now; she had to do what she could to protect her vines. First of all, she had to find the identical twin twenty-year-olds who were the Peine's sole remaining workers, and so useless as to be barely worth what little they were paid. In her opinion they shared a single brain, a small one at that, but they had brawn to spare, and that was precisely what she needed. They would all have to move quickly to get the *chaufferette* burners placed out among the vines in time to ward off the frost.

"Get off your fat bottoms, you lazy good-for-nothings!" Clementine exhorted the huge, bulky, ruddy-faced, blond dimwits Jean-Claude and Jean-Luc when she found them in the vegetable patch behind the winery, smoking cigarettes and drinking from an unlabeled bottle. "There's going to be a frost. We need to put out all the frost pots."

As she spoke, her curls retreated even closer to her head like high-speed snails drawing into their shells. Other *vignerons* did not yet have a sniff of what was to come and were probably planning a cozy night in front of the television or a game of cards with friends. But as well as wearing it on her head, Clementine could taste it on her tongue: the tang of pending catastrophe. It burned her cheeks and clogged her pores, agitating the deep reserves of irritation that sat constantly beneath her surface.

"Come on. I'm not paying you to lie around getting emphysema!" she scolded the two unapologetic workers. "I'm paying you to work!"

Jean-Claude or Jean-Luc, she never could tell the difference, looked at his twin and then at her, his jowls heavy with scorn. "Oh, no, you're not," whichever one he was drawled, loutishly taking another drag on his cigarette. "You're not paying us at all. Two weeks now, and your old man has yet to come up with our wages. So unless you have our money, you're on your own with your stinking frost pots."

Clementine tried not to show her dismay. She had known money was tight. René at the gas station had whined to her that their account was overdue, and the phone had been cut off again. They'd had cash flow problems before. Who hadn't? But was it possible they were now so broke they couldn't pay even these two lumbering incompetents their paltry dues? If this was indeed the case, she was up *merde* creek without a paddle because she had no one else to ask for help. Olivier had no real friends and had long ago burned any bridges on the neighbor front.

She glanced across the vines in the direction of the Geoffroy château next door, that old wound in her heart pulling like a torn muscle as she thought of Benoît Geoffroy, lost to her now for half a lifetime. No, there would be no good samaritan for the Peines. The only way they could get anyone to do anything for them these days was to pay. She looked at the dopey twins and considered pleading with them to stay and help her for free, but, in any case, she didn't know how to plead. Instead, she stamped her foot and swore, which only made them laugh.

"Well, if there's no bud burst, there'll be no grapes, and if there are no grapes, there'll be no champagne, and if there's no champagne, there'll be no more work for you at all. Had you thought of that?"

Jean-Claude and Jean-Luc got up and flicked their cigarette butts against the winery wall in unison. Cochon stamped his own tiny feet at this and flicked his tail with an angry swish. If he had been bigger than your average farm dog, this might have had more of an impact. As it was, it just made the oafs laugh harder.

"What difference does it make anyway?" one of them asked wheezily when he stopped sniggering. "This time next year the whole place will probably be owned by Moët or Veuve Clicquot or old man Joliet. Why don't you just relax? Go and join Olivier at Le Bois for a pastis or seven, heh? And take your little stallion of a boyfriend with you."

The two of them roared their idiots' laugh again, and Clementine's soon-to-be-frostbitten cheeks further reddened with rage. Cochon sensed this and skittered excitedly around behind her. He loved her anger even more than her humming. (It was quite often followed by pastries, too.)

"Get lost, then, you lumpish dolts," Clementine bawled, shooing the twins away with a furious hand gesture. "At once! And I hope your balls freeze off overnight!"

"Same to you," Jean-Luc or -Claude called back to her as the two of them stumbled across the courtyard, clutching each other and hooting with mirth. "They're more likely to. They're bigger, after all!"

A potpourri of anger fermenting inside her, Clementine stomped over to the barn and, sweating and huffing, started loading the trailer. The frost pots stood almost as high as she, and it was a struggle to maneuver them, but what choice did she have? She cursed the Jeans under her breath. There was only one thing worse than one great lump of lard, she thought, and that was two. Those useless, fat, ugly, horrid, ungrateful creatures! But her anger was tinged with something else, something that penetrated the marrow of her bones and chilled them even more than the oncoming frost.

The truth was, if Olivier could not pay them their paltry wages, the lumps were right: the House of Peine was vulnerable to takeover by either the bank or, worse in every way, old man Joliet. The oafs were talking rubbish regarding the big houses—the strict regulations of Champagne did not allow the Veuve Clicquots or Moëts of the world to swallow the smaller houses. But old man Joliet was a different matter. One small house could buy another, and for decades that old crustacean, an inferior winemaker but superior moneymaker, had been greedily eyeing the valuable Champagne land that the Peines had spent generations acquiring.

"Over my dead body," Clementine swore to herself as she hauled the trailer full of *chaufferettes* over to the cranky tractor. She would truly rather die than see a single centimeter of chalky Peine soil handed over to old man Joliet. Olivier, though? The acrid remains of her afternoon tea made another unscheduled visit to her throat. She was no longer sure she could trust her father with the necessary resolve to fight such an invasion. Once, maybe, when he cared more about the contents of their own bottles than the ones down at the *tabac*. But now she could not trust him to leave the house with his trousers on let alone battle for the reputation of their once legendary birthright. Now it was up to her.

She was the one with the weight of three hundred years of Peine *vignerons* resting on rounded shoulders that sagged even further as she realized just how alone she was.

"I have nobody," she whispered into the cooling air. "Nobody."

Cochon let out a rather insulted knicker at this, a noise which in a miniature horse sounds quite a lot like the whistle of a kettle boiling four doors down. Clementine's shoulders lifted a little. She appreciated the sentiment. Cochon was indeed her constant companion, and she was fonder of him than of any other mammal in the world, but he was also a case in point when it came to Olivier's unpredictability. Her father had won the miniature horse in a drunken card game during a heat wave a few years before. Clementine had woken up, hot and bothered, to find the tiny foal mewling in her bedroom and was only further bewildered when her father grunted at her later in the day: "Did you get the pig?"

"Pig?"

"The little pig I left you. I won it off that shithead Marant. Didn't you always say you wanted a pig?"

"A pig?"

"When you were younger, three or four, you empty-headed girl, you said you wanted a smelly little oinker, and now you have one. I won it fair and square. So there."

Clementine had spent the rest of the day looking for a pig, the tiny pony following in her footsteps on dainty wobbly legs. In the end, though, she had to concede that her father did not know the difference between the two and that the horse and the pig were indeed one and the same. She said nothing about it, though. The truth was, she had wanted a puppy when she was younger—desperately in fact—and had begged and pleaded and cried for something warm and fluffy to cuddle at night in her lonely cot. Olivier had not obliged. Being obliging was not what he was known for. But the fact that even a tiny kernel of what his daughter had one day longed for still rattled in his sozzled brain was almost overwhelmingly touching, so rare were such jewels. She simply called the horse Cochon and got on with it.

And to be perfectly honest, Olivier was not the only person to be confused by what exactly Cochon was. White with big chestnut patches and a short, fuzzy mane, he was not only a miniature horse but a dwarf of the species, destined never to stand taller than two and a half feet and to be constantly mistaken for a furry pillow or a cowhide hold-all. As far as Clementine was concerned, however, he was an excellent companion and, apart from the initial challenge of housebreaking him, hardly any bother. Yet for all his good points, he could not help her bottle champagne or shuffle *chaufferettes,* and on days like this, when loneliness combined with fear inside her to produce a bitter cocktail of hopelessness and burps, he was not much practical assistance at all.

Worse, this wasn't just any old hard day, long night, or bad week. This was the future. Clementine felt the sourness inside her growing more and more vinegary. It would choke her, she feared, if she just stood there and let it. It would drown any fighting spirit she had left.

Shaking off her dread, her doubt, she climbed aboard the ancient Peine tractor, an ugly belching creature whose temperament shared more than was ideal with Olivier. All night she drove around her vines, dragging the pots off the trailer, lighting them as she went, whispering words of encouragement to her canes, warning them of what was to come, pleading with them to be strong.

By midnight, word was well and truly out, and the still, cold air in the Marne Valley reverberated with the sound of neighboring *vignerons* preparing to battle the frost. Not a single person would be left sleeping through this one, not an elderly gran or a snotty-nosed child. Every helpful hand in every winemaker's house would be dragged out of bed and put to use. It would have been the same at the House of Peine had Clementine had anyone to wake. Instead, her father was no doubt passed out under a table at Le Bois. Even Cochon had forsaken her for a warm spot between two rotting bales of hay in the barn. She thanked God, possibly for the first time, for blessing her with the crinkly orange hair that had given her such a good head start against the elements.

By six in the morning she had moved from thanking God to cursing him and every last one of his pointless creations. Every bone in her body ached, the skin on her face felt rubbed raw by the cold, and her throat was hoarse from breathing in the harsh smoke that now clung to the rows of vines, drifting moodily across the valley like a low-slung mist, making eerie specters of the neighbors' crisscrossing tractor beams and the burning amber flames of the *chaufferette* smoke pots.

The frost was all around her, twinkling like fancy frosting on an ostentatious wedding cake. She had done all she could. Only time would tell if it had been a killer or not. Her instinct (and her hair) told her it wasn't the worst they had suffered, but who knew how much those unborn buds could withstand?

Exhausted, Clementine turned the grouchy tractor for its final run toward the house. Heading down from the wooded hilltop toward the château, her trailer empty now of frost pots and bouncing on the rough ground, she wished she had left some lights on inside despite the cost. The château loomed dark and sulky behind the screens of smoke that wafted in layers in front of her like sheets of finest oyster-colored silk. It had once been a beautiful home, greatly admired by centuries of valley *vignerons*, but those days were long gone, and in this light it looked threatening, abandoned, haunted. Clementine shivered in a way that had nothing to do with the temperature.

There was only one way to shake off the chill of a night such as the one she had just lived through, and at the very thought of what this was, she started to warm from the inside out, as surely as though someone had reached into her heart and flicked on a switch.

She returned the tractor to the barn, waking Cochon, who had not moved a muscle while she toiled, and scurried over to the winery, slipping inside, passing the grape press, and then lifting up the trapdoor that led down a narrow spiral staircase to the *cave* or cellar below. Previous Peines, like many other *Champenois*, had dug the *cave* out of the cool chalky ground hundreds of years before. The space resembled a four-digit hand, with a large open area in the middle where the barrels were stacked and four fingerlike alcoves leading farther into the chalk where the bottles rested.

Cochon, who had been blearily following his mistress, shuddered to a halt at the lip of the hatch and peered down the hole after her. Dwarf miniature horses and narrow spiral staircases were a near-deadly combination, as he had found out twice in his youth. At a constant 10 degrees it was too cold for him down there anyway, but it was perfect for champagne, and Clementine headed straight for the farthest finger, stopping at the end of a dusty rack and pulling out a bottle of the vintage '88.

Returning to the palm of the *cave*, she plucked a crystal flute out of Olivier's broom closet–sized office and wiped the grime off the glass with the tail of her loose shirt. (Champagne glasses should never be too clean anyway; it interfered with the bubbles. She had learned that when she was two.) Then, settling herself on the bottom spiral step, in the light of a single cobweb-covered lantern, she gently pulled the foil away from the top and twisted off the wire muzzle. Holding the bottle at its base she twisted it, pressing down on the cork until she felt it pressing back. Then, ever so slowly, she let it emerge until it came away with the gentlest of sighs, as though the relief of having her come along and remove it had been just what it had been waiting for all these years.

And with that the fear and panic that had built up inside her as she had worked through the freezing night to save her grapes released itself with a similar hiss.

She heard Cochon flop to the floor upstairs with a reluctant sigh. There would be no humming or pastries with a fresh bottle of the '88 just opened.

Clementine poured a little of the bubbly wine into her glass and held it up to the lantern so she could get a good look at it. The color was the perfect deep gold of a French queen's satin gown. "Luxurious" was the only word to describe it. She filled the rest of the glass and turned it again to examine the bubbles. They flowed upward in a continuous stream, like tiny magical pearls, rising quickly but in a stately fashion commensurate with their age and stature.

Next, she held the glass to her ear and listened to the bubbles chattering happily as they ascended. Such a sweet sound! She could listen to it all day. Then she put her nose to the glass and breathed in, deeply and happily. There were roses, yes—she could almost see them—and the smokiness of oak plus the roundness of freshly baked buttery madeleines. And was that a suggestion of citrus? A soupçon of earth?

She closed her eyes and took a long, loud sip. It was creamy and smooth with the bite of the bubbles tingling merrily on the roof of her mouth. The fruit lingered on her tongue, leaving a passion fruit aftertaste that reminded her of all the sultry afternoons she had never spent languishing on sandy beaches in Tahitian summers. But who needed a holiday on the other side of the world? There was nothing Clementine could not get from that glass of champagne. Well, almost nothing.

She smacked her lips together in pleasure, a smile spreading across her face. Only the spiders living in their own little lantern château could see it, but odds were even they were impressed. It was a face vastly beautified by adding a smile.

No sooner had her inner warmth reached her outer, however, than this rare state of contentment was shattered. Cochon heard the approaching footsteps first and jumped clumsily to his feet. Clementine sat on the bottom step, dead still, listening to see if it was her father, worse off for liquor and coming to shout at her. But the footsteps were too steady and purposeful for Olivier. If he was ever up at this hour, he was on his way home from somewhere and not up to more than a shuffle on a good day. But who else could it be skulking around her winery? No one ever visited the Peines unannounced. No one ever visited them at all. Clementine was sure the sound of her heart beating would deafen her as it bounced off the *cave*'s chalky walls. She held her breath. The footsteps grew louder, more purposeful, closer, and then a long dark shadow threw itself over the hatch and spread down the stairs, a following flashlight beam seeking out Clementine's frightened eyes and temporarily blinding her.

"Who is it?" she whispered, fear dampening her volume. "Who are you? What do you want?"

"At last I've found you," Marc Debasque, the local *gendarme*, boomed down the hatch. Relief flooded through her. She knew for a fact that Marc Debasque had wet his bed until he was fourteen and wasn't scary at all.

"You just about frightened me to death, you fool," she chided, shading her eyes and looking up at him. "What the hell do you want?"

"I'm terribly sorry, Clementine," he said, taking off his cap. "But there's been an accident."

Débourrement

"Typical," Clementine thought morosely three days later as a solid clod hit her father's coffin with the most unfriendly of thwacks. Aboveground, the seasons had taunted him with their fickleness. Belowground, they continued their insults. Winter had clung to spring just to kick Olivier in the seat of the pants one last time, to aggravate Gaston the lazy gravedigger's tendonitis, to burn his daughter's cheek as an icy tear slid down it. There had been no more frost since the night Olivier met his maker, but there had been no more sign of spring, either. The ground was still hard, the air sharp with chill.

"I'm so sorry, Clementine," murmured the nervous young parish priest, Father Philippe, as they turned from the grave. "He was indeed a complicated man."

But Clementine knew all there was to know about her father's complications. She certainly didn't need to hear any more from the priest. She shrugged off his pity, grunted a curt *au revoir*, and then headed down the grassy alley between the graves toward the churchyard gates where Cochon awaited, his little head pushed through the wrought iron bars.

Her coat did not fit well, her best Sunday shoes were worn away at the heels, but she had good ankles, Father Philippe and Gaston both noticed at the same time with matching embarrassed coughs as they watched her walk away. In fact, without the upholstery of her obvious unhappiness and those few extra pounds around her middle, Clementine was altogether a fine-looking woman.

Of course, she cared not a jot how she looked, particularly at that moment. All she could think of was putting as much distance as possible between herself and that hole in the unrelenting ground. Plucking her bicycle from its position against the hedge outside the church, she threw a leg over the saddle, cursing her sagging tights as they caught on the seat, and started to pedal away, Cochon breaking into a canter behind her.

Above the sound of his hoofbeats, however, and her tires crunching on the gravel lane, that mocking thwack of clod on pine kept ringing in her ears. The ceremony had been short and attendance sparse, consisting only of her, the priest, and the gravedigger, both of whom were there only because their jobs demanded it. No, you certainly couldn't say the townspeople were mourning Olivier's passing, and, really, why should they? Over the years he had turned on all his friends, invented feuds with all their neighbors, and mocked every innocent act of kindness ever visited upon anyone, his daughter included.

But still was there not one single person, Clementine allowed herself to think as she eyed a rhubarb tart in the window of the *patisserie*, who cared that she was now truly and officially all alone in the world? She still had blood flowing in her veins, after all. She was not yet frozen as her father had been three days before outside the video store. Was there not one single person who could have stood by her—without getting paid for it—as she farewelled him forever? Her feet pushed harder on the pedals as a streak of Olivier's bitterness swirled through her like cream in a *chocolat chaud*. What is it about me, she asked silently, that sucks the sympathy out of even the softest heart?

Even sappy Father Philippe had been short on appropriate words of comfort, twittering on instead about the lawyer, Christophe Paillard, saying she needed to contact him right away. What for? So he could trick her into selling her land to Joliet? Never. The land, the grapes, the champagne—that was all she had left. That was all she needed. The townspeople could go to hell, she decided, her disappointment melting into anger as she sped past the town square with its tattered tulips, around the *mairie*, behind Le Bois, and on through the village until she rounded the bend past the last house, home of Laure Laborde. And she could be the first one to burn, Clementine thought, eyeing the chirpy daffodils in the wretched woman's window boxes. The clothes of Laure's never-ending horde of ill-mannered children flapped in the sharp breeze. The woman's eldest was nineteen and at university in Paris, yet the youngest was barely out of diapers. It was disgraceful, her infernal breeding, thought Clementine, her stomach churning at the thought. Disgraceful. All those children. All those babies. She began to hum somewhat feverishly. This humming habit had once been strictly internal: a silent deflection of thoughts too painful to bear. But somewhere along the line, the odd practice slipped out into the world of sound where it did not really belong. Sadly for Clementine, there had been no one there to tell her to shove it back in again, and now it was like an aural tic over which she had little control.

The humming grew louder as Laure's youngest tumbled out the front door and fell onto her chubby toddler knees, golden curls tumbling down infant shoulders.

The trouble was, there were just so many thoughts that Clementine found unbearably painful.

Around the corner the road straightened, and midway along it stood Saint Vincent, patron saint of winemakers and a reason to stop humming if ever there was one. His stonily compassionate smile loomed sixty feet above her as Clementine cycled by, his arms benevolently outstretched above the valley. She had no particular fondness for him personally, but nonetheless as she passed him those motionless arms seemed to swing down and snatch away her anger, sweeping it from her like a matador's cape. This was hardly a religious experience; to her Saint Vincent was just a punctuation mark on the road from the village. On one side of him lay the close-knit community of which Clementine was not a part, full of the friends she did not have, the good times she had never enjoyed. But beyond him, to her right, marching neatly up the hillside like long lines of obedient brown soldiers, lay her true and faithful *amies*. Her grapes. In this case the robust and fruity pinot meunier. Whether bare or snow-covered as they stood in the winter, woody and hopeful as they were now, or green and heaving with late summer fruit, the first sight of the family vines always gave her the same pleasant burr of satisfaction.

Actually, other *vignerons*, especially in Champagne, might have gone so far as to feel joy at such a sight. They were in the business of making the world's famously effervescent celebratory drink, after all. But while Clementine had spent her whole life living, breathing, making, and, yes, drinking the glorious sparkling elixir that imbued the rest of the human race with gaiety and exuberance, and while she undeniably loved those grapes more than she loved anything else, she herself could not claim so much as a single bubbly bone in her body—not a bubble of any kind in any part of her for that matter. For reasons that stretched far into the past, Clementine was as flat as a glass of Marne River water. A pleasant burr of satisfaction was as good as it got. She simply knew nothing more.

She slowed the pump of her shapely legs on the pedals and let her bicycle cruise as her eyes lingered over the fruits of her labors. These vines up on the hill had been barely touched by the frost, and, anyway, pinot meunier was tough; it could take it. She wasn't worried about them. But in her other parcels of land at the bottom of the valley? Fear nipped at her satisfaction. Her pinot noir grapes did not have the resilience of their meunier cousins. They were not at all thick-skinned; they were sensitive and precious. You could taste it in the finished product. That's why the extra effort at mollycoddling them through to harvest was worth it, more than worth it. Still, thought Clementine, guiding those grapes through the minefield of seasonal aberrations was not a job for the fainthearted. She had no time to dillydally and feel a burr of anything. What was she thinking? Winemakers, when it came down to it, were farmers, working always against the whims of nature, especially here in the north. There was a good reason that no one else on the globe (except a small handful of Germans, some ninnies in England, and a group of upstarts in Denmark) attempted grape growing at this latitude. Unless you knew exactly what you were doing, it was a fool's game. Even when you did know what you were doing, you needed good luck in large quantities. And it could not be said that Olivier Peine had been known for his luck. Well, he was hardly having a good month.

Clementine sped up again, her muscles singing, and then looked down the hill to her left as another Peine plot near the river heaved into view.

This part of the Saint-Vincent-sur-Marne hillside may have looked to a casual passerby like one solid brown undulating blanket of grapevines separated only by the odd chalky pathway, but in fact it was no such thing. It was instead a monochrome mosaic of different villagers' grapes. If that same passerby looked closely enough, he might notice that the color, size, or material of the posts varied from plot to plot, that grass grew between some vines, tangled weeds between others, and that pruning clippings lay between the grapes over there, but the ground was bare between those ones there. So it was in Champagne. One *vigneron* might tend his twenty rows a certain way while his neighbor, not spitting distance away, might do it completely differently, and *his* neighbor, not half spitting distance away, might do it differently again.

The Peines had their nineteen separate parcels of grapes dotted along the hillside and down in the valley. They used metal posts and grew grass in the rows, which Olivier believed helped the vines grow deeper in the ground for extra nourishment. The Larbordes had a dozen plots, as did the Feneuils, the Geoffroys (the name flitted through her mind like a moth—would she ever not feel a lurch at the thought of it?) had seventeen, and there were many more village *vignerons* who didn't make their own wine but sold their grapes to Moët and Veuve Clicquot or, Clementine's heart skipped a beat, to Krug, the king of champagnes.

Oh, how she dreamed of producing just once in her life a vintage wine to rival Krug's Clos du Mesnil, probably the most talked about and least tasted champagne in the world. She had sampled it just once, at a tasting in Epernay many years before when she and Olivier were still included in such events. Sometimes to this day she woke up with the taste of those chardonnay bubbles on her tongue. And then there was the Vieilles Vignes Françaises, Bollinger's ode to champagne the way it was before the phylloxera louse got to most of France's native vines. She had tasted that Bollinger *blanc de noirs* only once, too, but she let a vigorous hum chase away all memory of that.

The thing was, Clementine considered, returning to the safe subject of her one true reliable passion, Peine champagne was good. She knew that. She knew it in the same way François Peine had known it when he first grew his grapes and bottled their juice back in 1697 when bubbles were still considered a mistake. She knew the modern Peine champagne was every bit as good if not better than that of most of the *grand marques*. Saint-Vincent-sur-Marne was a *cru* village, after all; every single grape rated near perfect on the official scale of quality.

They would never have the kudos of Krug or Bollinger, of course they wouldn't, but both those houses made their champagne using grapes brought in from independent growers. No big champagne house owned enough land to grow all its own grapes. Why, some big champagne houses owned no land at all. They bought every last berry from someone else! At the House of Peine, on the other hand, every last drop in every last bottle came from a vine tended by no other hand than Clementine's. She knew each row of vines by name and nearly every plant by character. She helped pick them, she pressed them, and she coaxed their juice into barrels and their wine into bottles. She choreographed almost every last bubble. She might never have the kudos of her famous rivals, but she truly believed she had a champagne that was every bit as good if not better.

Of course, her famous rivals had been busy pouring their resources into making sure the world knew about their superior product, which the House of Peine had not. Instead, Olivier had stayed in his underground *cave* chiseled out of the chalky earth where, never mind the world, there wasn't even a window. The rest of the universe was never going to find out about the deliciously nutty notes of the '98 or taste the strawberry highlights of the last rosé. Not with Olivier at the helm. The Krugs and Bollingers had left the House of Peine far behind in this regard, and Clementine knew she could never catch up. But she could at least start trying now that the House of Peine was hers.

Her confidence in this matter had grown, as it happened, since the night of the frost when her loneliness had closed in on her like a fog. In the few short days since Olivier's demise, Clementine had come to realize that without him the House of Peine actually had more of a future than she could ever remember. Her mornings were no longer hampered by her father's hungover mumblings, his brusque instructions; her afternoons were no longer pock-marked with worry about his humiliating her in the street or being squashed by a falling barrel.

It had slowly dawned on her that without the curmudgeonly obstacle of her complicated father, she could do whatever she wanted. And what she wanted was to see the House of Peine return to the glory days of previous centuries when Russian czars had begged for it, English kings had toasted with it, and her Peine ancestors had walked the streets of Champagne with their heads held high.

In fact, it was what she had been waiting for her whole long, lonely life. It was why her time on this particular square of often bleak and battle-scarred earth was not a waste. It was the reason she got up in the morning.

"Good-bye, Papa," she shouted into the crisp quiet air, tears drying on her cheeks before she could even feel them. "And good riddance!" The dark prince of Peine was dead, long live the queen!

At this she felt an infinitesimal pull on her handlebars, which seemed to point her in the direction of her little unborn berry babies down near the river. Clementine let the bike take her where it wanted to go, crossing the road and squinting down the hill toward her nearest plot of pinot noir. Could it be? Her heart skipped a beat. Was she imagining it, or was there an almost invisible green tinge to the dull woody brownness of her naked vines?

Her heart sped up again as she veered off the tarmac and into the vines, Cochon bringing up the rear. Her bicycle flew faster and faster down between two rows of Feneuil pinot, her body bumping and jiggling over the rough ground. The gentle breeze colluded with her downhill speed and picked up her orange curls, unfurling them behind her like a cartoon character as she bounced through the vines, her open coat flapping noisily and flirting dangerously with the greasy chain of her bike.

In her haste, however, she forgot about the stones that Olivier had recently moved after an entirely unnecessary argument with Henri Feneuil to mark where their grapes stopped and the Peine ones started. Her front wheel, its tire long due for more air, hit one such rock at just the right angle for the bike to come to an instant stop. Clementine was not so lucky. She flew through the air like a giant navy blue juggling ball, landing flat on her back quite some distance from her bicycle with a noise not unlike a hot air balloon in an emergency deflation.

She lay there for a moment, wondering if she was dead. Everything hurt, but she was pretty sure the whole point of being dead was that nothing at all hurt. Slowly, still winded, she attempted to sit up, turning around to face her pinot noir canes at eye level. At this the breath disappeared from her lungs once more, but her pain vanished, and a smile launched itself across her face once more, completely changing the nature of her looks.

To her pinot noir she looked beautiful.

And to her, so did they. Her eyes had not been deceiving her from the road. There had been the vaguest tinge of green. *Débourrement!* Bud burst! Each little knot on every single cane had broken into the tiniest of songs. All was not lost. The frost had killed nothing but Olivier. And now, on the very day his body had been committed to the ground, new life had been breathed into her vines.

Clementine collapsed back on the grass and laughed. How she laughed!

It was a sound the vines hardly ever got to hear. And it warmed them as much as the glorious spring sunshine, which chose that exact moment to make its first truly serious appearance.

Mathilde

Once spring had wriggled out beyond the clutches of winter, everything about the valley changed.

It could be a bleak place in the cooler months, prompting many a thin-lipped tourist who hadn't done his homework to murmur bitter asides to the effect that they didn't care how delicious champagne tasted, Provence was much nicer this time of year.

But come mid-May, the Marne Valley reeked of hope. Those dry, dark vines, having slept through the snow, survived the first frosts, and gone on to give birth to millions of tiny buds, now sent supple green shoots out into the world, turning the landscape from dull brown and off-white to a kaleidoscope of brilliant jades and emeralds.

Clementine was down in the cellar riddling: twisting and turning the resting champagne bottles to dislodge their yeasty sediment from the bottom of the bottle into the neck from whence it would eventually be disgorged. Once upon a time, riddling—or *remuage,* as it was known—had been a revered profession, passed down from father to son, but as with many of the old ways, those days were long gone. Now most the fathers were dead or arthritic, and the sons worked in IT in Paris.

There was still the like of old Nicolas Bateau over in Hautvillers if anyone looked hard enough, but it was common knowledge his hands were so crippled that he was merely wheeled out to rattle the bottles for goggle-eyed visitors. The Bateau champagne, like most, was actually riddled in a jointly owned mechanical *gyropalette*, which did in eight days what took human hands eight weeks.

As one might imagine, Clementine would not cross the street to spit on a *gyropalette*. Always a stickler for tradition, she riddled the bottles herself, yet unlike other *vignerons* who could not afford any alternative, she liked it. It gave her a chance to reacquaint herself with her grape juice, she felt. It had been pretty much ignored for the years it had lain in the *cave* inventing its own bubbles, after all, and deserved a bit of one-on-one attention.

Standing there in front of the *pupitres* full of bottles, arms outstretched as her hands moved back and forth, and up and down, wrists flicking in perfect harmony, she often felt like a passionate conductor leading her favorite orchestra in a movement of enormous importance and beauty.

After more than three hours on the trot, however, the noise of the bottles clinking as she turned them was no longer music to her ears, which was why on this particular perfect spring day she decided a little something custardy was required to help her through to lunch. With the off-key melody of her bottles still ringing in her ears as she emerged into the courtyard, she stopped for a moment just to feel the sun on her face, to breathe in the fresh air, and then she jumped on her bike to head for the *patisserie* and whatever Bernadette, the *pâtissiere*, had on offer. Cochon, hearing the bicycle start its noisy trip across the courtyard potholes, shook himself awake from his position under the kitchen table and started after her.

At the bottom of the drive, however, they struck a snag. The once magnificent gates to the House of Peine refused to open, and Clementine was moved to get off her bicycle and clatter and jangle them for quite some time, employing a smorgasbord of different expletives as she did so. This excited Cochon beyond belief—he so enjoyed a temper tantrum—but just when she was thinking she would have to go back to the kitchen and settle for a stale baguette with a dollop of thyme honey, the gates begrudgingly creaked open and let them out.

Once on the other side, having heaved them shut again, she dropped her bike and stood back with a critical eye. Cochon, who was in the mood for a little pastry something himself, flopped huffily onto the ground at her feet, one black eye rolling upward as it followed her line of vision. The same old gates, as far as he could tell, but for Clementine it suddenly seemed that now there was the possibility—no, the promise—of change in the wind; she was seeing all the same old things in an entirely different light.

The entrance to a home was like the cover of a book, she decided, standing there with sweaty hands on sturdy hips. No matter what anyone said, it told you all you needed to know about what lay inside. And looking at the entrance to the House of Peine, well, truthfully, the story was a sad one, most likely titled "Has Seen Better Days." The ridiculously ornate gates stood five meters tall, delicate curlicues fanning extravagantly far above her. Once a particularly becoming shade of sky blue, rust was now the predominant shade, the paint long since bubbled and flaked off into the ether. What is more, the artisan ironwork stretched for five meters on either side of the gates but then ran out to be replaced by an anemic hedge that had once been tall and lush but was now crippled and spare with big bald patches where whole herds of animals or people could step through if they wanted to, which of course they didn't.

The château, half a kilometer back up the bumpy gravel drive, was another picture that painted a thousand words and told a barely happier story. Clementine squinted through the gates at her home for the past forty-four years. It was golden brick and stood three stories high if you counted the attic floor with its cheerful collection of chimney stacks and dormer windows. From a distance the bones of the house were as good as they ever had been, but close up the impression was far less flattering. Nearly half the upstairs windows were boarded, the glass long since broken with no hope of being repaired. Many of the shutters hung crookedly off their hinges, and grassy weeds grew enthusiastically out of the blocked guttering. The original front door had been in disrepair for decades, old slats from wooden packing crates nailed haphazardly across it to stop cracks from getting bigger and to keep drafts at bay—a losing battle as far as Clementine could fathom. Up closer still there was not even a door handle, just an old screwdriver in an empty geranium pot that one poked in the hole and wriggled to gain entry. There was no bell, no door knocker, either, although Olivier had long ago scared away anyone who might come to visit, and Clementine did not have the skill or the inclination to get them back.

All this would be lost on that thin-lipped Provence-preferring tourist should he happen to pass by, it must be said. In many ways from a distance the House of Peine looked like the perfect French fairy-tale castle: a grand dame of a château draped in the rich green cloth of her vines. That tourist might even forget his disappointment about the general lack of charm in this part of the country and pull over to the side of the road, commenting that he thought he saw something just like this house in the *New York Times Magazine*. Or he might take a photo through the gates to catch the color of the shutters so he could go home to his London flat and paint the outdoor furniture that exact shade.

From where Clementine stood, having lived there all her life and planning on staying, it looked more like an abandoned ship that had been looted by pirates and left, full of nothing but ghosts, forlorn and becalmed on a luscious green sea.

Still, it was afloat, wasn't it, she thought? The promise of her future brought a smile to her face as she reached down and grabbed the handlebars of her bike, Cochon jumping daintily to attention. And it would sail once again. She might even get a sign put up, a notice to the world that she was seriously back in the business. She had to cellar the recently bottled champagne first, of course, keep riddling the previous year's, disgorge it when she had time, cellar that, take stock of Olivier's reserves, look at the accounts—about which she knew absolutely nothing—and sort out some help to replace those useless twins. Actually, the sign would have to wait. She had a lot of work to do before the end of September and the *vendange*, the harvest.

No wonder I am starving, she thought happily, licking her lips. But before she could throw that strangely graceful leg over her saddle and head toward Bernadette's tarts, Christophe Paillard's bright red Renault careened around the corner, veering wildly into the loose gravel beside her as he threw on the brakes, a cloud of dust enveloping her and her little horse.

"Mind what you are doing, you stupid oaf," she growled as he cut the motor. She had met the lawyer many times before. He had too much chest hair for her liking; it poked up above his shirt collar like an unmowed lawn, but worse than that, he was a lackey of old man Joliet, who sent him around periodically to sniff out the chance of a land sale. "And for the last time the answer is no." She slapped furiously at the grime on her clothes, coughing and half-blinded as she heard him open and close his car door. "No, no, a thousand times no. How many times do I have to say it before you get it through your thick skull?"

Another door opened and shut, this time with a sharp slam. "Well, well, well," purred a velvety feminine voice, "will you look at what we have here? All these years, Clementine, and you still look like something the cat dragged in."

Clementine's blood ran cold. She stopped brushing away the dirt, her hands falling uselessly to her sides. Surely it couldn't be . . . No. It was impossible. She was dreaming. But that voice, that tone, the tension that tingled in the air between them. She peered through the billowing dust, blinking stupidly, at the vision of sophistication that had stepped away from the car and was standing still beside it, a tall, rail-thin blonde in caramel stilettos, a cream trench coat belted tightly around her tiny waist, arms crossed in front of her, red nails gleaming, and red lips gathered in a perfect contemptu-ous smirk.

There was no doubt about it. "Mathilde," Clementine breathed. She had not seen Mathilde for eighteen years, not since the evil wench had ruined her life in more ways than she would ever, could ever know. And while the skin may have grown over those wounds and hardened into scars, Clementine felt that she was splitting open in all the same places, as though no time whatsoever had passed, let alone almost two decades. "Whatever you want," she cried, "you're not having it. Go away!"

"Jesus, what the hell is that thing?" Mathilde, ignoring her, pointed an elegant finger at Cochon, who was pig-rooting in the dust beside his owner. "Monsieur Paillard, you didn't mention she'd spawned."

Clementine felt a panicked hum rising in her chest but fought the urge to succumb to it. "Leave!" she cried instead. "Go away. Go on. Get out of my sight before I call the police and have you arrested for, for—"

"Ladies, please," implored Christophe. "Is this really necessary?"

"Have me arrested for what, exactly?" Mathilde smiled languidly as she patiently inspected a large diamond ring on her slender wedding finger.

"For being a filthy tramp and a thief and a trespasser, that's what!" Clementine exclaimed. "You're nothing but a—"

"Now, now, Clementine," Christophe said, more forcefully this time. He stepped toward her and waved a pudgy hand in the air as if attempting to slow traffic, but Mathilde, unconcerned, just laughed her old tinkly laugh.

"Don't worry, *monsieur*," she said soothingly. "If I remember rightly, she just needs to let off steam every five or six minutes. You know, like a big, fat, old black kettle."

Eighteen years, and like that she could bring tears to Clementine's eyes—tears that usually were tucked down neat inside her, buried beneath the tune of turning bottles, the click of pruning shears, the chatter of dancing bubbles.

"Tramp," she mumbled, turning around, refusing to give Mathilde the satisfaction of seeing what effect she had had. "Thief." Like a vampire, if Mathilde knew what blood she had already drawn she would not stop until the last drop was sucked out. Abandoning her trip to the *patisserie*, Clementine dragged her bike clumsily over to the gates and attempted to open them, Cochon bringing up the rear so closely she could feel his enthusiastic nose against the back of her leg. "I don't want to see you," she said, her hands shaking as she fumbled with the rusty gate. "I don't know what you're doing here, but you're not welcome in my home. You had your chance, Mathilde, and you didn't want it. You threw it away. All those years ago you threw it away, and nothing has changed since then. Nothing will ever change. Just go away and leave me alone!"

But the gates would not oblige to allow her a dignified escape. Instead, they remained stubbornly closed as she desperately rattled them, her bike sliding off her hip to the ground and Cochon nudging her bottom just to add to her humiliation.

Christophe slipped in beside her, using his squat hairy bulk to assist her with the recalcitrant ironwork.

"It's not quite that simple, I'm afraid, Clementine," he said gently. "It's not a matter of taking chances or throwing things away, as you must well know. Your sister and I—"

"Half-sister!" Clementine corrected, twisting around and ending up with her face pressed very nearly in his sweating armpit. "Half-sister!"

"Very well," Christophe agreed patiently as the gate finally relented and allowed itself to be pushed open. "Your half-sister and I need to come inside and talk to you. That is, I need to come inside and talk to you both. I'm sorry, Clementine, really I am. I thought perhaps Father Philippe might have prepared you for this. I spoke to him as soon as I made contact with Mathilde but—"

"Father Philippe? What do you mean?" Clementine demanded, her teeth starting to clatter, her fear out in the open, naked and undisguised. "Prepared me? Prepared me for what?"

"I'm sorry," Christophe repeated, "but I've been trying to reach you. I've called, I've sent letters." He noticed at that moment the soggy pile of unopened envelopes lying on the grass inside the rusty gates where the postman had no doubt flung them rather than wrestle with the gate—or Clementine. "Really, this need not have come as such a shock."

Quatre Quarts

There were few situations in Clementine's experience that left her without an appetite, but being told she had to share the House of Peine with her long-lost (and happily as far as she was concerned) half-sister Mathilde was definitely one of them.

The creamy tarts and luscious pastries that had been dancing about in her head as she riddled now slithered to a slimy heap at the bottom of her mind with all the appeal of a freshly steaming cow pat.

"I don't believe it," she said in a dull, empty voice to Christophe as he sat in the kitchen, having just revealed what felt distinctly to her like the final slap on her stinging cheek from the hand of her dead and now decomposing father. "I just don't believe it."

Mathilde, sitting awkwardly across the table as though her tightly toned buttocks were repelled by the mere thought of what scum lay on her chair, rolled her eyes.

"Your father never talked to you about what would happen in the event of his, um, demise?" Christophe prodded. "You never discussed the possibilities?"

"He hardly talked to me at all," Clementine replied in a daze. "We never discussed a single thing."

"Yes, but you knew that Mathilde would always have the right to—" Christophe started, but mention of that name catapulted Clementine out of her stupor.

"The right?" she repeated. "*The right*? How dare you talk to me of rights? What right has she to any part of the House of Peine? What? Tell me! What? It's *me* who has been working here with Olivier all these years. Not Mathilde. Not anybody. Just him and me. And most of the time lately just me. Who has been out there in the vineyard training the vines and tasting the grapes? Who spends hours down in the winery riddling the bottles and calculating the *dosage*? Who wets the barrels and prunes the canes and battles the infernal bloody grapeworm, hm? It's me, Christophe, me. I'm the one who's lived with him all this time. I'm the one who's put up with his moods and his silences and whatever demons had him howling in his room at night if he hadn't passed out on the kitchen floor. I'm the one who's put up with his meanness, who's sacrificed my friends and any chance of a normal life for our grapes and our champagne. I am! Yes, me!" There was no point trying to get a word in. Christophe just bit his tongue. "He never even spoke her name again," Clementine continued, pointing at Mathilde. "Not once since she was here the last time. And you talk to me about her right? It's inconceivable that she—no, worse than that. It's criminal that she has any right. What has she ever done to deserve it? There must be a law against this, Christophe. There must! If there's a God in heaven, then the House of Peine should be mine. I know it, you know it, everyone knows it. You're the expert, so what can I do? Tell me! What can I do? Don't just sit there staring at me—tell me!"

Christophe tried opening his mouth to speak but was nowhere near quick enough.

"Oh, don't get yourself so excited, Clementine," Mathilde leapt in. "I'm hardly jumping with joy at the prospect of splitting my inheritance with you, either, but you don't see me making a song and dance routine out of it."

Clementine stood up from the table so abruptly, her chair clattered to the ground behind her. "Don't speak to me," she cried, one trembling hand flying up to her face to shield her eyes from the very sight of her sister. "Don't you dare even speak to me!" Cochon, who had not been showing his usual enthusiasm for a skirmish, skittered out from beneath the table at that point, his rounded rear flanks quivering as he skidded on the smooth stone floor.

"You let that overgrown whatever-it-is inside?" Mathilde demanded, a disgusted look on her face. "Why couldn't you just collect cats like a normal madwoman?"

But Clementine was too distressed to bite back, turning instead, with uncustomary desperation, to the lawyer. "There must be something you can do," she begged him wretchedly. "Anything! Please, Christophe, anything. You must help me. It's just not fair."

"Come on, Clementine," he reasoned, not without sympathy. "Is this really such a surprise?"

"She should renounce it!" cried Clementine. "That's what she should do. That's what anyone else would do. What does she want with champagne, Christophe? With Saint-Vincent-sur-Marne? With me? It's just not fair!"

For a moment Christophe felt real pity for her. She was right.

Life had not been fair to Clementine. It had stuck her in this dilapidated empty hole with Olivier Peine, to whom reason was a foreigner and rationale an enemy, as far as Christophe could make out. The old man had been the same ever since he could remember. Frankly, the Peine sisters should be grateful the law protected their birthright because the old reprobate could otherwise have left the whole sorry business to old man Joliet just to spite them or, worse still, signed it over to the Oeuilly donkey refuge.

"Well, don't just sit there, you great fat lump!" Clementine's desperation was short-lived, quickly stirring itself into the usual mélange of Peine anger. This was a drop that Christophe had sampled on many a previous occasion and that somewhat overwhelmed the appetizer of compassion he had only just tasted.

"Well, it might be criminal, but it is perfectly legal," he said brusquely. "Your sister—sorry, half-sister—has made it abundantly clear that she does not wish to renounce her share in the estate, and there's not a thing you or I or anyone else for that matter can do about it. Plus, I'm afraid there's—"

"Why, that miserable piece of shit," Clementine bawled, still standing, hands clenched, her foot now stomping furiously on the cold slate floor. "That drunken selfish pig. That poor excuse for a human being. That imbecile!"

"And he spoke so fondly of you," Mathilde drawled sarcastically, still sitting wrapped tightly in her trench coat, her disdainful eyes on the croissant flakes left over from her sister's breakfast.

"It is hardly your father's fault," Christophe insisted, noisily straightening his papers against the tabletop. "He is required by law to leave the bulk of his estate to his children, which brings us—"

"He did not speak fondly of me." Clementine forced her eyes

to rest on Mathilde, her voice low and hoarse. "He did not speak fondly of anyone. Not me, not you, not his lawyer, not our neighbors, not our pets, not a thing, no one."

"Well, I don't have any pets, and he was probably right about the neighbors, so I don't care. I'm just here to get my share of his precious champagne house."

"Please, Mathilde," Christophe attempted yet again, "you really should—"

"*His* precious champagne house?" cried Clementine over the top of him. "I've poured my whole life into this place, and now I'm expected to hand it over to a trumped-up city floozy who knows nothing about grapes, nothing about wine, nothing about—"

"I knew enough to get in one month what you'd been desperate for your whole pathetic life," said Mathilde, "and probably still are, you stupid fat cow."

"Ladies!" Christophe, who had two highly strung daughters aged four and seven, could spot a brawl brewing from a mile away. He leapt to his feet just in time to stop Clementine from clocking Mathilde over the head with the bread board.

"You horrible witch," Clementine bellowed, tears of rage squirting from her eyes. The bread board fell noisily to the floor, further alarming Cochon, who was huddled against the coal range, the whites of his eyes still rolling in the direction of Mathilde, about whom he had a very bad feeling. "Why did you have to come back? Didn't you do enough damage last time? Why do you have to do this to me?"

"I'm not doing anything to you, you ridiculous creature," Mathilde answered calmly, not a hair on her perfectly coiffed head ruffled as Christophe continued to physically restrain her enraged sister. "Why don't you save yourself the bother of an aneurysm and get used to the idea that I'm simply here to rightfully claim what is mine: one half of this crumbling old house, one half of that dreary spread of grapes, and one half of the contents of Olivier's cellars."

"But, *madame*," Christophe grunted with some force, pushing Clementine back toward the chair he had righted for her and attempting once more to take control, "that's what I have been trying to explain to you." Mathilde uncrossed her long, sheer denier-clad legs and then crossed them again, which made it extremely hard for him to concentrate.

She smiled to herself. Men, really. They were quite ridiculous. "Explain what, Monsieur Paillard?" she encouraged in her silkiest voice.

"That it's not half," he replied, feeling sweat develop on his upper lip that was not altogether to do with the promise of what lay at the top of those never-ending legs. He should have gotten this part out of the way sooner. What had he been thinking? Women! Would he ever understand them?

"Not half? Ha!" cried Clementine, a tremor of relief rumbling through her despair. The French succession laws were so complicated, she had never fully contemplated them, but of course there would be loopholes for situations such as hers. Of course. "Thank God!" She collapsed back into the chair, her rage deflating. "He did care," she said softly, picking at a pastry crumb on the table. "He did. I knew he did. He had to."

Mathilde's poise wavered slightly, and Christophe felt a surge of nausea as a steely glint flashed in her eye. For all Clementine's faults, among them extreme rudeness and truly terrible taste in clothes, she lacked the scent of danger that lurked deep in the chic Mathilde. Certainly, those American legs of hers had bewitched him for a while. He had found himself comparing his wife's short stocky ones quite unfavorably earlier in the car, wishing that she would dress more like a Parisian and less like a provincial mother of two. But his wife took in stray kittens. She cooked him *truite ardennaise* after a bad day at the office (hopefully, she would make it for him tonight). His wife delivered homemade raspberry jelly to new neighbors, even foreign ones, and chose his ties and ironed his shirts. His wife loved him to pieces and spent nearly every moment they were together showing it. Mathilde would do none of these things, he suspected. There was something missing in her.

The Peines were altogether a sorry bunch, he thought. Sorrowful by name and sorrowful by nature. The best he could hope for was that his part wouldn't take too much longer and he would escape without the need for surgical attention. Thus recognizing the urgent need to get a grip on himself and the business at hand, he swung into his well-practiced professional mode.

"I'm afraid that what I have to say will come as something of a surprise to you both," he said boldly. "I'm not sure how best to tell you, so I'll just come straight out with it."

Two sets of eyes bored fervently into him.

"Your father had another daughter."

A gasp, in stereo.

"Her name is Sophie Laroche. She was born in Paris in 1979 to Josephine Laroche, or Fifi as she was more commonly known. You might remember her, Clementine. She worked at Le Bois here in Saint-Vincent-sur-Marne for a year or so until . . . Well, anyway, your father was in limited contact with her for a while after the birth of the child, but Mademoiselle Laroche's whereabouts are currently unknown. My colleagues in Paris, however, are following a strong lead regarding young Sophie. I am expecting to hear from her anytime soon, and you should be prepared for the same."

Clementine had been struck dumb, but not Mathilde. "What the fuck are you telling us, you gibbering idiot?" she demanded, whipping her charm out from under the lawyer's feet so adeptly that he felt like a wobbling teacup on a magician's table. Oh, how right he had been to sense danger.

"I'm telling you that your father did not leave the House of Peine to you two," Christophe answered swiftly. "He left it to you three." The last word reverberated around the room like a horseshoe ricocheting off the pale brick walls. For the first time in nearly two decades Clementine and Mathilde met each other's eyes with something other than loathing. "Sophie, too, inherits an equal share," Christophe added with as much good cheer as he could fake.

"Why, that miserable piece of shit," Mathilde breathed.

"May he rot in hell," Clementine fumed.

"And may it take a long, long time."

"May it take forever!"

"No, forever isn't long enough. He should rot longer than that. For an eternity. For two eternities!"

Christophe felt an even more urgent need to go home and lavish his daughters with love and affection. You reaped what you sowed; the two disgruntled harpies sitting right in front of him were evidence of that. It was not their fault, he knew. Olivier was the tree; they were just the *pommes* that had not fallen far. Still, he did not want to be around them a moment longer. It was leaving a rotten taste in his mouth.

"A quarter of his kingdom," he said, standing up and patting his pocket for his car keys, "to each of his three delightful daughters. It's what your father wanted."

"Hang on, you," Mathilde said quickly, her voice bereft now of anything even approaching silkiness. "A *quarter* of his kingdom? To each of his *three* daughters? What about the remaining quarter? Who gets that? And if you tell me it's tiny Tonto here"—she flicked her perfect hairdo in Cochon's direction—"I will snap your head off at the neck and kick it into Epernay."

"Under French law," Christophe said, backing toward the hall now, his flat feet itching to break into a run, "your father was entitled to leave the remaining quarter to whomsoever he chose."

"And whomsoever did he choose, you silly little twerp?"

"He chose his grandchildren," Christophe answered, fervently hoping there would never be any. Then, before they could turn on him, he was gone.

Clementine and Mathilde stayed on opposite sides of the kitchen table, each frozen in their separate thoughts. Clementine's future, so rosy only hours before, had turned back to the same gray sludge as her past. Grayer, perhaps. More sludgy, definitely. She had to share her world with not just the heinous Mathilde but an entire other sister? And their *children*? She started to hum, quietly at first but with increasing vigor.

Mathilde, who had been so confident when holding the upper hand, was visibly rocked by this news of a wildcard sibling. The opportunity to come back to Saint-Vincent-sur-Marne had provided her with an escape hatch precisely when she needed one, but she did not require the added complications of a surprise Peine. As for the subject of children, had Mathilde been prone to humming, she might have done so with vigor herself.

Instead, she got up and went to the kitchen cupboards. "What do you have to drink around here?" she snapped as she slammed the cupboard doors open and closed. Cochon slunk around the outside of the room to get away from her, his dark eyes radiating deep suspicion.

Clementine ignored them both. The appetite that had abandoned her upon finding out her birthright had been carved into pieces returned most enthusiastically when she learned that her particular piece was little more than a sliver. She stopped humming, went to the ancient refrigerator, and pulled out a lump of moldy goat cheese and the crumbling remains of the *citron* tart she had been on her way to replace when her life had turned to ruin. Mathilde, meanwhile, found a bottle of Olivier's pastis and poured herself a healthy slug. She knocked it back in a single mouthful and poured another.

"How can you eat at a time like this?" she asked, grimacing as she watched Clementine combine the cheese and tart and head it toward her mouth.

"I told you not to speak to me," Clementine replied. "But since you mention the time"—she indicated the clock; it was not yet midday—"only wastrels and whores drink before lunch."

"Aren't you forgetting your father?"

"*Your* father," Clementine shot back.

Mathilde knocked back another swig. "Yes," she said sourly. "Our father. Who art in heaven."

La Racine

Olivier Peine, when it came down to it, was all that Clementine and Mathilde had in common, and it wasn't much to be getting on with for many reasons, not the least being that their separate experiences of the same person had been a million miles apart.

Mathilde had spent just four weeks out of her thirty-five years with the man, whereas Clementine had been stuck with him ever since her mother's death when she was a baby. The circumstances of this tragic passing were never discussed; in fact, Olivier would not allow any mention of her name (Marie-France), nor did he possess a single picture of her. To Clementine she was little more than a secret, rarely whispered word: *maman,* a blurry hummingbird of a presence that fluttered vaguely in the darkest recesses of her memory.

She could dimly recall other bustling shadows from her early years in the world: a grandmother who smelled of lavender and wet socks and whose sudden demise plunged the House of Peine even deeper into gloom; a whiskery old priest who never spoke at more than a murmur; a kindly neighbor in whose doughy bosom Clementine's toddler cheek had pressed itself.

Mostly, though, she remembered being on her own, the frightening sounds that came from her father's bedroom at night, the cold, the darkness, and the loneliness.

But when she was seven, Olivier, much to her surprise and no doubt everyone else's, had married again, this time to a young American college graduate who had come to Champagne to work the *vendange*. Clementine remembered Ann MacIntyre as a pretty, gangly, vivacious blonde. She had been in awe of her, this sudden intruder into her sheltered life, but had welcomed her. Some light, for a while it seemed, had filtered back into the House of Peine, and what a pretty place it was when that happened. Draperies were hung, quilts were patched, and floral posies appeared on clean, dusted surfaces. It was a blessed relief for such a serious, silent little girl, but still Clementine worried what Ann—sweet, foreign, happy Ann—could possibly see in the dry, moody, dark Olivier. And she was right to worry because whatever it was, it didn't take long for Ann to stop seeing it. Over two wet, misty Saint-Vincent-sur-Marne winters, Ann's vivaciousness leached into the chalky soil where depression only too readily took hold and blossomed in the ideal conditions of bone-chilling damp and seemingly eternal darkness.

For Clementine there was an unexpected upside, for in her wretchedness Ann sought the warmth she was no doubt being denied by Olivier. She would spend hours holding Clementine, hugging her close, rocking and weeping into that head of bright red untamed curls. Clementine, such a stranger to affection, misguided or not, silently soaked it up. Such was her own happiness that never in those last few months did she notice the bump that grew under Ann's sweater in direct proportion to the flow of her tears. Then one day a gray-haired American couple turned up at the house and took their miserably pregnant daughter back to New York, and that was the last they ever saw of Ann MacIntyre-Peine.

Clementine had been inconsolable, but Olivier merely shrugged and disappeared into the vineyard, and wordlessly Ann became just another name that was never to be mentioned again.

Not a year after she disappeared off the scene, though, a photo came, a photo of a fat, smiling, redheaded baby girl: Mathilde. Clementine had found the picture underneath a bottle lying next to the garbage can outside the kitchen and had squirreled it away in her underwear drawer. For a long, long time during her bleaker moments she would take that picture out and stare at it, imagining how much happier her life would be if only her little sister was there to share it.

As it was, happiness eluded her through her school years and past her teens. A trifle plump but pretty with eyes the color of chardonnay grapes, she was hindered by a shy disposition that disguised itself in the gruff family armor. Friends were a luxury she could not seem to afford. The closest she ever came to anything remotely resembling joy was on her own out among the vines, feeling the heat of a spring ray of sunshine, smelling the balmy summer fragrance of flower turning into fruit, shading her chardonnay eyes from the glare of the naked plants covered in a twinkling blanket of January snow.

Then one summer morning, not long after her twenty-sixth birthday, Olivier, more foul-tempered than usual, announced that the little sister he had never mentioned was coming to stay with them. Clementine, although taken aback, allowed herself a tingle of excitement. Could it be that at last the little Mathilde she had spent seventeen years dreaming of, that chubby, smiling baby, was about to come to life, to her life?

The creature that subsequently stepped moodily out of Olivier's rust- and apricot-colored *deux chevaux* was far from chubby and certainly not smiling. She was thin and exceptionally sulky. In fact, she took one look at the House of Peine, said, "What a fucking shit hole" in loud American, and then flounced inside, leaving Clementine to lug her bags upstairs to her room while Olivier melted into the winery. It became apparent soon after that she had been schooled perfectly in French and was just as colorful in that language.

It also turned out that Mathilde had been expelled from her smart Manhattan school for lewd behavior, and her mother, Ann, in desperation and to appease her most recent husband, had packed her off to France to make her someone else's problem for a while. There is no way the sisters could have known that they both battled the same stifling insecurities, that what had turned Clementine shy and clumsy had turned Mathilde caustic and hard. Clementine thought Mathilde unspeakably ungrateful for shunning the warm, comforting arms of her mother; and Mathilde thought Clementine a dowdy spinster in the making who had turned their no doubt potential Prince Charming of a father into the dark, uninterested force he appeared to be.

Worse, upon her arrival in Saint-Vincent-sur-Marne, Mathilde made it perfectly clear that she had no interest in grapes, wine, champagne, or certainly in Clementine, of whose existence, she claimed, she had been totally unaware until seeing her standing "all fat and sweaty" outside the crumbling house when she arrived.

A more robust adult might have recognized the psychology of a resentful teenager and ignored it, but the thin-skinned Clementine was cut to the quick. On cold nights she could still feel the warmth of Ann's arms, yet the woman had failed to mention so much as her name to Mathilde? Oh, yes, Mathilde assured her. Her mother loved and left stepchildren all the time. It was really no big deal in the United States.

For the first week or two Clementine fought nonetheless to find common ground, but Mathilde made sure there was none. The only thing she was truly interested in was sex, and this was a problem because sex was in short supply in Saint-Vincent-sur-Marne. Clementine of all people knew that because she had never had it. And she wanted it. Desperately and secretly.

With Benoît Geoffroy, the boy next door.

The only child of another sixth-generation *vigneron*, Benoît was two years her senior. A dark-haired, dark-eyed, solid young man of a serious nature, he loved the grapes and bubbles of Champagne every bit as much as Clementine did. Day after day the two worked at identical tasks in their neighboring wineries and on their adjoining plots of grapes dotted about the hills and valley, but both were so crippled with reserve that little more than embarrassed looks and the odd "more rain" or "another frost" had ever passed between them. This didn't stop Clementine from dreaming of more. She dreamed of it often in her creaking oak bed with the window open and nothing but fresh air and fantasies between herself and the object of her desires.

And she had dreamed of it more often than usual just prior to Mathilde's arrival because she had come the closest she had ever been to having her feelings for Benoît requited. She had sat five rows behind him at church one previous Sunday, totally transfixed by the back of his neck: the way his shirt was caught in the collar of his jacket, the downy confusion of his hairline, the tips of his ears. Afterward, outside on the steps as she shuffled into the sun with the rest of the congregation, she had felt a strange heat radiating from behind her, and turning toward the source had found it to be the man of her dreams.

His cheeks had burned instantly, and while he held her gaze for only a second, he had asked—well, it was more of a mumble, really—if she was going to the Saint Vincent's Day Parade that year.

Now this might seem an insignificant inquiry to a regular person, but remember that Clementine was far from regular. She had never been asked anywhere by anyone, let alone the man of her dreams, so although all she could do at the time was nod vigorously and scuttle away, the memory of his smell, his voice, and the soft little clutch of hairs he had missed shaving on his cheek kept her warm night after night after night.

Sophisticated Mathilde, used to leaving a trail of brokenhearted Manhattan boys in her wake, picked up on Clementine's weakness for Benoît straightaway, but to begin with did nothing more than file it for future reference. In the end, it was nothing more than boredom, sheer and simple, that one sunny afternoon prompted the taunt that would set in motion a devastating sequence of events, the aftershocks of which would resonate for years, were resonating still.

"I'd have him licking my toes in a minute," Mathilde had drawled upon catching Clementine gazing longingly at Benoît across a dozen rows of chardonnay. She had been idly watching her sister thin out the unripened bunches, leaving the vine to better nourish the ripening ones. It was mind-numbing work for most, but for Clementine it was a chance to further mother her canes, to encourage them to look after their healthy, fat, sweetening grapes, never mind the ones that stayed small and hard and green on shoots that had come too late to the party.

Mathilde was supposed to be helping but instead had been lying in the grass between the rows, smoking cigarettes and listening to a tape on her Walkman. It was only curiosity at what was so clearly distracting Clementine that got her to her feet where she followed her sister's adoring gaze and saw Benoît mirroring her bunch-thinning activities just a stone's throw away on his own plot.

Clementine ignored what her sister had said about Benoît's toe licking, her fingers continuing to move smoothly through the velvety leaves, but her heart hardened against her sister.

Mathilde was not the first setback of Clementine's life; far from it. But the chasm between what she dreamed of in a sister and the reality of it was so vast, it took disenchantment to a whole new level. Mathilde, for no apparent reason, loathed her and possessed that lethal combination of a sharp eye, an acid tongue, and a cruel streak that made it almost laughably easy to make another life a misery. The life she had chosen in this instance was Clementine's, and Clementine knew it but seemed powerless to fight it.

"Don't just stand there," she snapped nervously at her younger sister that day as she plucked one innocent stunted bunch off the vine a tad too viciously.

"Oh, I'm not just standing," Mathilde answered her, still looking over at Benoît, her head coquettishly tilted to one side, the tip of her moist pink tongue running itself around her practiced pout.

Clementine was hardly an expert in matters of seduction, but she recognized a full-fledged flirtation when she saw one. "He wouldn't be interested in you," she said, trying to sound casual and assured, but her panic was obvious even to her. "You're too young." Mathilde stood in front of her, hand on hip, one slender shoulder exposed, the curve of her breast rising and falling under her thin top, a sinful smile on her glossy lips.

Clementine had felt inadequate before but never more so than at that moment.

She had always known she wasn't a beauty queen but hadn't really noticed until Mathilde showed up exactly how frumpy, how uninviting she was in comparison. Mathilde would not leave the house without spending an hour applying perfect makeup to her flawless features. Clementine had one single lipstick that after nearly a decade of sporadic application had not even worn itself to a point. Mathilde blow-dried her hair every morning, whereas Clementine washed hers only once a week and even then couldn't always get a comb through it. Mathilde threw outfits together and looked like a fashion model; Clementine threw outfits together and looked like someone else had been doing the throwing.

She glanced down at her baggy brown skirt and oversized man's shirt, the vines forgotten for a moment. Was that why Benoît had done little but glance and mumble at her all these years, she thought? The inadequacy rumbled inside her. Had she been deluding herself that one day those mumbles would turn into conversations, the conversations into feelings, the feelings into marriage and motherhood and a whole new blend of champagne? Had he truly been asking her to the Saint Vincent's Day Parade or just politely inquiring if she was going? She had been so certain there was something between them, but now suddenly . . . Was it she in whom he would never be interested?

Mathilde exhaled her Gauloise smoke and watched all these

doubts unfold across the landscape of her sister's face. Clementine was very badly practiced at hiding her emotions, whereas Mathilde was an expert. She had seen three stepfathers come and go, and watched her mother's roller-coaster self-esteem rise and plummet with each one—and paid the price. There had been countless stepbrothers and -sisters (she hadn't been exaggerating about that, although her mother always grew far too fond of them). There had been more bedrooms than she could remember, a change of school most years, a change of friends most months. There was no point letting anyone get close, Mathilde had learned, because the moment you had everything you wanted, it could all be whisked away from you in the blink of an eye, the drop of a tear, the whistle of a coffee cup flying past an ear. It was better not to give anything away, to keep the world at arm's length, to show it a little of what you had but not let it get close. It was better that way. Her real father, Olivier, was plainly an expert at this, and she liked that—if nothing much else—about him. But Clementine, thought Mathilde as she watched her standing among the vines with her big moony eyes and her sad-sack body, wore her heart on her sleeve, which was no place for it. In her opinion, the big lump needed toughening up.

Mathilde stubbed her cigarette out in the grass with her foot, threw her Walkman into her shoulder bag, and then swinging her narrow hips with exaggerated grace, sauntered slowly past her older sister and down through the grapes, crossing the hillside and stopping on the opposite side of the row Benoît was pruning.

Clementine kept pulling at her own bunches, trying to be gentle, trying to pretend she hadn't noticed, which was quite ridiculous. How could she not notice? So many times she had wanted to saunter up to Benoît herself but had never had the courage. Trust that precocious little madam to make it look so easy! But surely Benoît had more sense than to be sucked in by a bony young shoulder and too much eye shadow. *Please, God*, prayed Clementine, *let him have more sense*.

She tried to keep her attention on her chardonnay grapes but could not, looking up just in time to see Mathilde fling her long skein of strawberry blonde hair in a single sweep from one side of her back to the other. A peal of her flirtatious laughter wafted across the hillside like tiny autumn leaves being scattered in the cool north winds. She was swiveling in a girlish fashion, both hands clasped innocently behind her back, and Benoît had stopped what he was doing, was standing up, wiping his brow, grinning foolishly.

"Ouch!" In her anguish, Clementine had nicked herself with the pruning shears. A bright red blob of blood dropped from her finger and wobbled on a quivering leaf before sliding lazily to the ground. Mathilde's laughter rang out over the vines again. The tiny autumn leaves turned to crystal and fell, brittle and shattering, at Clementine's feet. The wind carried another harsher sound then, a hearty boom, across the vines toward her. She dragged her eyes away from her bleeding finger and looked across at Benoît. His head was thrown back in obvious delight, and he was laughing as though he had never laughed before—which for all Clementine knew he had not. It was certainly not a sight she had yet seen nor a sound she had ever heard.

The clouds that up until then had been scuttering energetically across the blue sky seemed to freeze, the temperature plummeted, and the sound of her unrequited lover's amusement faded to an almost inaudible whisper. The words, the feelings, the dreams and desires that Clementine had secretly harbored for so long swirled out of her heart in one swift gurgle and were sucked down a deep black drain. It was unbearable. She bobbed down into a crouch, shame and rage burning her cheeks, and tears of humiliation springing to her eyes. There was a rip in her now bloodied skirt that she hadn't noticed before, and beneath it her pale leg was freckled, a patch of wiry golden hairs catching the sun. In that moment she hated herself almost as much as she hated Mathilde.

It was a monumental moment.

Nobody would argue that Clementine had led a grim life, but up until then she had not been a hateful person. She had felt sorry for herself, of course, with no mother, a difficult father, few friends, and a lot of hard work to do. Yet, despite this, her feelings had been turned inward. She felt unlucky, definitely; lonely, always. But it was a private matter as far as she was concerned, plus she had champagne—champagne that had flowed through Peine veins for centuries. And she had hope. Until the afternoon that Mathilde Peine-Myer-Stephenson-Burroughs sauntered past her with a wiggle in her walk and a glint in her eye and made Benoît Geoffroy laugh like a carefree schoolboy, she had hope.

She stayed crouched between the vines until her leg cramped and that torturous laughter faded to nothing but a cruel memory. When she stood up again, they were gone, and nothing would ever be the same.

Sophie

Weeks after delivering one poisonous Peine to the other, the two of them were still weighing heavily on Christophe Paillard's mind—and ringing in his ears. The sisters had undertaken a separate and random program of making extremely lengthy and unpleasant phone calls to his office in Epernay.

"Yes, yes, I'm terribly sorry, but there's nothing I can do. Please listen to me, Clementine. Please." He was currently attempting to extricate himself from one such barrage, but it was proving difficult. "Yes, well," he finally said over the top of her acrid combination of pleas and threats, "thank you, and the same to you. Good-bye." He hung up, which only made him feel more of a toad than he already did.

The worst thing was that he could not honestly begrudge her such anger. He didn't like it, of course. Who did like being called a stunted hairball with the scruples of a gutter rat? But he understood it. Deep down he truly understood it. She had labored over those eight hectares of grapes her whole life. She probably knew the composition of every square centimeter of soil, could tell you how much rain had fallen during each of her forty-four years, and possibly counted the bubbles in every bottle, knowing her. The

House of Peine was not just her home, it was her life, and while having to share it with one sister should truly not have derailed her quite so monumentally, divvying up with a third—well, the shock of it all, the disappointment, he could imagine how much that would hurt. Her frustration had to come out somewhere, Christophe supposed, and down the line to his ear was as good a place to unload as any, although he cursed the phone company for reconnecting the Peine line.

Mathilde's rage was a different matter; it was much harder to put a finger on, not that he wanted to put a finger, or anything else for that matter, anywhere near her. He had learned his lesson there. No, what puzzled him about Mathilde was that she already had a home, a career, a life—a successful one by all accounts—in New York. What did she care if her share in the House of Peine was smaller than she had anticipated? It was still a bonus to her, surely, whether it was a half or a third or a quarter. If he had known she was going to react so violently to news of Sophie, he definitely would have told her sooner despite that being contrary to Olivier's instructions, but he had wanted to tell Mathilde and Clementine together. In fact, he had assumed they would be pleased to find out there was another sibling. An only child himself, he had imagined how happy he would be to find out there was a secret sister for him out there somewhere—as long as she wasn't like either of the Peines, of course. Christophe felt a shiver run up his spine. What if Sophie was cut from the same cloth as those two? It didn't bear thinking about. The witches of *Macbeth* would have nothing on such a trio of harridans.

He looked out the window of his tidy little office at the bright spring sky and sighed. He had been trying to concentrate on conveyancing documents for an English couple in Montvoisin when Clementine had rung to shout at him, but the truth was he had been thinking of her anyway; he could not get the whole sorry Peine business off his mind. It wasn't just the calls; the matter had been haunting him ever since he drove his Renault down their dusty drive as though being chased by the ghost of Olivier himself.

And in a way he felt he was. That was the problem. It wasn't just the sour-as-boils sisters that irked him. They were only in this situation because of their miserable father. And it was thinking about that disagreeable old man that left Christophe with the nastiest flicker of—he coughed with embarrassment even though he was alone in his office. Yes, there was no doubt about it—guilt. That was why he could not shake off this dismal affair quite as easily as he might have wished.

It was not a lawyer's job to question a client in these sorts of cases; he knew that, especially when the client was a cantankerous old soak like Olivier. Why, you couldn't bid the man a simple *ça va* without getting an earful about the unsavory weather conditions and the beleaguered state of this and every other nation. But now Christophe wished he had paid more attention to what Olivier was doing with his will, offered some advice to the old curmudgeon. He should have made more of an effort, maybe, to warn Clementine what lay around the corner, to alert her to the existence of young Sophie. It wasn't his job; it wasn't his business. But if her own father wasn't going to tell her that she was being sidelined, who was?

Plus, now that there was absolutely no chance of being able to do so, Christophe found himself wanting to ask the old man what good could possibly come of combining his three alienated daughters around his crumbling near ruin of a house and a once grand winery on the brink of collapse. It went against the laws of nature to wish that kind of disaster on your progeny. And the old barnacle had not only wished it, he had orchestrated it, tying the tortured troika together for yet another generation. It was monstrous, really.

Christophe was jostled out of this depressing reverie by a timid knock at his office door. His so-called secretary was not in for the week because of some family drama, of which she had a seemingly endless supply.

"Come in," he called tiredly, pulling at his shirt collar. A scruffy boy in tartan trousers carrying a weathered rucksack slipped in through the doorway and stood nervously against the wall.

"Monsieur Paillard?" He realized then that it was not a boy at all but a girl, a young woman. "I have your business card," she said, holding it shyly in the air. She was very thin with jet-black hair that was cut short and stuck straight up from her head in chunky spikes. Her wide violet eyes were circled in thick black kohl, and her translucent skin gave her an erotically innocent look despite her dark purple lipstick and a cluttered collection of rings in one ear. The punkish camouflage did not toughen her at all, Christophe thought. Quite the opposite. She seemed to him as delicate as a pearl.

"How can I help you?" he asked, intrigued. "Is it a police matter?" She was wearing a tattered leather jacket and biker boots in a tiny size. People who dressed like her rarely landed in his office without its being a police matter.

"No," she said shyly, "I'm not in any trouble. I'm Sophie Laroche. Or Peine, I suppose. The lawyer in Paris told me about . . ." She faltered. "It's about the champagne house, you know? He said I should come to you."

Christophe's heart sank. The House of Peine truly was haunting him today. This strange little chick was Sophie? Those gargoyles over in Saint-Vincent-sur-Marne would chew her up and spit her out in no time at all. She was no match for them despite her tough nut visage. Not by a long shot. He could tell that just by looking at her.

"Of course. I have been expecting you," he said kindly, standing up and beckoning her. "For some time, yes. Although I thought you would call, but still it's a pleasure to meet you. Please, please, come in." She glided across the floor and settled herself in a leather chair facing him. She took up hardly any space in it at all.

"So what can I tell you?" he asked.

"Everything," she replied earnestly. "I want to know everything."

He smiled. "All right. Let me see. Where should I start? Well, you've spoken to my colleague in Paris, so you know that you have inherited one quarter of the House of Peine, and that your two sisters between them a half?"

She nodded. "Clementine and Mathilde," she enunciated clearly as though she had been practicing their names. Christophe, shuffling the Montvoisin conveyancing documents, did not meet her gaze.

"Yes, indeed. And you know that the House of Peine comprises eight hectares of grapes planted in chardonnay, pinot noir, and pinot meunier; the winery where the grapes are pressed and the wine is made; the cellars where the bottles are stored as they age; and the family home?" She nodded again, solemnly.

"Then you know all there is to know, really." Christophe spoke with a chirpiness that was not entirely authentic. "There's not much more to say. Unless there is anything in particular . . ."

"You must have known him," she said quickly. "My father. Olivier. I would like to know—well, it seems a strange question to ask—but . . . what was he like?"

This took Christophe by surprise, and he cursed himself for being so crass as to forget the offering of any commiserations. "Please accept my condolences. I'm so very sorry for your loss," he said, trying desperately to think of something nice to say. "Your father was, um, let me see. . . ." His mind drew blank after blank until he recalled that his mother, rather oddly he felt, had always thought kindly of crusty Olivier.

"He had a lovely head of hair," he grasped from the recesses of his memory. Sophie waited for more, but all that followed was an uneasy silence. Christophe pulled again at his collar, feeling sweat break out on his forehead. His summer vacation in Normandy suddenly seemed a long way away, and never had he felt more in need of it.

"Monsieur Paillard?" The quiver in Sophie's voice was enough to snap him back into business mode.

"Yes, yes," he said, sitting up and trying to act more professionally. "I'm sorry. I was just remembering the excellent champagne your father made, Sophie. Delicious always. He was a master blender, you know. He could get those three champagne grapes singing and dancing in perfect harmony, even after a disappointing harvest and in vintage years, well, many believe there is none better. His '88? I had the pleasure of tasting it only once, a business lunch at Les Crayeres." (He recalled a divorce settlement in Reims that had gone particularly well.) "But I remember the taste of it to this day—the way the pinot noir lingered on the tongue. Ah. Perfect with the beef."

Sophie was sitting forward, hanging on to his every word, and he desperately wanted to keep telling her things that would keep that glimmer in her beautiful eyes. But he remembered the scorching regret he had felt at waiting too long to deliver bad news to her sisters. It would be better to get it out of the way at once.

"Listen," he started briskly, "obviously I've already been to Saint-Vincent-sur-Marne and had a talk with Clementine and Mathilde about the contents of your father's will." Could she have even the vaguest clue what lay ahead, he wondered? "Sophie, I must be honest and tell you that your sisters did not take the news very well. Clementine worked with your father all her life, you see, and is having trouble adjusting to the thought of sharing the House of Peine with anyone else. As for Mathilde, well, she is perhaps not quite so emotionally attached, but she is, um, how would you say? Firmly attached nonetheless." He saw he was losing her; she was looking bewildered. So he stopped and took a deep breath. "They did not know about you, you see, so it's been something of a shock to learn they must split their inheritance with you. In fact, if I may speak frankly, Sophie, you should probably be prepared for some hostility. I don't want to be disrespectful in any way, but the truth is that your father, despite his lovely head of hair and magnificent skill as a *vigneron*, was toward the end of his life and even, truthfully, in the middle of it and perhaps also at the beginning, although I didn't personally know him then, something of a difficult man, and I think his daughters have inherited some of that. His other daughters, I mean. Your sisters."

Sophie flinched, and Christophe berated himself again for not treading more carefully. "Well, not so much difficult perhaps as complicated," he added quickly. It was the obvious one-size-fits-all choice of word when it came to describing any one of the Peines. "I'm sorry. I don't mean to distress you."

"Oh, it's not that," Sophie assured him. "It's just that I didn't know about them, either. I've never had sisters before. The word seems . . ." She searched for a way to put it. "Funny. Not related to me." She failed to get her own pun. "I mean, for all I know all the sisters in the world are hostile and difficult and complicated. And all the fathers." She allowed herself a sigh. "It's just so strange to think that the first I ever see of him he will be in a hole in the ground covered with dirt."

You don't know how lucky you are, Christophe thought. And before the day is out, you're probably going to wish your sisters were in there with him.

"I suppose you're on your way there now," he said brightly. "To Saint-Vincent? Do you have a car?"

Sophie laughed. "No, but I have a thumb." She held it out in a hitchhiking gesture, and Christophe looked shocked. What harm would come to this little poppet before she even got to her sisters?

"I won't hear of it," he said. "Wait until four and I will give you a ride there myself." He was expecting a call from the Montvoisin husband, otherwise he would have taken her straightaway. "A young girl like yourself out there on the roads, even here in Champagne, it's just not safe."

Sophie stood up and smiled at him. "Thank you all the same, but I think I'll go now," she said. "You don't need to worry about me, you know, Monsieur Paillard. I'm not a young girl, and I can look after myself. I've been doing it for a long time, and I'm really quite good at it." There was not the slightest suggestion that he should feel sorry for her. In fact, her tone was quite upbeat and optimistic. But he remembered the bread board fast approaching Mathilde's head and wondered just how long she would stay that way.

"If you're sure," he said, "but please promise me that you'll be careful. And if there's ever anything I can do for you, well, you have my card. Will you call me?"

She nodded. "There is one thing," she said awkwardly. "I don't have a map, and there doesn't seem much point in buying one since I only need to know the way to Saint-Vincent-sur-Marne once."

"Oh, there are plenty of road signs," Christophe told her. "Just head for Oeuilly, and once you're past it, you will see the statue of Saint Vincent up on the hill to your left. Take that turn, and the House of Peine is on the main road just before you reach the town. It has very grand blue gates, although a little past their prime."

"So that's west?" she asked.

"Yes, yes, take the N3."

"Off the roundabout with the wickerwork sculpture?"

"The N3, yes, as I say, but please be careful, Sophie. It's been a pleasure to meet you. Take care and good luck. Yes, indeed, the best of luck."

Floraison

A house painter from Saint Thierry dropped Sophie at the gates of the Peine property some time later that afternoon. She stood on the roadside marveling at them. She didn't notice the rust or the threadbare hedge, just the beautifully ornate ironwork and the neat rows of lush vines that grew on the gradual slope leading up to the château.

With a quickening heart she slipped through the gates (not recalcitrant for her at all: quite welcoming, in fact) and tramped up the drive, stopping in front of the badly patched front door to catch her breath and collect her thoughts.

Eventually, she rapped timidly on the boards, but when no one answered, she applied herself more robustly again and again until she finally heard high heels clicking their way toward her.

"What do you want?" Mathilde demanded upon wrenching open the stubborn door. She looked Sophie up and down and clearly found her lacking. "We have enough problems here without the village urchin showing up to scrounge for cash. Shoo. Get lost." And she slammed the door in her face.

But it was not the first door that had shut swiftly within an inch of Sophie's nose, and she had more reason than most to want it to open again. Once more she knocked. And once more. And once more.

"I've already told you," Mathilde said angrily when she finally jerked it open a second time. "Go away, or I'll call the *gendarmes*." She was about to slam the door again when Sophie stepped forward and put one small booted foot in the way.

"But I'm Sophie," she said, "the other sister."

Had she been expecting a warm welcome, a joyful embrace, an instant clasping into the family bosom, she would have been sadly disappointed. Luckily for her, she arrived on that doorstep not only armed with Christophe's recent warning but, thanks to her experience in life so far, with no assumption that anything would work out in her favor.

She felt nervous, of course. Who wouldn't? Barging into a totally foreign world belonging quite rightfully to someone else would churn up even the sturdiest of innards, and hers were no exception. However, Sophie approached this threat of danger as she did all others: with expert watchfulness.

Mathilde, she saw instantly, was one of those spoiled wealthy women who had everything but happiness. She had met many such matrons in Paris, and they all had that same expression on their faces, one of smoothed surgical satisfaction, yet there was a hunted expression in the eyes that suggested all was not as it should be and probably never would be. Mathilde was very thin, very beautiful, spent a lot of money on her hair, and was used to being loved but didn't feel the need to return it. There would be a rich husband somewhere, Sophie imagined, who adored her but most likely sought affection elsewhere.

Clementine was in some ways harder to categorize. After fol-

lowing Mathilde down the imposing hallway of the big house to
the kitchen, Sophie came upon her eldest sister sitting hunched at
the table feasting on a thick *mille-feuille* while a strange dog sat at
her feet waiting for pastry flakes.

"Sophie," Mathilde said rudely by way of an introduction,
adding a disdainful raise of her perfectly plucked eyebrows. "The
other sister. You know, the one we have been wanting so desperately to meet."

Clementine looked at the newcomer, her eyes dark and distrustful, as she stuffed another bite of the custard slice into her mouth
with weathered hands. The dog scrabbled out from under the table
and turned out to be a tiny horse. Sophie laughed delightedly, and
the horse trit-trotted straight over to her and rubbed the flat space
between its eyes on her leg by way of a welcome.

"Cochon!" scolded Clementine, but the horse kept rubbing.
"Cochon!"

A horse the size of a dog that was named for a pig? Sophie
could not help her amusement, but it was clearly not infectious.
Clementine did not look amused; she looked positively terrified.
But of what? Of whom? She was unhappy, too, but her unhappiness lay deeper, much deeper. She didn't wear it like a prickly
shield the way Mathilde did. What she did wear, though, was
not much of an improvement. She dressed like a person much
older and larger than she was, with layers of lumpy loud pat-
terns doing nothing for a passable figure. Untamed curls and no
makeup turned a pretty face into a bland canvas decorated only
with discontent. Clementine was not used to being loved. She had
no husband and knew nothing of affection. Sophie could see that
straightaway. Such misery!

67

Of course, she had every right to be miserable, and so did Mathilde. Their father had died, after all. Sophie felt unhappy about this herself, and she had never even met him.

"I know this must be a terrible time for you both," she said, gently pushing the little horse away and apprehensively sitting herself on a wobbly chair at the end of the kitchen table.

"You're not kidding," said Mathilde who was making her way through a bottle of pastis. "How did you get to be so small? What was your mother, a circus freak?"

Clementine snorted involuntarily and helped herself to another custard slice from some bakery paper on the table. She did not consider for a moment offering any to anyone else.

"She was a barmaid," Sophie answered pleasantly. "Medium-sized, pretty much."

Clementine snorted again and kept eating. An awkward silence mushroomed. Cochon retreated under the table again.

"This is a tricky situation, I realize that," Sophie eventually said. "Your not knowing about me, that I was even born, let alone . . . Well, anyway, I don't know anything, either. I mean absolutely nothing. Could you tell me, do you think?" It was like speaking into an empty well, but she had nothing to lose, so she kept on going. "I forgot to ask the lawyer in Paris. It all came as such a shock, and then today with Monsieur Paillard . . . So I don't even know. What happened to him? Olivier, our father. What happened?"

Clementine stopped chewing and stared rigidly at a spot on the opposite wall. Mathilde sensed her distress and moved instantly to exploit it.

"He was trying to mount a life-sized cardboard cutout of Juliette Binoche down at the local video store," she informed Sophie, "although they were on different sides of a pane of glass at the time—an important factor your father failed to take into account when he launched himself at the poor woman."

Sophie was stunned by the delight with which Mathilde was telling this woeful tale. "My father?" she asked timorously. "Yes, of course, you mean our father. But . . . Juliette Binoche? The actress? I don't understand."

"It's always about sex!" Clementine was on her feet, pastry flakes cascading down her worn checked shirt. "With you," she shouted at Mathilde, "it is always about sex!"

"No, Clementine, that is not the problem," Mathilde answered unfazed. "The problem is that with you it is never about sex. It never has been. And it probably never will be."

"Bitch!"

"Virgin!"

"Slut!"

"Virgin!"

"I hate you," shrieked Clementine, quite unhinged. "I hate you. How could he do this to me? That wicked old man. You can have him! You can both have him!" And with those shrill words she ran from the room, down the dark hallway, out into the courtyard, and into the rows of chardonnay that grew around the house, tears streaming down her cheeks and a roll of pale flesh popping out above her skirt as yet another reminder of how her awful life only ever got more awful. What is more, the traitorous Cochon stayed behind with the new sister, although it could have been the remaining *mille-feuille* that kept him glued to the kitchen. Still, to be abandoned by the only thing that ever showed her any fondness? It was too cruel. Clementine wailed a great gutsy sob, inhaling a huge gob of air in preparation for another one.

And then it hit her.

She stopped in her tracks and took in another deep breath through her nose. Yes, yes, yes! A thousand times yes. There was absolutely no doubt about it: the air out among the vines was ever so slightly greener, sweeter, than it had been before. Clementine swallowed her sobs, wiped at her wet cheeks, and moved toward the closest vine, Valentina, the fourteenth. At such close inspection her hopes were confirmed. Her tears dried, her paunch tightened, and her heavy heart lightened and fluttered. The vines had started flowering. Their journey from shoot to fruit was beginning!

This was a magical moment for a *vigneron* because *floraison* determined everything about the harvest. A poor flowering, and it would be *bonjour* Joliet; a healthy flowering, and the House of Peine had a shot at a future.

She had been expecting it, of course, the sooner the better, but she had been so bogged down with hard labor in the winery that this monumental leap forward had all but escaped her. The flowering of a grapevine was not the most sensational thing to see, after all. In fact, it was all but invisible to the casual observer and so unspectacular as to escape the notice of even the local bird life. The only truly sensual aspect of flowering was that smell: a sweet, pungent odor that Clementine could always detect ahead of anyone else in the vineyard. She breathed it in again, the hysterics of just minutes before forgotten as she scuttled up the rows inspecting her canes, congratulating them on their itty-bitty bunches, and savoring the promise that now danced in the air.

Volonté

Sophie, stuck in the kitchen with the moody Mathilde, knew nothing of the change in temperament occurring outdoors. Clementine's hysterics had shaken her, and she had seen plenty other hysterics in her time. She had stood as her eldest sister fled, uncertain as to what she should do. "Should I go after her, do you think?" she asked Mathilde. "She seems so upset."

"She is upset, you idiot," snapped her sister. "But it's nothing to do with 'our father' and his tragic passing if that's what you think. It's because she thought she was going to end up with this whole dump all to herself, and now she has to share it not just with me but with you—whoever you are."

Sophie sat down again. She felt hopelessly out of her depth and sorry for these two sad cases into whose lives she had parachuted. On the bright side, at least there were no knives involved. She had found herself in the middle of fights worse in the past and even had a ten-centimeter scar down one thigh to prove it. She may as well simply plow on.

"So did he cut himself?" she asked, returning to the subject of her unknown father. "After hitting the pane of glass? Is that what happened?"

"No, he didn't cut himself," Mathilde answered in a bored voice. "He fell and then was too drunk to get back up again, and no matter how loudly he called for Juliette Binoche, she simply refused to come and help him. Those screen goddesses can be very selfish like that, you know, especially the cardboard cutout ones. Instead, it was the frost that came and got him. Yes, it was the frost that killed Olivier Peine." She started to laugh, which further bewildered Sophie.

"You think it's funny?"

"I think it's hilarious! Frost is the enemy of champagne," Mathilde answered. "Even I know that. I just didn't realize it was the enemy of the *Champenois* as well."

Sophie didn't know how to respond. She found Mathilde frightening: thought she preferred the hysterical Clementine. But weren't you supposed to like all your sisters equally? Not pick favorites? Or was that just mothers and children? She felt wretchedly undereducated in the business of being part of a family.

"You have a strange accent," she said to Mathilde by way of changing the subject. "Where are you from?"

"Mind your own business. I'm from here now."

"I'm sorry, I didn't mean to—"

"And I suppose you're from here now, too? Well, no surprises there. It would be too much to hope that the daughter of a drunken *vigneron* and a slut of a barmaid would ever amount to anything. You certainly don't strike me as someone with a lot of other places to go."

Sophie blushed more with shame than anger. Mathilde was right. She had not amounted to anything and had nowhere else to go.

"Well, I'm sorry—" she started to say.

"Don't apologize to me," Mathilde cut her off, throwing back what was left in her glass and standing to leave. Cochon scrambled to his feet again and warily eyed her stilettos, causing Sophie to wonder if in the past he had perhaps felt the point of a shoe in the spongy pad of his rump.

"I didn't mean to—"

"I said save your breath," snapped Mathilde. "Really, I don't give a shit. You can do what you want, whoever you are, wherever you're from. You are of no interest to me, none at all. I could not care less." She turned on her heel, snatched the bottle off the table, and teetered out of the room.

Sophie had been made to feel small before, many times, and she felt small to begin with, so she needed whatever size she could lay her hands on. But to have Mathilde belittle her like that, dismiss her like that, well, it hurt. She had no expectations of her sisters in particular, but she had expectations of people in general even if they were low, and while cruelty certainly figured, it was usually delivered by someone of no fixed abode in response to an act of drug-induced treachery. From a sophisticated beauty who was actually flesh and blood it cut deeper than any knife ever could. Had Mathilde guessed that Sophie's biggest fear was that she was of no interest to anyone? Not another living soul? That she lay awake at night trying desperately to gather together in her head a collection of people who cared whether she lived or died?

Sophie slumped forward, her head on the table, and turned so her cheek lay flush against the cool wooden surface. Then with her hands lying flaccidly in her tartan lap, she cried.

What an idiot she had been to come on her own! She didn't know what to do, how to handle such a situation. She should have brought her friend Francesca or Xavier, her ex-boyfriend, or even

Rico, the boyfriend before that. They all had families even if they had chosen to leave them. She, on the other hand, had not even been able to hang on to her mother, a softhearted catastrophe who had hurtled from one misfortune to the next, be it a boss, a boyfriend, or a crooked slum landlord, until finally disappearing off the scene altogether when Sophie was twelve.

Since then, Sophie and families had not worked out that well. She had been farmed out to a succession of foster parents, but the story was always the same. First, there would be trouble in the classroom, and then in the playground, and before long there would be trouble at home, too. At fifteen it just seemed easier to melt into the backstreets of Paris and go her own way. The friends she made there were more like her; there were fewer expectations, fewer disappointments. Life was just a matter of day-to-day, hand-to-mouth existence. Hunger, foraging, food. Cold, foraging, warmth. It wasn't complicated. And if sometimes she was hungrier or colder than she wanted to be, at least she was never hungry or cold on her own.

For a while there she had even had a job at the Guerlain counter in Le Bon Marché department store. Francesca worked there and had managed to get her a few hours a week restocking the shelves. Then one day when Francesca was out having a long lunch, Sophie had stepped in to do a makeup job for a particularly persnickety client who had been quite enamored of the results. The Guerlain manager, a frosty fifty-something who had earlier hissed at Sophie to stay hidden so her gothic ragamuffin look didn't scare the customers, had changed her tune when other persnickety clients started asking for her by name. Sophie was promoted from part-time in the basement to full-time on the shop floor.

She had loved that job with all her heart and soul, had loved getting up every morning and having somewhere to go, somewhere like Le Bon Marché where just eyeing the tiny pastries in the chic customer café gave her the greatest of thrills. And there was the Guerlain counter: all those colors, all that bronze and gold and scarlet and primrose and purple, those shimmering eye shadows and lip-licking glosses. A hundred different shades of flesh! Fourteen different blacks! Surrounded by such a living kaleidoscope of blushes and hues, she was in her element. In fact, she discovered what her element was.

After her first few paychecks she had even moved into a proper apartment, a tiny overcrowded five-story walk-up in Montparnasse but, still, she had actually started to think maybe she could live a normal life like the customers on whom she applied her exquisite makeup. Daring to even dream this was a big step for Sophie because up until then she had assumed that her lot in life had already been carved out for her and that it did not involve a comfortable bed, dry walls, regular meals, and belonging.

It was the belonging that thrilled her the most. Belonging to the working crowd. Before, when she had walked the passageways of the Métro in her old uniform of ripped clothes, worn boot soles flapping, passersby would avoid her eye. It was clear from the way they stepped away from her or pulled their clothes closer to their bodies what they thought: filthy vermin, homeless orphan, beggar, thief. But when she took the very same subways in her black jacket bearing her gold name badge, her fellow Parisians looked at her and smiled, thinking, "Oh, she's from the Guerlain counter at Le Bon Marché." It was a marvel for Sophie. Too good to be true, she often suspected. And she was right.

One afternoon the frosty fifty-something discovered money missing from the till, and Sophie, with her vagabond's police record, had seemed the ideal candidate to blame. Her employer did not recognize her talent enough to believe her pleas of innocence. The job was history. So was the apartment. So was her dream of a normal life.

She had been back on the streets almost a year, had felt the rush of air in front of many a door being slammed in her face since then, had been just about to give up hope for the first time ever when a man in a suit, a lawyer, appeared out of nowhere and told her she had inherited part of a champagne house and two sisters.

Naturally, she had assumed he was joking. But he had a fistful of official documents and had been most persistent. He had bought her three hot chocolates, one after the other, at Angelina's on the rue de Rivoli, insisting: "It's true. Trust me, it's true."

And so Sophie had headed for Epernay and the office of Christophe Paillard, and now here she was in a home—yes, a home—that was partly hers, yet she was more clueless and lonely and afraid than she had ever been before.

An oversized tear dripped onto the ancient oak table and slid woozily between two worn beams. She felt so small, she was certain she could slip in there with it, as temporary as a teardrop, as insignificant as a microbe of dirt.

But the wonderful thing about having a history filled with low moments was that Sophie knew this one, like the others, would pass. There was simply nothing to be gained from clinging to them. If she had learned that great expectations were never worth having, she had also learned that just when life seemed at its most appallingly grim, it got better.

"That's bullshit," Francesca had once told her. "You just get used to how much it sucks so that it *seems* better." Which in Sophie's eyes was exactly the same thing.

She had been crying on the Peine kitchen table for less than two minutes when she felt the warmth of Cochon's flank on her leg as he slumped beside her chair. A germ of optimism started radiating in her belly.

A heartbeat later her tears ran out. She dried her eyes and helped herself to the rest of Clementine's *mille-feuille*. It was delicious.

Eté

Remuage

It was a magnificent day in the Marne Valley, the sort that gave summer a good name, but far from enjoying it, Clementine was hiding in the darkness of the winery *cave*, hyperventilating quietly at her *pupitres* as she riddled with trembling hands.

Forty-four years she had lived in the Peine château, and in all that time barely one speck of dust had changed, yet now she hardly recognized the place. It may have been a broken-down old hovel full of drafty holes and fur balls, but that was the way she liked it.

Now there were two sisters injecting their presence into her home like arsenic—slowly, in small amounts, so that no single dose was lethal, but after all these weeks, Clementine was choking. All these weeks? She clutched at the riddling rack to steady herself. It seemed inconceivable.

Mathilde had arrived with such a small suitcase, Clementine had been certain her visit would be sour but at least short. Yet here she still was, invisibly tidying and straightening the house behind Clementine's back, arranging the kitchen crockery by color; sweeping the familiar grime from the stairs, and lining up her empty bottles in a uniform fashion outside the kitchen door instead of throwing them out the window the way Olivier had.

Unconsciously, Clementine had shifted her routine to avoid her sister. She skipped the bathroom when she knew Mathilde would be using it, stayed in her bedroom when her unwanted guest was in the kitchen, and returned from the winery only when she could see from the courtyard that the upstairs lights were switched on.

When their paths did cross, Clementine found herself so twisted with pent-up rage that should she open her mouth to speak, her recriminations stayed lodged in her throat like pebbles. Mathilde had wafted past her one evening wearing a peach-colored peignoir, everything about her impeccable, clean, glowing, and all Clementine could do was stand there openmouthed and quivering. She could suddenly feel the dirt beneath her fingernails, the cobwebs in her hair, and the unplucked sprawl of her own eyebrows. But she could not speak. All she wanted to know was when Mathilde was going back to her life in America, but the more time passed, the more she was afraid of the answer, and the less she found herself able to ask the question.

Then Sophie had turned up.

Clementine's hands froze on the two bottles she was turning as she fought to catch her breath.

The littlest Peine had been there for weeks herself now, flitting around like a frightened moth, picking things up, putting them down, fluttering in and out of Clementine's eye line. It was . . . well, Clementine didn't know what it was. She was a prisoner of her own ineptitude. Her torment sat heavily on her chest like an old cat, drooling and ugly. She could not move it. How could she bring herself to talk to that little *mademoiselle* when there was another bigger madam with whom she already had not dealt?

One day not long ago she had gone out to the washing line to hang up her week's worth of large threadbare underpants only to find Sophie's tiny, tatty thongs already hanging there next to Mathilde's fancy silks and satins. This had seemed to her the last straw, and she had bawled like a calfing cow, tears of pain and frustration coursing down her cheeks as she fell to the ground, beating it with her fists until she felt her arms would break. Cochon was the only one who witnessed this. Actually, it was the high point of his day.

After this Clementine started to recognize even more signs of someone else with no plans to move on: the leather jacket always hung on the rusty nail inside the back door, and the same chipped green cup used day after day. The odd little something from Bernadette's *patisserie* even turned up here and there. It was infuriating, of course it was, this invasion of her privacy, but perhaps it was less infuriating than the unwelcome military neatness Mathilde was imparting. A symmetrically intimidating stack of Italian *Vogue* magazines on a repolished hall table was one thing; a jam jar of wildflowers on the kitchen table was another.

In truth, Clementine had to admit that the littlest Peine did not exude anywhere near the same poison as the middle one, but this did not mean she could or would speak to her. She wanted nothing to do with either of these two interlopers!

A sob escaped her, and those hands, usually so steady, lost their rhythm. A bottle fell to the floor, painfully hitting her foot and rolling, unbroken, away from her.

There was only one reason that her sisters were still there, and jam jars of wildflowers or not, she was a fool to keep ignoring it. They weren't there for the champagne, of that she was sure. Mathilde claimed it gave her a headache, and Sophie had probably never even tasted it.

Money. In the end, it was going to be about money.

Clementine had been tending her vines these past few years, but, as she had recently discovered, Olivier had not been nurturing the family finances. She had tried to make sense of his office but didn't need to decode the scribbled messages and random calculations in his wine-stained ledger to see just how close to ruin they were. Unopened bank statements littered the floor, unpaid bills decorated the desk, and countless pieces of correspondence suggested that many customers who had faithfully ordered Peine champagne for years had more recently stopped bothering. There were letters of complaint at gross delays, mix-ups over addresses, and clear evidence that order after order had simply not been delivered and thus not paid for.

In other words, there was no money.

Enough payments limped in from sales of the existing stock to keep Clementine from starvation, but if her sisters wanted to be bought out, there was no way on earth she could manage it—not without caving in to old man Joliet. Selling off chunks of her carefully tilled Peine soil to that old *mec* would be the only way she would ever come up with the money required.

Pictures of her Peine ancestors crowded Clementine's jumbled mind. They had battled the likes of Henri Joliet for centuries—and won—and would roll in their graves and most likely seep out from the Saint-Vincent-sur-Marne churchyard and haunt her into her own should she be reduced to selling off any of her precious plots. And, anyway, how would she ever choose which grapes to sell and which to keep? It was an impossible task, like choosing which child to hand over to enemy soldiers.

Another bottle crashed to the ground through Clementine's shaking fingers, this one shattering, its lively *mousse*—the teenage bubbles—confidently forging tiny instant pathways in the *cave*'s uneven floor.

Flawless Mathilde would probably ruin them just for the fun of it, but Sophie looked like someone truly in need of money. She had a few cents to her name, obviously, which were funding her trips to the *patisserie*, but her clothes looked about to disintegrate, and there was barely enough meat on her bones to keep out the chill that clung to the walls of the house even though summer had arrived in the outside world.

Clementine's sobs gained momentum as she watched the spilled champagne travel farther away from her. All at once she was desperate to escape the cool air of the winery and abandoned her riddling, scuttling up the spiral stairs to seek comfort in the warm open arms of her vines.

Outside in the courtyard she all but fell on top of Patric Didier, the cooper's son, who was chatting animatedly with Sophie. The Didiers had been producing barrels longer than the Peines had been producing champagne—it was a sign of the house's once great reputation that they kept returning—but on this occasion, in her angst, Clementine had forgotten they were due.

"My father can't be here today," Patric told her after she burbled a muffled greeting, hiding her face with a series of eccentric hand gestures so that no one could see her tears. "He's asked me to mend your barrels, and your delightful little sister here says she's going to help me."

Clementine felt fury chase her anxiety from the tips of her toes to the top of her head where it escaped into the air with a sharp crack through the crinkles in her hair. That little minx! Only here five minutes and no doubt throwing herself at poor Patric. She knew from the unpaid bills on Olivier's desk that the Didiers were owed for the last three years of Peine cooperage, so if Sophie put one finger wrong . . .

Sophie heard the crack, or at least picked up on her anger. "Unless there's something you would like me to do for you, Clementine," she offered, her violet eyes wide and innocent.

Half-strangling an anguished cry, Clementine pushed rudely past the young pair and scurried over to her bike.

"She's a regular charm school graduate that one," remarked Patric. "What a fright you must have gotten to discover she was your long lost sister."

"Oh, she's not so bad," Sophie said charitably as she watched Clementine pedal away. The truth was, she did not think that she had discovered Clementine at all. In fact, she still knew very little about either of her sisters despite finding herself living in the same house as them. They acted as if she was invisible, so she acted that way, too, hiding herself in a gloomy little bedroom with a sagging but nonetheless cozy bed, creeping around close to the walls of the ramshackle house like a beaten puppy, slinking in the shadows of the winery, sniffing the vats, and running her thin little fingers along the rows and rows of bottles in the *cave.*

She had loved exploring the old house and was entranced by its nooks and crannies, its rooms full of forgotten furniture, its bookshelves heaving with old volumes and aged magazines. She loved the different creaks on the staircase, the rattles in the walls, the echo of leaking water hitting bare boards somewhere up in the attic. These sounds were not reminders to her that the house had seen better times. She simply rejoiced in hearing the same thing day after day, in seeing the same whorls of dust collected in the same corners, the same dead fly in the same abandoned spider's web.

This was how a home spoke to its inhabitants, she assumed, how it murmured lightheartedly of its aches and pains. It just wanted its occupants to know how it felt, to keep them in touch. She took to patting the peeling walls as she climbed the stairs, as if to say, "All right, I hear you." She wanted the house to keep her.

Unsurprisingly, perhaps, the room she loved most was her father's. The smell of the tobacco he had smoked in there seeped out of the walls, and she could not breathe in deeply enough when she first slipped inside the door to hunt for any sign of the man he might have been. There was none or at least very little. He smoked roll-your-owns, drank pastis, was not allergic to dust, and didn't feel the cold. All this she picked up from the evidence left beneath his bed. There were papers, ash, bottles, and dust balls the size of tumbleweeds but no slippers. It wasn't an awful lot to know about a person, she had thought that day as she straightened up and looked around the room.

She had wondered a lot about her father over the years. Of course she had; everyone who grows up without one does whether they admit to it or not. She had gathered from her mother that he was not exactly a knight in shining armor, but on the rare occasions when Josephine had spoken of him, and never by name, she had seemed to feel more pity than anything else. All men were bastards, apparently, but Sophie's father no more or less than any other.

"You certainly couldn't say he ruined my life," Josephine had said more than once. "It was ruined already."

Anyway, Sophie had been lurking around the shadowy corners of her new home (what a luxury that thought) and surrounding vines for quite some time and was hungry for conversation when Patric Didier drove up to the door. He was easy on the eye, the cooper's son, a little younger than she, perhaps, and tall, fair, slim, with sparkling blue eyes and a slightly wicked grin. She felt it the moment she looked at him, that jump in her chest, that chemical jolt igniting a spark of hope. But something in his wicked grin, the way he looked at her without really seeing her, stopped her from being too drawn in. She had been drawn in by the likes of him before, after all, and it had rarely gotten her anything but heartache, which she could ill afford at that moment. When he suggested they meet later in the day at Le Bois, she simply smiled and shrugged her narrow shoulders.

Désespoir

Mathilde swatted at the faded pink curtains as she watched from her window while some lanky lout flirted with Sophie in the courtyard. Something about her younger sister pulled at her insides, adding to the anger that swirled there already. She reached for a Xanax, tossing it down with a mouthful of pastis, trying to drown out that feeling, whatever it was.

Down below she saw Clementine emerge from the winery like an old crab, recoiling at the sight of Sophie and the boy, waving her pincers around madly in the air and then heaving herself onto her bike. That silly fat creature with her ugly hair and frumpy clothes, thought Mathilde, her discomfort easing as she did, she was just so easy to loathe!

She stepped away from the window and slumped into the rickety wooden chair, the only piece of furniture in the room other than the bed and termite-ridden armoire. She kicked off her high heels, stared at the water-logged ceiling, and waited for the Xanax to start working its magic. Numbness. That was what she craved. What was taking it so long?

Her eyes slid down the once pretty rosebud wallpaper to her suitcase sitting on the floor and next to it to her cell phone, its battery flat, its charger still in her case. She had been keeping in vague contact with her office using her BlackBerry but felt the importance of work drifting away from her. She had thought it would be a struggle, letting work go, but it hadn't been, not at all. They could cope without her; that was what she had decided. And it was about time, too. She had mollycoddled the overpaid namby-pambies far too long.

Home, though, that was a different matter. She had thought letting go of that would be a blessed relief, and to some extent she was right. Just twice she had called, both times when she knew no one would be there, and had left businesslike messages saying there was much to be done at the House of Peine and she couldn't be spared in the circumstances and didn't know when she could be. She had felt a surge of power after each of those phone calls, but in its wake had been the beginnings of that nagging itch she couldn't quite understand. Wasn't this exactly what she had been dreaming of these past years? Wasn't this what she had been so desperate for?

Mathilde closed her eyes with an irritated sigh. She had imagined her escape so many times, but until that call from Paillard, it had seemed impossible. Thanks to him, though, or thanks to Olivier's stupidity at the video store, she had actually been able to do what she had longed for all this time. She had found the perfect excuse. Remarkably, when it came down to it, she had been able to shrug off her old life as easily as an Armani coat.

Her eyes flickered spasmodically beneath her closed lids. She had done it, she had fled, she had succeeded. Yes, the tiny voice that belonged to the nagging itch was saying, you got what you wanted. So why, it whispered with a determination she could not fail to hear, do you still feel *the same*?

"Fuck you," Mathilde said out loud, standing up and slipping back into her shoes, deciding to take her aggravation elsewhere. "Fuck all of you."

A little while later, out among the vines, Cochon leaped nervously to his feet and started dancing on the spot like a tiny Lippizaner as the familiar rattle of the family *deux chevaux* drew nearer. Clementine stopped what she was doing, her eyes growing smaller and darker as the car stopped and Mathilde climbed out, stepping daintily through the pinot meunier to reach her.

The miniature horse did not wait around to see if she had her pointy stilettos on; he simply turned and headed for the hills. "Cochon!" Clementine called after him, but she couldn't really blame him. Had she been able to move that quickly in the opposite direction to Mathilde, she would have. "Don't worry," she whispered, consoling the cane she was working on, Cecile, the eighth. "But don't listen, either." She had yet to share a civil word with her sister and doubted she was about to start now.

"That chandelier that used to hang in the living room," Mathilde demanded without preamble. "What happened to it? I want to . . ." Her jaw dropped open as her eyes moved down her sister's body. "Clementine, what the hell are you wearing? Didn't we used to have a chaise covered in that pattern? We did. Yes, we did. My God, you look like a sofa!"

Clementine felt tears form instantly behind her eyes. She had made the pinafore she was wearing with material she had found in the attic. Maybe the old chaise had been covered in it. Maybe that's why she liked it. But she didn't want to look like a sofa!

Nobody before had ever noticed or cared how she looked. Why did Mathilde take such pleasure in bringing these things up?

"Can't you see I'm busy," she gulped, clipping at some heavy leaf growth that was hindering Cecile the eighth's berry formation. "Just go away and . . ." She scrabbled for a clever aside, a cutting jibe, the sort of tongue lashing she could normally dish out so easily to total strangers. ". . . file your nails or whatever it is you do." As usual, Mathilde's very presence sucked her dry of any semblance of wit.

"Yes, that's right, Clementine. I got to be head of my own PR company just by filing my nails. That's how it works in the real world. Just ask my clients. Calvin Klein, heard of him? Oh, why am I bothering? Look, just tell me where the chandelier is and—" Something distracted her, and she looked over Clementine's head to the hillside beyond, shading her eyes and peering dramatically in that direction.

"Is that . . . ? Oh, my God. Benoît? He still lives next door? Yes, I suppose he does. Why, he's hardly changed a bit. Just look at him. It's as though time has stood still!"

This was simply too much for poor Clementine. It had been such a worrisome day, and she was already at the end of her tether. The tears she had been resisting since the sofa taunt burst their barriers and began to flow down her cheeks.

"Well, that's not very neighborly of him," Mathilde continued, quite unaware of her sister's distress, "not even coming to visit in all this time. How rude. And us so tragically bereaved. What's going on, Clementine? Have you had a falling out?"

Clementine could not speak, but Mathilde was still not looking at her and did not notice.

"Well, there's only one way to get to the bottom of this," Mathilde said, and once again those narrow hips just sashayed right past Clementine's round ones, taking her long lean legs in the direction of Benoît Geoffroy.

This time Clementine did not stay to watch. She would rather take her pruning shears and slit her wrists. Instead, she apologized brusquely to Cecile, jumped on her bicycle, and with one hand stuffed in her mouth to stifle the wail that was trying to escape, she pedaled home as fast as she could, her sofa dress billowing in the wind like a giant beanbag chair, her face unrecognizable as she battled tears that felt as if they would flow forever.

It was happening again. The worst day of her miserable life was being repeated with the exact same cast of characters. Of all the possibilities she had imagined in the past years, she had not even considered one as unbearable as this. And she had spent many long, lonely nights considering.

It was Sophie who found her several hours later lying in the *cave* behind the oak barrels of Olivier's 1999 reserve pinot noir, widely considered to be his last great work. She was sobbing still, teetering on the brink of a hysteria that comes only when a well-preserved stew of suffering is stirred up with a pinch of fresh pain.

When her eldest sister missed lunch, Sophie thought it odd, but when supper time came and went and still there was no shuffling of old scuffed boots, no clinking of the cutlery drawer, she became concerned and went looking for her.

Once she found the discarded bicycle lying by the vegetable patch, with clippers and a half-eaten pastry spilled from its basket, it didn't take long. She heard the sobs from the open hatch in the winery floor where Cochon lay slumped and sad, and simply followed the wretched noise to where she found Clementine lying in a crumpled floral heap in a cramped dark space behind the '99.

In her short but colorful life Sophie had been witness to many a heart in the process of breaking. She could recognize the signs from a hundred paces. And she could tell that this was not the sound of a fresh break. Whatever horror lay at the bottom of Clementine's pit of despair had been there for quite some time she was sure.

Far from launching a dramatic rescue, Sophie simply crawled in beside her sister, just a hairsbreadth from touching her, and, sitting squashed up against the cellar wall, she pulled her knees to her chest and hugged them. She said nothing, just watched that desolate body heave with misery, waiting for the right moment, if it came, to do anything more. She wasn't sure at first if Clementine even knew she was there, but eventually the heaving receded to more of a hiccup and the hoarse weeping to a staccato moaning the sound of which echoed eerily around the chalk walls of the *cave*.

This took maybe half an hour, but Sophie was a patient soul. She filled in the time observing the way the colors in the flora on Clementine's dress changed with the rise and fall of her sobs, the pink turning to mauve, the lavender to indigo, and the purple to black as it caught and lost the dim light at different angles. They were hydrangeas, the flowers, Sophie thought—full and lush and beautiful like the ones she had seen so often at the market on boulevard Edgar Quinet in the sixth *arrondissement*. She imagined choosing a scarf from her friend Enrique's stall, a green one, perhaps, to pick up on the little bits of foliage scattered over Clementine's crumpled form. Or a lilac one to bring out the flowers' prettiest color. She would wrap it up in tissue paper the color of clotted cream, tie a soft pink ribbon around it, and thread a bouquet of dried lavender through the bow. She would give it to Clementine.

At this she realized the moaning had drifted into a lull of sorts; the hydrangeas were not moving as far or as fast. She wriggled ever so slightly closer, sat there for a few silent moments, and then reached her small hand over to Clementine's rounded shoulder and gently, gently, gently lay it there, as soft as a feather.

Clementine's body resumed its shuddering under Sophie's caress, but she did not shake her sister off or shout at her to leave. Whatever unhappiness lurked deep inside her was so desperate to escape, Sophie could all but feel it frantically clawing under those hydrangeas. She just kept soothing, her strokes getting longer, her palm pressing gently but firmly on that unhappy garden, until she managed to draw out each of her sister's anguished breaths for a moment longer than the last.

Soon Clementine was calm. The *cave* was almost noiseless, so black, so still, and so dense it felt to Sophie—who had spent many cold winter afternoons huddled in the chapels of Saint Sulpice—almost like a confessional.

"I had a baby," Clementine whispered into the pool of darkness still occupied by that thought. "Amélie." She murmured the name so softly, it was like rain falling in the sunlight; you could only be certain it was there if you caught it at the right angle. Even then, despite its being only a fraction louder than silence, it was the loudest she had ever said it. *Amélie*. The word bounced around the great empty cavern of her heart, chasing away any possibility of the hum she usually relied on to keep such things well buried.

Then came the memory of delivering that perfect squealing little body all those years ago. She had blocked it out for so long that she had started to believe it had all been a dream, a misty half remembrance of somebody else's tragedy, but in uttering that one little pink fleshy word, she brought that baby, her baby, back into her life. In that clear, honest moment Clementine felt the loss like a wound and recognized the sore that festered inside her, poisoning everything; she saw her womb empty, weeping, useless. She started to howl again.

Sophie moved closer so that she was pressed firmly against Clementine's back. She smoothed her sister's crinkled red hair, tucking it behind her ear, and kept her silence. A baby? Clementine? She couldn't begin to imagine whose it was or what had happened to her or where the baby was now or how old she was or who the father was. They were questions that Clementine would not want asked, Sophie was pretty sure. And who else knew about it? Clearly not Mathilde, with her constant arsenal of nasty virgin jokes. What a dreadful, harmful, hurtful secret for her eldest sister to keep and to have kept. And what a price she had paid. This was the misery that reeked from every pore, that pulled her mouth down at the edges and kept her eyes swiveling from side to side, afraid to rest on anything pleasant or peaceful other than her grapes, her children, thought Sophie, and her gentle heart swelled. It was such a good heart. And perhaps Clementine, in her despair, felt it beating with extra vigor on her behalf because her howling started to subside into a less tortured form of grief and eventually evaporated into a mere whimper. Soon after, her breath started coming deep and even. She was asleep.

Sophie stayed for a while before slowly extricating herself. There was nothing more she could do. She knew that, and she also knew that Clementine would probably not want her there when she woke up.

Out in the courtyard the sky was dark, the odd misshapen cloud moving halfheartedly in front of the stars, the moon not yet high in the sky. Sophie took her sister's despair and tucked it away deep inside where she treasured such confidences, and then she hugged herself, the beginnings of a smile warming her pretty face.

Veraison

The Peine berries grew fat and sweet as the summer lived up to its early promise, each sunny day lazily sliding into a balmy evening and returning with another clear pink sunrise. The smell of ripening fruit hovered in the air every bit as thick and obvious as the famous winter mists but bringing none of that dreary claustrophobic gloom, just the pure certainty of great possibilities.

The vines had a more luxurious look about them, too; a deeper palette was creeping across the hills. *Veraison* was under way; the grapes, all born the same shade of green, had started to change color, the pinots taking on a dark red tinge and the chardonnay tending toward a paler yellow.

The grapes weren't the only things growing fat and sweet and changing color, either. Sophie, thanks to the consistent advantage of having a roof over her head and food at every meal, had started to lose her urchin look and take on a healthy country glow. Her jet-black hair had faded under the northern sun; her translucent skin had turned a honeyed gold. Gone were the purple lips and the heavy black kohl. That disguise for the moment discarded, those violet eyes radiated only contentment.

The hospitality could not claim full responsibility for this improvement in her demeanor, though, for remarkably that was due to Clementine.

Something had changed between the two sisters after the night in the winery when Clementine had released her secret into the yeasty blackness. It wasn't momentous or earth-shattering, the change; they weren't suddenly the best of friends sharing every little thought and spending cozy nights gossiping in each other's rooms as they painted their nails. But there had been progress of sorts.

One small step for most other families; one giant leap for the Peines.

To Sophie it felt a little as though the most delicate thread had been spun between her and Clementine when they huddled there in the dark behind the reserve pinot noir. It was fragile, that almost invisible strand, but it was still a bond where before there had been none. And Sophie clutched it with delicate fingers. She wound it daintily around her slender wrist until she felt the faintest tug and then let it pull her in Clementine's footsteps as she did her rounds of the vineyards and the winery.

The older woman, while not at first going so far as to exactly acknowledge her, at least never chased her away or scuttled into the foliage at the sight of her. Before long she had actually grown used to her little shadow—expected it to be there, as a matter of fact—and eventually found herself gruffly explaining what she was doing with words that had until then lain uselessly inside her. As long as the conversation did not stray outside the subject of her champagne, she felt quite comfortable. Incredibly, after a while she came to realize that the feeling she got while chatting—yes, chatting—to Sophie about her work was something akin to pleasure. Gradually, even the gruffness disappeared, leaving nothing but her enthusiasm for her work peppered with just a little of her trademark grousing.

"See, these little berries here are growing in a tight bunch, just the way I want them to," she might explain one day, "because this row, Dorothée, got extra attention from my pruning shears this year. As if I had the time! But Dorothée has always been needy."

Or "Pasqualine has too much leaf coverage. Can you tell? We'll leave her be for the moment. It'll keep the berries from getting burned, but later in the summer, before the *vendange,* she'll need plucking. It's the sort of thing I might actually have trusted those useless twin oafs with, but no chance of that now, hm? Typical!"

And "Look at the fruit on greedy Antoinette! Those poor canes must be working overtime trying to feed all her berries. It's bunch-thinning for you, Antoinette, and I know how much you like that, but, really, didn't you listen to a word I said last year?"

As time went on it became clear that Clementine, too, was flourishing. She was standing straighter, and the misery that usually upholstered her face was, if not gone altogether, then at least substantially remodeled. The edges of those lips were not headed quite so far south, and there was a light in her often distrustful eyes that had not been there before.

So taken was she with her little sister's company that she decided to allow her to help with the riddling: a huge chore she treasured but could not tackle alone. Yet just looking at all the inverted oak Vs full of holes into which the bottles were inserted and twisted seemed to cause Sophie to lose concentration and become atwitter with nerves.

"There are three steps to *remuage,*" Clementine instructed her. "You twist the bottle about an eighth of a turn to the right like so, give it a quick shake to stir up the sediment, and then tilt it slightly as you replace it in the slot. We'll turn every bottle every second day—once to the right and once to the left—and when the bottles are all directly upside down, the sludge will be gathered in the neck and then, voilà, *dégorgement*! Once we've gotten rid of the sludge, the cork goes in and the champagne is ready to sell. Come on, Sophie, now you try. Shoulder-width apart. No, shoulder width, same row. Same row! And twist. To the right. Your *right*. *Your right*. Oh, for pity's sake! We'll be here for months if you carry on like this. The old *remueurs* turned fifty-thousand bottles a day, but you won't get to fifty!"

Mind you, having even fifty turned by wrists other than her own would be a help, so Clementine eventually left Sophie to it and made her way along a different row of *pupitres*, both hands flying, the musical rattling of glass against timber soothing her the way it always did.

If the eldest and youngest Peines were blooming in the sun, however, Mathilde was shriveling in the shadows. She had been doing her best to medicate that itch of hers, but still it nagged. Whenever she closed her eyes nowadays, she saw her Upper West Side apartment: the Tiffany lamp in the dining room, the tangerine sofa in the den, the stand in the hall holding her coordinated collection of caramel- and chocolate-colored umbrellas and the one annoying pink one with little love hearts on it.

Had she done the right thing?

There. That was it. Doubt, a thousand times worse than guilt. Guilt she could choose not to feel. With doubt she was struggling.

The thing was, she admitted to herself in a lucid moment one sleepless morning when the pastis had worn off but the Xanax had not yet kicked in, she was the one who had left. It had been her choice, her wish, her blessed relief—so why was it that she felt so *abandoned*? She hated that word. It stank of weakness, and she could not abide weakness. Besides, to be abandoned you had to be in need of whoever had abandoned you, and this was not the case in her situation. She didn't need anyone. She wasn't forsaken in any way. She was the one who had gone. But the truth was she could have tracked herself down in a nanosecond, so why the hell couldn't they? Couldn't *he*? Or, more to the point, why *hadn't* he? All this time and not so much as an angry letter, an accusatory phone call, or a desperate plea to return to the States.

George. She rolled her husband's name around in her head, the American way, seeing him standing in their bedroom wearing any one of his pastel-colored cashmere sweaters, staring at her the way she so often caught him doing, a look that made her want to slap him so hard his teeth rattled.

They had hardly enjoyed the romance of the centuries, but the arrangement had suited them both extremely well. She had been very happy to marry someone wealthy and successful, and he had certainly never complained about her looks, her style, and her great ability to get the right people together in the right room. It was an equal marriage, reasonable in many respects, and most definitely better than any of the unions her poor deluded mother had attempted. Even so, Mathilde had spent the past however many years wishing he was dead or she was dead or that one of them was on the other side of the world. And now she was. So why, why, why, she asked herself, was she spending so much time wondering why he hadn't chased after her?

For a while she had escaped these irritating notions by flirting with Benoît Geoffroy again. It had been a relief to let her hormones lead her for a bit, but she lost interest when he resisted her charms—first out among the vines and then again, more robustly, when she turned up at his house wearing a low-cut top and bearing a bottle of single malt.

She had then set her sights on straightening up the Peine chateau, but without going to Paris and spending a fortune, it was a fruitless task, and since no one but herself had the slightest inkling of style, what was the point? Clementine trailed mud across the rugs like an old plow horse, and Sophie's idea of interior design was plonking a pile of matching pebbles next to a jar of dried twigs.

The Peine family finances, now they were another matter.

This was a project into which Mathilde could truly sink her teeth, and so she did. The paperwork was nonsensical, true, and all she knew for sure was that once the taxes were paid, the House of Peine would be so in the red that she and those two fools to whom she was allegedly related would for all intents and purposes be the joint owners of nothing but an enormously painful headache that would require a complete decapitation unless they could turn the business around.

Still, still, still. Turning it around was not impossible. For all Clementine's nutty eccentricity and infuriating social incompetence, the dullard had clearly done a capable job of taking care of her precious grapes, and the land, after all, was the family's major asset. If Mathilde could just rescue the finances, stave off payment of the monies owed until the House of Peine was in better shape, then there was a chance to make some cash.

All she needed in the absence of a secretary, a financial controller, and the slew of dewy-eyed males she was used to charming into doing the dirty work was an assistant.

"Sophie, I need you today," she said briskly as she walked into the kitchen one morning. She filled a cup with coffee from the pot on the stove and lit a breakfast cigarette. There was no one here to tell her what a disgusting habit it was and how passive smoke could kill. This was France! "There's office work to do, and I can't do it on my own."

Clementine and Sophie both froze: chunks of baguette spread lavishly with Mirabella plum jelly were halfway to each mouth. Cochon, upon hearing Mathilde's shoes clicking across the stone floor, jumped to his feet with such speed that he banged his little head on the seat of a chair.

"What do you mean 'office work'?" Clementine finally said at the same time that Sophie stammered, "But I'm riddling."

"Yes, well, it comes as no surprise to me that you are not familiar with the accounts, Clementine, or we wouldn't be in this state. But someone around this festering heap has to pull her finger out and confront the mess we are in and I've decided it's going to be me. I just need a filing clerk to sort out the books, and Sophie will do nicely."

"But I don't know about filing," Sophie cried, and even Clementine was surprised by the panic in her voice. "I don't know about accounts."

"If you can learn to twist stupid bottles, you can learn to file," Mathilde said impatiently.

"She still hasn't learned to twist the bottles," Clementine argued, meaning that she needed more time to teach her, but Mathilde pounced on this logical flaw straightaway.

"Well, if she hasn't picked it up by now, she's hardly going to. Come on, you," she said to Sophie, pulling out her chair. But Sophie clung to the table, white knuckles shining, like a toddler being sent to bed for not eating her dinner.

"I don't want to," she cried. "I want to riddle with Clementine."

"Oh, don't be such a sap," Mathilde snapped. "It's only filing, for Christ's sake. It's as easy as ABC." She saw the terror then in Sophie's eyes, and her clever mind clicked instantly, an incredulous laugh flying straight out of her.

"I don't believe it," she said, letting Sophie go. "I've read about people like you, but I never thought I would have one in the family." She ignored the tug in her smooth flat stomach at that thought and felt a further hardening in the callused muscle of her heart.

"She still hasn't learned to twist the bottles?" she asked Clementine. "Let me guess. She gets confused between left and right? Has trouble following your directions? Can't do it with both hands?"

Clementine nodded dumbly, clueless as to where this was leading. Mathilde picked up one of her fashion magazines and tossed it in front of Sophie. "Read it," she commanded.

"I can't," whispered Sophie, barely glancing at it. "It's in English."

Mathilde laughed humorlessly. "It's in Italian, you stupid girl."

"Well, maybe she can't read Italian," Clementine interjected. "We didn't all go to fancy schools like you, Miss America."

"Can't read Italian? She can't *read,* period, Clementine. The little tramp has obviously never been to school at all. Just my luck, not one idiot sister but two."

With an anguished cry, a scraping of her chair, and the spin of her coffee bowl on the table, Sophie leaped to her feet and ran from the room in much the same way that Clementine had done the first night they met. The eldest Peine half-stood to follow her but was out of her depth. Sophie couldn't read? Her mind was a muddle. It was unusual in this day and age, certainly, but what was the big deal?

She turned to look at Mathilde, who wore a proud smirk as though she had just won the grand prize at the Champagne awards, and at this her elusive eloquence calmly slipped into place. "You are too thin," she told her sister. "You are a soak like your father. You haven't a drop of kindness in your dry old body, and I thank God you don't have a family of your own because they would feel about you the way you obviously feel about us."

Mathilde stood there and let the insults penetrate, ignoring the clenching in her entrails, concentrating on the adrenaline pumping through her body as she felt the straightforward passion of hatred blending in her veins.

"You know," she drawled slyly, picking imaginary tobacco off her perfectly made-up lips, "you could have told me Benoît was married."

Clementine's chest collapsed as the wind was sucked out of her lungs, but she fought to regain her composure. "You didn't think he was waiting for you all these years, did you?" she demanded, but there was a fear in her voice no one could miss. "Like everybody else in the world, he had better things to do with his time."

Again Mathilde laughed her joyless, brittle laugh. "It's just that if he was going to settle for a rotten sow like the one he's with now, Clementine, he may as well have married you."

Mathilde flung her words with the casual skill of an Olympic archer and hit, as she knew she would, the bull's-eye.

Clementine's already crumbling world had shattered completely years before when she heard the rumor that Benoît was seeing another *vigneron*'s daughter. But that devastation was nothing, *nothing* compared to how she felt when she found out that it was

Odile Joliet, daughter of old man Joliet, a plain-looking woman a few years older than she with a harsh face, brassy blonde hair, and what was generally described as an unfortunate manner. Of course the union made sense in a way because the Geoffroys didn't have enough pinot noir and the Joliets didn't have enough chardonnay, so together they were both better off. But for Benoît to marry the odious Odile?

"Why not me?" Clementine had indeed cried into her pillow. "Why not me?"

The memory of those tears, of waking up to the smell of goose feathers soaked in the sadness that leeched out of her as she slept and of what came afterward, ground the gears of Clementine's confidence as she stood across the kitchen from Mathilde all those years later.

"I hope you . . . you get that disease . . . the one that makes your nose fall off and . . . you go bald . . . and you just *die!*" she stuttered. It was the best she could come up with, and then she, too, fled the room.

Peine

Sophie was behind the reserve pinot, which was exactly where Clementine headed. She crawled in next to her, not even bothering to stop and feel resentment at finding her there. In fact, she surprised herself by being mildly pleased. Sophie's face was still wet with tears, but she managed a feeble smile at the sight of her sister.

"I just couldn't learn," she said. "No matter how hard I tried, I just couldn't learn."

Clementine wanted to comfort her but didn't know how, so she just shimmied as close as she could until her round hips were settled flush up against Sophie's bony ones.

"The teachers always called me stupid, and so did my foster parents. They thought I was doing it on purpose, not trying, not understanding, but I didn't understand! Something was always wrong. I felt as if I had missed the very first bit that everyone else was told, the bit that you absolutely had to know to be able to do it. I could pretend for a while, but then the pretending got too hard. The letters just danced in front of my eyes, Mentine. They still do. They don't settle into words or the words into sentences. They are always juggling themselves, juggling, juggling, juggling."

She sniffed and wiped her cheeks with a ratty sleeve. "Mathilde is right. I hardly went to school at all. I'm stupid now, and I'll be stupid forever."

"A lot of stupid people can read perfectly well," Clementine pointed out meaningfully. "It doesn't count for anything. Look at Mathilde!"

Sophie laughed, or tried to, and the sound heated the chalky cellar. "She's not stupid, though, she's clever," she said. "But mean. She's so mean! Why is that, do you think?"

Clementine shrugged. "I don't know why," she said. "She was like that when she came here last time and ruined everything."

"What happened then, Mentine?" Sophie asked, her low moment gone and on its way to being forgotten. "Between you."

A low hum started in the back of Clementine's throat.

It was so odd, this humming, thought Sophie. She had noticed it plenty of times before and knew it started merely as a noise, but as the droning continued, it seemed to her that her sister disappeared somewhere no one could follow. Her eyes grew distant; her face became slack and pale. One moment she was there right in front of you, and the next she had vanished into the Marne Valley mist.

"Mentine," Sophie whispered, tugging gently at her sister's sleeve, "come back."

The humming stopped, and life returned briefly to Clementine's face, but her eyes were so full of terror, of pain, that again the mist descended and the humming returned.

"Come back to me, Mentine," Sophie urged again, taking her sister's hand. "I'm here. It's all right. I'm here." This time when the fog disappeared from her sister's eyes, Sophie was ready. She held that frightened look with her own unyielding gaze and squeezed her sister's hand, willing the mist to evaporate and take the humming with it. Clementine's lips wriggled as she strived to keep hold, and soon there was silence.

Sophie let go of her hand and leaned back against the cool chalk wall, hugging her knees and waiting to see what would come next.

"All my life," Clementine eventually said into the blackness, "I thought I was going to marry Benoît Geoffroy."

There it was: her broken dream just thrown out there and left hanging in the air like a kite dangling from a tree. What was it about this spot behind the six-year-old reserve that turned it into a confessional?

"I hadn't done anything about it," she soon continued, shrugging as though with the wonder of her own foolishness. "Just thought it. Like you might think, 'One day I will paint the kitchen' or 'One day I will replant those woody geraniums.' It just felt as if it didn't need attention right away but that it was going to happen. We lived next to each other, we did the same job, and we both loved our vines, and our grapes, and our champagne. The House of Geoffroy made a good drop, too. Not as good as ours—we have a little more sunshine, more pinot noir, a bigger mix of soils. But together? Who knows what we could have done. We seemed like a natural combination. Anyway, that's what I thought. It was just taking time. We were resting on our lees, waiting until we were ready."

It was amazing to Clementine herself that she could suddenly speak at such length on the subject about which she could not bear to even think for long. More startling still, the admission felt good, as if the pressure within the overfilled balloon of her heart was finally, mercifully being released.

"Then Mathilde showed up." Her voice dropped and became flat; the balloon filled up again. "Her mother sent her over here when she became troublesome at home, but she was horrible even then. And when she realized I felt something for Benoît . . ." A single fat berry of a tear sprung out of her eye and rolled down her cheek. "She just took him. One afternoon when I was sure we were close to being together, Benoît and I, she just saw him out there among the grapes, and she went right over and took him.

"I got a bottle of Bollinger Vieilles Vignes Françaises, the 1975. Such a good year. I had been saving it for . . . Well, anyway, I brought it down here," she continued bleakly, "and I drank it. It tasted like gold, I remember that, but I still thought I was going to die. Then I drank more, a bottle of our own vintage '75, which was foolish. Such a magnificent wine usually but compared to the *blanc de noirs* of those old Bollinger vines . . . It was silly of me, a waste."

Sophie let the silence swirl around them again.

"Then when it was dark," Clementine finally whispered, "I went and found him."

"Benoît?"

The beginnings of a hum curled up the *cave*'s dark walls, but again Sophie scrabbled in her sister's lap for her hand and once more squeezed, as though pulling her closer to the ground, anchoring her to sanity. "It's okay, Clementine," she soothed. "It's okay."

"It's not okay," Clementine cried, a string of berries now trailing her smooth pink cheeks. "It was never okay."

"What happened?"

"Benoît! I went and found Benoît in the winery over at the Geoffroys. He was disgorging their '83, not a good year but certainly not their worst."

"And what did you do?"

"I shouted at him, Sophie. Me, who had barely ever had the courage to talk to him in a whisper! I screamed at him. I swore. I was so angry that he had fallen for Mathilde's trickery like that. She was so obvious. So common. So young! So beautiful! It all seemed so . . . unfair."

"And then?"

"And then . . ." Oh, how the memory hurt now that she had dredged it up. How it battered in her chest like the pummeling of an angry fist. And her mind, so unsympathetic to her all these years, had another cruel trick still to play on her. For when she recalled that terrible night, it was not the innocent, angry twenty-six-year-old Clementine who let her clothes fall to the ground and who threw herself at him, it was the forty-four-year-old she was today, her body loose and folded like an old sack, her face painted with her heartbreak as she stepped toward him, weeping, holding out her arms, and begging him to do to her what he had done to her sister.

"And he did?" Sophie asked gently.

Clementine was nodding, her lips wriggling again, trying to keep control of herself.

"And afterward?" Sophie wanted to know. "The next time?"

"There was no next time!" Clementine shook her head so violently that the tears flew off her face in angry arcs. "I never spoke to him again," she cried, saliva gathering in the corners of her mouth, thickening her voice. "I was so ashamed. It was so awful. I was so awful. And then . . . the next day . . ."

"What happened the next day?"

"Over and over again I have asked myself, but really there was no other way. Look at me!" she cried, clawing pitifully at her breasts. "Just look at me! It would never have been me if Mathilde had stayed here. Never!"

Sophie held her hand even tighter then, trying to quell her anguish, to still her.

"There's nothing wrong with you, Clementine," she said. "Nothing at all. You are ten times the woman Mathilde is."

"I told Olivier," Clementine wept.

"About you and Benoît?"

"No. About Mathilde and Benoît. She was only seventeen, remember. That's probably nothing in this day and age, but then for a man of twenty-six to be with a teenage girl, especially in a small town like this, it was a disgrace, a scandal. She was sent home straightaway. And I hid from Benoît because I was ashamed of everything I had done, but still I somehow thought it would be all right, that in the end we would be together, the kitchen would be painted, and there'd be fresh geraniums. And while I was thinking that, he married Odile Joliet. His father insisted. That's what they said, but what did it matter? It wasn't me in the end anyway, you see. After all that, it wasn't me. It was never going to be me."

"And Amélie?" Sophie prodded softly. "The baby?"

Clementine was quiet for a long, long time, but for once she let the memory of that little pink squirming creature wriggle into her mind and settle there.

"I didn't even know myself until she was nearly here," she finally said. "And by then it was too late to tell Benoît. He and Odile were already . . . Besides, how could I tell him? What words would I use? Why would he listen? In the end it was Olivier who helped me," her voice cracked, "the night she arrived and who arranged for her to be taken away. Some family in Bordeaux, I think. Winemakers. We never spoke of it."

"Oh, Clementine," Sophie said, tears in her own eyes, her full little heart bursting, "I am so sorry."

It was the first time Clementine had ever considered that someone other than herself might indeed be sorry. And as she realized this, she also felt a glimmer of the pain Sophie must have suffered over her own dark and torturous secret, and this hurt even more. Racked with such anguish her body began to shake uncontrollably. Sophie twisted around so that she was kneeling and then took her big heartbroken sister in her two small arms and held on with all her might. She squeezed her eyes tightly shut and hoped against hope that somehow Clementine would learn what she herself had: that this awful time would pass, that there was light after dark, and that things could only get better.

Une Invitée

As the warm sunny days continued, the vines grew more and more lush, hugging the hills of the Marne in their obedient rows like a rich green corduroy suit. The grapes were as fat and sweet and juicy as anyone could remember, prompting much wistful talk of the bumper crop of '76. Given this splendid state of affairs the *vignerons* of Champagne were in good spirits. Save a freak storm or—not that the word was so much as whispered—hail, the *vendange* would be a good one.

All this was of little interest to Mathilde, of course. The grapes could have turned pink and started whistling "Dixie" as far as she was concerned. She cared not a jot for berries or bubbles but was definitely making headway with the House of Peine accounts.

The collecting of what few documents there were and collating the figures had been a crushing bore, true, but it was a challenge nonetheless and one that kept her mind off whatever ailed her.

She had also had early success at the bank in Epernay, instantly relieving the worst of the family's financial pressures and securing an overdraft extension by way of charming the pants almost literally off the bank manager. He was desperate to take her to Paris to a discreet little hotel he knew in Montmartre, and she had indicated that there was every chance he would indeed be able to. The foolish man did not suspect that the exact moment she would be in a position to go with him would be the same moment she no longer had the slightest bit of use for him and so would not be inclined to oblige. He might one day indeed be rummaging between crisp white sheets, the bells of Sacré-Coeur ringing in his ears, but it would be with a far less crafty soul than Mathilde.

Anyway, it was a balmy afternoon, and she had just come back from a surprisingly successful trip to Reims, where she had secured agreements from five different restaurants and three wine stores to start selling the Peine backlog of vintages and the traditional *brut*.

She had expected it to be a hard sell and had dressed with extreme care: a skirt that was short but not too short, the same silk blouse that had failed to wow Benoît but nevertheless did great things for her bust, and a pair of spiky heels that she knew made her ankles irresistible to the average red-blooded male. She had spent two hours doing her makeup so that she looked beautiful but not intimidating and had taken great care in employing a few drops of her cherished Clive Christian perfume.

She had even gone to Paris on the train earlier in the week to have her hair styled and colored, and had been to the library to research what had been written about Peine champagne in its heyday. She had prepared a spiel about family traditions and the renaissance in artisan produce and had spent a fortune getting a laminated portfolio made up that tracked the company's rather romanticized-for-this-purpose history over the generations with pull-out quotes (minus the dates) from the wine magazines she had found. Olivier had actually kept tasting notes for each of his vintage blends. This was strange considering that the rest of his record keeping was so haphazard, but Mathilde had found the notes in an old tin trunk lying underneath what looked like a horse blanket in his tiny cluttered office. This was greatly appreciated because it meant that she did not have to speak to Clementine on the subject other than to request that she put out a few bottles of whichever champagne best reflected the house style for Mathilde to take to the buyers.

She had seen Clementine struggle with this demand, her face rippling like a pond on a windy day with the effort of not telling her to climb to the top of the house and jump off the roof. They had barely spoken since Mathilde had taunted her about Odile, but Peine champagne always came first for Clementine. Always. Mathilde knew this and so had not been at all surprised to find two dozen bottles of carefully selected champagne stacked at the bottom of the stairs when she was ready to leave for Reims.

As it turned out, she need not have troubled so much with her hair, her clothes, the world's most expensive perfume, and even the laminated portfolio because without exception the buyers licked their lips and started salivating, not at the sight of those slim long legs of hers or that buxom cleavage but at the label on the bottles bearing the family name in gold lettering and the château in its glory days.

"At last!" the *sommelier* at Le Millénaire had cried. "The Peine is back! Oh, you have the '99? Please, *madame*. I'll get the glasses."

It had been the same at each of her appointments. She had barely needed to open her mouth. The champagne had spoken for her. Mathilde had worked with many prestigious clients during her career, but rarely had any one product required so little PR. It was encouraging to say the least.

Flushed with this success, she was in a good mood when she got back to the house, but she was hot and sticky—the sun roof being the *deux chevaux*'s idea of air-conditioning—and desperate for a long bath and a glass of something with a lot of ice in it.

Her plans fell somewhat apart, however, when she opened the door to her room and found a small, dark, extremely wrinkled old woman lying in her bed and feeding chocolates to Cochon, who was curled up—rather contemptuously Mathilde could not help but think—on the floor atop her La Perla negligee.

"What the hell is going on?" she demanded, sweeping into the room and registering that someone had been through her suitcase and, by the looks of it, the armoire as well. "Who the hell are you?"

The woman was ancient. Her skin was so crumpled and dry it looked cracked, as though she were the subject of an old master's oil painting. She was slight, from the size of her wizened face, yet wore so many layers of clothing that it was impossible to tell how big or small the rest of her was. She had long gray hair that was coiled up behind her head in an extravagant plaited arrangement. It looked thick with grease, like some sort of industrial rope. And while Mathilde was thoroughly aghast at the sight of her, she was not at all perturbed by the sight of Mathilde. She barely took her eyes off the little horse, in fact, as she continued to feed him chocolate by chocolate over the side of the bed.

"Did you hear me? I said what the hell is going on?" Despite her anger, something kept Mathilde from going too close. The old woman did not smell as fresh as she could have, and even the little horse had a confidence that Mathilde could usually suck out of him with just one glance. She felt hot all of a sudden and unusually flustered as she stood with arms crossed in front of her chest at the foot of the bed.

"Mathilde, heh?" the old woman said, although her singsong accent was spiced with the history of some faraway place, and it took a few moments for Mathilde to decode her own name. "You didn't bring them with you?" the old woman asked her.

"What?" Mathilde seethed. "You are in my bed, old woman, and I would like you to get out of it."

"It's my bed now," the old woman cackled, grinning to reveal a mouth only half full of teeth. "You should find another one. I'm in no hurry to move, having just got here. And you should have brought them with you."

"I'm not finding another anything," Mathilde retorted. "This is my bed. This is my house."

"But you have another house," the wrinkled gargoyle chortled from the bed. "And in it are two people who should be here."

Mathilde froze. Who had sent this old harridan? "Did that fat cow put you up to this?" she demanded. It must be Clementine's work. Surely it couldn't be George. He didn't have the imagination, and, anyway, why would he? "Who the hell are you?" she asked the old woman again.

"No, Mathilde," the object of her disdain shot straight back. "The question is who the hell are *you*?"

Mathilde opened her mouth to say something, but absolutely nothing came out. The nagging feeling that had been repeatedly scratching at her empty belly erupted then with such violence that her knees started to shake, and she had to sit down on the rickety chair, her thin arm holding on to the wall for support, her world spinning around her.

"If she's anything like you were when you were young, I'm not surprised you've run away," the old woman said, gnawing at one of the chocolates before handing it on to Cochon to finish. "But it's not the answer. It's not the right thing to do. A smart girl like you must know that, heh? That you have to fight for anything worth having. It never comes free. Good little pony, here, try this one. And in my experience it never comes cheap, either. Is this strawberry flavor, do you think?" She held up another half-chewed chocolate, this one with a bright pink center, but Mathilde was still speechless. "I don't care for strawberry flavor," the old woman said, wiping her nose on the duvet cover. "Strawberries themselves, now that's another matter."

Mathilde stood abruptly and bolted out of the room and down the stairs. Who was the old witch? And how did she know so much? She fumbled in the kitchen for the pastis, poured herself a stiff drink, and slugged it back, feeling the alcohol warm her chest and calm her panic. Or did she know anything? She poured another drink and took a gulp. It could all be some horrible coincidence. The shriveled old prune could be quite mad. Yes, that was it. Why else would she turn up in a stranger's bed and start feeding that spotty little pig with finest Fauchon? She was deranged. Someone's nutty granny who had escaped from the retirement home or, worse, a local loony bin. She was talking utter nonsense, Mathilde decided. There was nothing in it, and, besides, it was breaking and entering and theft and so out of order and annoying that her hands continued to shake after she drained her drink.

She jumped at the sound of a distant cackle and the skittering of Cochon's hooves on the upstairs floorboards. Then she slammed her empty glass down on the counter so hard it cracked and fell apart in two even halves. She stared at this, her mind racing, and then spun around and stalked outside, climbed back into Olivier's overheated rusty car, and drove angrily down the dusty driveway.

La Petite

The eldest and youngest Peines were working in the vines on a steep slope behind Saint Vincent. Clementine was checking the grapes' sugar content by tasting them—pinot meunier at that moment, and how delicious those berries were, too!—and teaching Sophie how to green prune, or throw away the stunted unripened grapes so that the healthy plump ones could continue to prosper.

They stopped what they were doing when the *deux chevaux* skidded to a halt and disgorged an irate Mathilde into the long grass and scattered violets at Saint Vincent's feet.

"You need to come home at once!" she shouted up to Clementine. "There's a wrinkled old hag in my bed, and you must get rid of her."

"The old soak has been into the pastis again," Clementine grumbled to Sophie. "Tracking us down just so she can yell her vile nonsense at us.

"Come back when you've sobered up," she shouted down the hill.

She couldn't quite make out the particular swear words with which this was greeted. She just shrugged and kept moving along the row, tasting a big juicy grape here, plucking at a shriveled little bunch of them there, waiting all the while to hear the rattle of the 2CV starting up again.

"Look," said Sophie, pointing with her clippers. "She's coming up." They both stopped again to watch Mathilde negotiate the steep incline in her heels. It was quite a sight, that short skirt and those skinny legs maneuvering their way over the steep, uneven ground. If Clementine's eyes were not deceiving her, there were dark patches under her arms and down the front of her shirt, too. Who would have guessed that Mathilde could sweat?

"For Christ's sake, it's your house, too," the perspiring Peine panted when she got to the top, quite disheveled. "I thought you would care about that if nothing else, you useless heffalump."

"You obviously want something from me to have come all this way, Mathilde, so I can't be that useless, can I? But regardless of that, whatever it is, the answer is no. That's what you get for calling me a heffalump."

Something about being out there among her chosen vines with Sophie was giving Clementine a little extra va-voom. She could feel it, and she liked it.

"For God's sake, this is not about you being a heffalump," Mathilde protested. "It's about—"

But Clementine turned away. "Come on, Sophie. We don't need to listen to this. There's work to be done. The mannequin can come back when it has a civil tongue in its head."

The mannequin did not appreciate this. Her head looked very angry, and her tongue was ripe for distributing a decent lashing.

"Well, you may not care about some smelly old witch taking up residence in my bed, but I do, and what's worse is that she is feeding your great fat roundabout reject my precious Paris chocolates!"

Sophie hunched her shoulders and prepared for the situation to explode. Mathilde never tired of baiting her sister about her pet, probably because she never failed to get a rise out of her.

"Would you mind telling me what it is that Cochon has ever done to you?" Clementine predictably combusted, miffed that her little friend had slipped off without her even noticing. He had been there just minutes before, hadn't he?

"Apart from choke on my underwear, crap wherever I seem to want to step in the outside world, and offend me with his far too small and extremely pointless existence, *nothing!*"

"You are truly despicable," Clementine said, her lips white and narrow. "Come on, Sophie. Let's go down to the river. The pinot noir could do with some attention."

But Mathilde stood in her way. "Screw the pinot noir," she said. "Screw your stupid horse. There's an old woman in my bed, and you need to come and get rid of her."

"What sort of an old woman?" Sophie dared to inquire, her interest piqued.

"You should really wait until at least three before you start tippling, Mathilde," Clementine said as she moved to push past her. "You're seeing things. There's no old woman that I know of . . ." Her voice trailed off. "What sort of an old woman?"

"How many sorts are there?" fumed Mathilde. "She's a thousand years old and smells like compost."

"Does she have long gray hair all piled up on top of her head?"

"Yes! God knows what's nesting in there! And she's in *my* bed. I think she might even be wearing *my* clothes. Who the hell is she?"

Clementine did know someone who answered this description.

"La Petite," she murmured. But La Petite usually arrived the day before the *vendange* began, never, ever any sooner. And Clementine had just tasted the chardonnay. It was the first to be picked and was at least a week away. "How strange."

"Who's La Petite?" Sophie wanted to know, further intrigued. "What's strange?"

"Apart from the old trout festering in my bed, which, by the way, has my own personal Frette linen on it?" Mathilde complained.

Clementine ignored her. "*La Petite Noix*," she told Sophie. The Little Walnut. It was a good name—even Mathilde could see that—for the old woman did indeed look like a wrinkled nut. But the moniker had long ago been shortened to just La Petite. "She's a grape picker," Clementine continued, but she was more than that. Much more. For as long as Clementine could remember La Petite and her extended family of Romanian gypsies (or were they Lithuanian? No one was sure, not even the gypsies) had descended on the House of Peine for the harvest.

She could not fathom how they knew to do so, but they would turn up just in time for the grapes to be picked, would work for the week or ten days it took, and then would disappear again. The next year they would swarm back, never exactly the same bunch but always exactly the same number. Sometimes a husband would be missing and a cousin would be there instead, or a mother would be nursing an infant and her eldest daughter would be picking for the first time. The only person who remained constant was La Petite, the matriarch of the family, a tiny crumpled bundle of burning energy and intuition.

Where they were before Champagne—Alsace, someone had once suggested—or where they went after, Clementine did not have a clue. She had known La Petite all her life but could barely remember a single conversation with her. This was not really as strange as it seemed since the world was full of people with whom Clementine could barely remember a conversation—and that was the world right at her doorstep, too, not the big wide one. Until Sophie came along she just didn't converse. Olivier, on the other hand, had always had a soft spot for La Petite, whispering away to her late into the night in the days before he spent all his time at Le Bois. And in recent years Clementine was pretty sure La Petite had joined him there. Her father had a lot to say to the old woman, it seemed, although she could not imagine what.

For her to turn up in Mathilde's bed though? That was very odd. She had certainly never stayed in the house before. She usually had one of her brood build her a little shack just below them in the hawthorn bushes beneath Saint Vincent. A nephew or a cousin of a nephew had once told Clementine that she liked being downwind of such a great big holy person.

"She is foul!" Mathilde was saying. "And she's mad! Insane! Talking all sorts of drivel. And she's feeding your stupid pig all my chocolates, and he's dribbling on my peignoir."

"What is she saying?"

"Who cares?" Mathilde snapped. "I just want the haggle-toothed old crone out of there now, so go and do something about it!"

Clementine put her finger to her chin and looked up at the sky as though seriously deliberating this possibility. "No," she finally said. "Do it yourself. It has nothing to do with me. Besides, I don't care if she is in your room. She can stay there forever as far as I am concerned."

Actually, Clementine was, if not frightened of La Petite, at least wary. There were lots of rumors about her, and even the other gypsies spoke in hushed tones about her "evil eye." She knew things that no one else could possibly know, they said, and whether or not this was true, Clementine had on many a previous occasion felt the heat of those little black raisin eyes boring into her flesh. Whatever her skill or power, there was definitely a patina of mystery smothering the old bird; there always had been. And hers were not feathers that begged to be ruffled. Clementine meant it: if La Petite wanted Mathilde's room, she was welcome to it.

"Oh, Mentine, please, can't you help?" Mathilde's voice was so sweet and delightful and the change so abrupt that Sophie nearly choked stifling a laugh. "I've been in Reims and got so many orders for your champagne that I'm really quite exhausted. I had no idea you were so talented. The restaurateurs, the wine sellers, they just could not get enough of it. You really are such a clever thing."

"Do it yourself," Clementine told her again, not falling for this at all. "I've already told you, it has nothing to do with me."

"You useless fat cow!" Mathilde cried, whipping around to start the perilous walk back to the car. "I hope your stupid stunted pony gets diabetes. And why are you throwing those grapes on the ground? That's money in the bank, you know. I'm not playing footsie with the bank manager just so you two useless sluts can throw it all away."

Clementine's jaw dropped to her chest in amazement. It was a well-known lament of the winemaker that the grape grower was reluctant to throw away the green berries to help plump up the ripe ones. It was the age-old battle of quality versus quantity, and it raged in plots like this one all over the globe. She just never in a million years would have expected Mathilde to give a damn.

Oh-là-là!

When Clementine and Sophie got back to the house in the early evening, Mathilde was sitting at the bottom of the stairs with an empty glass in her hand and a murderous expression on her face.

"That old sow won't even let me in now," she said. "For God's sake, Clementine, do something!"

Clementine looked halfheartedly up the stairs. Sophie, too.

"Or if you won't, get your forlorn little shadow here to do it. Isn't it time she made herself useful?"

Clementine looked at her forlorn little shadow and felt such a pleasant rush of something delicious that she could not help herself. She smiled, a great huge grin that smoothed out her creases and took ten years off her age.

Sophie, seeing this, basking in it, grinned right back.

"Okay," she said quite happily. "I'll do it." And she leaped up the stairs, light as a feather, taking them two at a time.

In the hallway outside Mathilde's room she knocked gently at the door, and it swung open to reveal La Petite sitting up in bed and applying the last drops of Mathilde's fancy perfume to the insides of her elbows. Cochon was curled up on top of the covers, his head on a pillow.

"Ah, the little one," La Petite cackled, clearly delighted. "Come in, come in. Sit down. I've always wanted to meet you."

Sophie was bewildered. "Me?" she asked, looking behind to see if either of her sisters had followed her up.

"Of course, you," La Petite said, patting the bed beside her with a tiny crooked claw of a hand.

"You know about me?" Sophie asked, going straight to where the hand had patted and sitting down in that spot. On the other side of the bed Cochon lifted his head off the pillow for just a moment before flopping back down with a miniature sigh. He had chocolate on his chin and looked extremely pleased with the way his afternoon was turning out.

"Of course," La Petite said. She lifted that curled claw toward Sophie and stroked her cheek. Her wizened hand felt so much softer than it looked, and La Petite's black eyes twinkled as she gazed deep into Sophie's. "You remind me of your grandmother," she said softly. "She had a heart just like yours."

Sophie could not hide her shock. Tears filled her eyes and wobbled above her lower lashes. In the evening light of the bedroom they looked like lavender-colored lakes, which made La Petite smile. Actually, it seemed more to Sophie like a severe case of indigestion (especially since there was definitely a burp involved), yet she was immediately flooded with a warm rush of emotion. In an instant she trusted the old woman with all the aforementioned heart.

"I don't know anything," she told her, the words tripping over themselves in their hurry to get out. "About any of them. Not a thing. My grandmother? I've never heard a word about her. Nor really about Olivier. Nothing nice, anyway. I mean, what was he like? Was he always so . . . complicated? That's what everyone tells me, but I'm not sure I even understand what that means. Am I like him at all? Even in the slightest?"

La Petite waved her little bird hand to slow Sophie down. "Hush, hush," she said. "All in good time." She hauled herself up in the bed, eliciting a series of trumpeting sounds from beneath the covers. She laughed delightedly. "Beans!" she cried and then pulled the covers up to her chest and wriggled back into the pillows. "I was sorry to hear that your father had passed," she told Sophie. "Truly I was. But not sorry for him. No, not at all. Was he like you? Well, once, I think, he also had your heart, little one. Just not the armor for it. And one's no good without the other, heh? When Marie-France went . . . poof, so did he. It's a shame, no? But sometimes with great love that's just the way it is. He saw something in the middle one's mother that might have saved him, but, ah, I think the damage had already been done. And your *maman* probably brought him his last bit of happiness, but she had troubles of her own, and that's a while ago now, heh? It's a long time to be unhappy, and he never wore it well or kindly. It's been hard, I think, for the fat one, especially."

Sophie sniffed away her tears. "She's not really that fat," she pointed out loyally. "She just dresses funny."

There was a muffled snort from outside the bedroom door where Clementine had been hiding and listening, Mathilde—just then poking her in the ribs—right behind her. At the sound of their scuffling La Petite laughed uproariously, which sounded a lot like a very old boiler finally giving up the ghost.

"That always gets them!" she cackled in a spirited aside as

though she were constantly catching out corpulent siblings. "Come in, Mentine. Let me look at you."

There was no point pretending she wasn't there, so Clementine just slunk into the room, head down, her face beetroot red.

"Hello, La Petite," she mumbled, giving Cochon her own version of the evil eye when she saw his head on the pillow. But when she shifted her look instead to the old woman, she forgot about the horse. She had always been ancient, La Petite, but now she appeared to have moved on to a whole different level. She was so tiny in that bed, in her skin. It was as though she had somehow abandoned herself. "Are you all right?" Clementine asked with genuine concern.

"It depends on what you would call all right," La Petite answered wheezily but cheerfully.

"But the *vendange* . . ." Clementine's concern was first and foremost for the harvest.

"I'm sorry, Mentine. I have picked my last grape," the old woman said mournfully. "I knew it was a bad sign when I looked at a beautiful vine heaving with petit verdot down in the Medoc, and all I could think of was sitting down with a pipeful of tobacco and a cup of elderflower tea. Don't worry," she said, seeing the woeful look on Clementine's face, "I won't be leaving you in the lurch. The gang will be here in time. I just came on ahead because I need a comfortable spot to stop for a while, and I like this one. These sheets are so soft! And maybe where I'm going there'll be more of this perfume, hm?"

There was another muffled sound from outside the bedroom.

"Yes?" called La Petite, winking at Clementine and Sophie. "Can I help you?"

Mathilde strode through the doorway again, glaring at her sisters. "You're falling for this crock? You two really are stupid!" She turned to La Petite. "Get up and get out."

La Petite fixed her with a stare that instantly stripped away her anger, leaving only the vaguely unfamiliar sensation of fear. It was a while since she had had a drink, and her bravado was diluted. She recalled what the old woman had said to her earlier and regretted coming into the room.

"You are right to be fearful, Mother dearest. It's the only way forward," La Petite said with a hint of wickedness.

"You see!" Mathilde, cheeks burning and heart hammering, turned to Clementine. "She is mad! We should call the police and have her thrown out before she says another word. Get the *gendarmes*!"

"Scared of what a sick old woman has to say, heh, Mathilde?" La Petite suggested slyly. "Afraid that I'll remind you once more of the daughter who pines for you at home?"

Clementine and Sophie both turned around, openmouthed, to stare at their sister.

"You have a daughter at home?" Clementine asked, feeling sick.

"What would you know?" Mathilde spat at the old lady. "And, anyway, she won't be pining for me."

Sophie looked at Clementine and read her fear. "How old is she?" she asked, but Mathilde didn't hear her. Her face was screwed up in a small, unattractive pinch, and she was pointing her finger at La Petite.

"You'd listen to the mad ramblings of this old crone? You're both as crazy as she is!"

La Petite made a big drama of counting on her bent old fingers. "She must be, what, ten by now?" Clementine and Sophie shared a look of great relief. At least this meant Benoît was not the father. Clementine felt almost giddy for a moment. Then incredulity crept in. "You've been here all this time, and you have a ten-year-old daughter at home?"

"Edie, yes. And a husband," La Petite pointed out helpfully. "George. Olivier told me all about them."

This stopped them all in their tracks. "*Olivier?*" All three women asked at once.

"Your father," La Petite agreed nonplussed. "You do remember him, don't you? Good-looking. Red hair. Liked a drink."

The Peine sisters swapped astonished looks. It didn't happen that often and felt quite strange. Mathilde noticed for the first time that Clementine actually looked younger than her age. Clementine noticed that Mathilde's eyes were a pale yellowy green, the exact color of ripened chardonnay. Sophie noticed that if you took away Clementine's redness and plumpness and Mathilde's blondness and tightness, the sisters actually looked quite alike.

"I certainly wouldn't call Olivier good-looking," Mathilde said eventually, which was somewhat beside the point.

"He talked to you about Mathilde?" Clementine asked La Petite. How could he keep hurting her like this, that wicked old man?

"Of course," said La Petite. "And her daughter. And you," she added coolly after a dramatic pause. "And your daughter." After another one.

Sophie's hand flew out and clutched Clementine's arm just as her eldest sister started to sway.

"*Your* daughter?" It was Mathilde's turn to be incredulous. "You have got to be kidding me."

"Leave her alone," Sophie warned.

"How the hell would you ever have a daughter? I mean who—"

"Don't you dare!" shouted Clementine. "Do you hear me? Don't you dare. I won't have it. I just won't have it!" She was quite hysterical, slapping away at Sophie's soothing hands as though she were a gnat, her eyes crazed.

Mathilde started babbling at her just as Sophie started babbling at Mathilde, while Clementine launched into a spirited hum. La Petite witnessed the whole ridiculous scenario as though it were the funniest part of her favorite TV sitcom.

Then into this uproarious cacophony walked quite the best-looking specimen on which any of the Peines had ever clapped eyes.

They fell silent in an instant.

He had smooth dairy milk chocolate skin and shiny dark hair that fell in delectable waves around his ears and halfway down his neck. He was tall with broad shoulders but slim hips, and when he smiled, he had the most beautiful mouthful of straight white teeth and lively brown eyes that twinkled like disco balls.

The three healthy hearts in that room (not counting Cochon's) all stopped beating while they drank him in. La Petite (whose heart had indeed seen better days) saw this and felt supremely content.

"Hello," the best-looking specimen said, lavishing them all with a separate and somehow secret look. "I'm Hector, La Petite's great-grandson, or something like it." He turned to the grinning imp in the bed. "Can I get you anything, La Petite?"

The Peine sisters, in their hurry to keep this gorgeous object in their eyesight, to feast on him some more, all turned around at the same time but in different directions, banging into each other and getting in a clumsy tangle that required the eldest to stand on the middle one's toes and the middle one to reciprocate with a well-placed pinch on that plump rump.

Sophie simply stood in the midst of this tussle totally goggle-eyed. She could imagine herself in this dark one's arms so vividly that it felt embarrassing to have anyone else in the room. It would happen, she just knew that. She always knew it. It would happen, and it would be lovely, and then it would end. He would take a little piece of her away with him and leave her with nothing. And she would settle for that. Happily.

Clementine, too, felt a strange squirmishness in her groin just looking at Hector, but it turned almost immediately to resentment that no one like him would ever give her the time of day, let alone throw his toned brown arm over her naked skin in the warmth of her bed down the hallway. She would never get within an inch of that delightful flesh. She was too plump. Not pretty enough. Sophie was right; she dressed funny. She didn't dare even dream that the likes of Hector would curl up and spoon her. There was no point.

Mathilde, on the other hand, had great faith in her ability to take that lithe muscular body, wrap her thighs around it, do whatever she felt like, and then send it packing. She licked her lips and turned slightly away from the young Adonis so that the bone of her hip jutted out and made her legs look even longer than they already did. She could teach him a thing or two, she thought to herself, and it had been a while, so she might even bother. If there was one thing Mathilde liked, it was a well-built ship in the night. She would happily cut a slice or two off young Hector and send him sailing. It was just the way she liked it.

La Petite watched all this on the faces of the Peine sisters and smiled to herself. He was a good boy, Hector. Strong but sweet and obliging. He would help her do what Olivier had asked of her. She had waited, as she had promised, until he himself was gone and his daughters were together, and there was much to be done. But right now she was hungry.

"Who can cook in this place?" she asked. "Hector loves *magret* of duck with potatoes *dauphinoise*, don't you, Hector?"

Automne

La Vendange

By the first day of the new month the *vendange* was in full swing. La Petite's flock had descended as promised, and the whole of the Marne Valley rattled and hummed with the happy sounds of a bumper crop about to start its magical transformation into the sparkling drink of kings and queens and anyone else with a lick of taste.

In the vineyard the pickers, sun-ripened like berries themselves, deftly snipped off the bunches and put them in their handbaskets, while the carriers collected the baskets and emptied them into bigger *stampes,* or crates, at the end of the rows.

Clementine then drove the *stampes* to the winery in the cranky old tractor and watched with a careful eye as the berries were tipped into the wooden press.

Every stage in the champagne journey was a crucial one but arguably none more so than the pressing of the *must,* the juice that would go on to be wine. There were many strict regulations to satisfy before the berries even got to that point, and while this prompted many a *vigneron* to complain until their ears bled, which had once been the case with Renaud de Vallois over in Fontaine-sur-Aÿ, they were also what protected the reputation of champagne—what stopped any other bubbly wine from being called that.

For a start, La Petite's bevy of dark-skinned chatterboxes could not just go out there among the vines and pick as much as they wanted: there was a limit to how many grapes could be harvested per hectare. This amount was decided every year by the Champagne authorities, and woe betide anyone who tried to pick more. They would be tattled on by a worker or a neighbor. Remember, the plots were all out there right next to each other, and it didn't take a mathematical genius to work out who was cheating: there would be trouble for sure.

Once this preordained amount of grapes had been picked, there was no chance for the pickers to sit down and enjoy a baguette stuffed full of spicy sausage or a glass of non-vintage *brut*, either. If the fruits of their labors didn't make it to the winery within a few short hours, the grapes were deemed unusable and dumped, something no grape grower ever wanted to see. Arnaud d'Ablois in Champillon had seen it twice in one harvest a few years back when half his pickers had come down with a stomach bug. After witnessing such traumatic waste, the poor *vigneron* quite lost his senses, disappeared for three days, and then came back wearing a purple suit three sizes too small for him and smelling strongly of aviation gas. He had not been quite the same ever since, and it had been a lesson to all *Champenois* to steer clear of Madame d'Ablois's fish soup.

Once the grapes were deposited safely in the press, the regulations still did not ease up. The berries were squeezed just twice, with only the clear juice of the first delicate pressure actually being used for wine because it was highest in sugar and acidity, the two ingredients most prized in champagne. This pressing had to be done very gently in order to extract a clear juice from the two dark-skinned pinot grapes. No winemaker wanted to see the slightest suggestion of pink unless it was some months later and she was tinkering with a rosé!

At the House of Peine the juice, once pressed, gurgled down through a pipe in the floor to the cellar below and straight into a vat that was marked with the name of the plot from whence those particular berries had come. All plots were pressed separately, and all *musts* were kept in different vats to protect their characters. That was essential for the blending process. The blend? Clementine tried very hard not to think about this just yet as she simply did not have time to disappear into the mists of her hums.

The juice was only a day in the vat before it was racked off, clear now of any unwanted debris, and then she added her special yeast and sugar concoction to hurry along the juice's transformation into alcohol—its first fermentation. Yet another crucial stage.

Actually, anyone who knew Clementine well (so small a group as to barely exist) might have picked up something of a transformation in her.

The *vendange* was always an exciting time for a committed winemaker such as Clementine: there was always the hint of a glint in her otherwise dim demeanor during the harvest, but this year she almost sparkled. Those mad wiry ringlets looked positively glossy and had loosened into an almost relaxed curl, the faded red tones revived to a glorious copper. Her skin, too, seemed more lively somehow: it shone with a glow she didn't usually possess, and on several occasions she had been heard whistling as she worked in a lighthearted fashion. She looked for all the world like someone who was in the advanced stages of, if not happiness, then something mighty close.

Unfortunately, the only person who might have noticed this, the chairperson of that almost nonexistent group of people who knew Clementine well, was too preoccupied to give it much thought. Sophie, too, was reveling in what the *vendange* had delivered. It turned out she had an indispensable part to play in the process, and she was unfamiliar enough with being indispensable to feel highly impressed with this state of affairs. She was not such a good picker, the movements up and down and along the vines being a little too focused for her, but she was an excellent carrier, and the grape pickers warmed to her as their leader in a way they might have once to Olivier but, sadly, never could to Clementine. This had a remarkable trickle-down effect because dealing with the pickers could be time-consuming if they were in a churlish state of mind and the clock was ticking.

With Sophie in charge, though, the valley rang with the sound of their laughter, the click of their cutters, and the tumble of grapes from their baskets. They picked quickly and happily, and the whole operation ran more smoothly as a result. There would be no skintight purple suit and aviation gas for the Peines this *vendange*.

Under such conditions Sophie, too, continued to thrive. Her hair had grown longer and was curling prettily around her slender neck, the harsh jet black fading and a rich burgundy emerging at the roots. There was a happy flush to her honeyed cheeks, and those violet eyes sparkled. Certainly the hours were long and the work exhausting, but still she flourished. The Guerlain counter at Le Bon Marché seemed a long, long way away. This was truly belonging.

Mathilde had not once been sighted in the vineyard—she just didn't have the clothes for that sort of work—but to everyone's astonishment she had appeared in the *cave* on the first day of the *vendange,* holding a clipboard and a Montblanc pen, and proved to be extremely organized in recording what was going where and for how long.

Clementine, distracted by everything else that was going on, had ignored her at first—their relationship worked better that way—but after a couple of days she had to admit (although never out loud) that Mathilde was actually helping quite a lot. Not only was she recording which *musts* were where, but she had reorganized the *cave* in a more logical fashion so that the bottled wine still resting on its lees was well out of the way, the oak barrels for the new wine were close at hand, and the riddled stock ready for *dégorgement* was somewhere in the middle where it would be easy to get to once the harvest was over.

If Mathilde was enjoying this work, however, it did not show. In contrast to her blossoming sisters, she looked as though every bit of enjoyment had been thoroughly wrung out of her on some earlier occasion, leaving her a desiccated shell of her former self. Her hair was limp, there were bruised bags beneath her eyes, and her dull skin was drawn tight over her sharp cheekbones. If Clementine and Sophie appeared full of the joys of life, Mathilde looked as if she had been emptied.

As it turned out, there was a very good reason.

"Hector," La Petite rasped from her bed one evening about a week into the *vendange,* "what are you doing to these women?"

Hector had come in to read her the latest celebrity gossip from *Paris Match*, which was usually a great treat for La Petite, but on this occasion she was impatient to discuss matters of a more pressing nature.

"Don't worry, Petite," he assured her with great confidence. "I know what I'm doing."

"It's *who* you are doing that worries me," said La Petite with a cough. She was fading, that was certain, but not as quickly as she had anticipated. Her spirit and flesh were colluding to keep her in good shape for the task ahead, there was no doubt about it. She couldn't go yet even if she wanted to.

Hector laughed and leaned over to place a tender kiss on her withered brow. "I don't much care for the middle one," he told her. "But that's what you wanted, isn't it?"

"Yes, of course. But both the others?"

Hector shrugged and shook open the magazine.

"It's all going according to plan," he said unapologetically. "My plan."

La Petite eyed him critically through her lizardlike lids. In this instance she could see that his sweet and obliging nature was perhaps being overruled by his strength. Ordinarily, she would have been angry, but just at that point she could not truthfully summon the energy. Besides, she trusted Hector. She had to. He was her successor, after all. Her kinky blend of genetics had been copied and passed down the line specifically to him, and she believed that he would do a great job of leading the family into the next century as long as he didn't eat too much red meat or smoke tailor-made cigarettes. She should expect him to flex his own muscle, she reasoned; it was good, it was a start, and she was not going to be there much longer to tell him what to do anyway, so he might as well stand on his own two feet.

La Petite lay back on her pillows with a sigh, scratched one itchy armpit like a little monkey, and remembered the first time she had exercised her own will with her own great-grandfather (or something like it). He was bedridden at the time, just the way she was now, and preparing to pass the family mantle down to her.

It was so long ago that she could only recall it in scratchy black and white as though her memory was a wartime newsreel. Horses were pulling carts of wine barrels—she could recall that much clearly—and a woman's ankles were a rare sight, her own included. But she had most enjoyed displaying them for the first time ever to a lonely, pockmarked riddler by the name of Claude whom she had loved out of a dangerous depression; she had saved his life, just one of many. Claude! She gave a dreamy little chuckle. Oh, how he had soaked up her touch, that man, how his heavy heart had lightened, how his hands had flown over bottles whereas before she worked her magic they had been stiff and heavy.

Of course, it wasn't really magic, not in the miraculous sense. Her great-grandfather had always been perfectly clear about that, and she hoped she had made it plain to Hector as well. The *vignerons* might have whispered that she had some sort of mystical power, but while she never quashed those rumors—in fact, she liked them; they never failed to give her a good cackle—they were not true.

She was no more than one of life's ordinary citizens but just a bit more clued in when it came to the power of *amour*.

Where La Petite and her ancestors came from (not that anyone could recall quite where that was), money had little currency and happiness counted for everything. This understanding was God's gift to their family and the world, she had been led to believe, particularly the champagne world. "Never mind Saint Vincent," her great-grandfather had told her. "We are the patron saints of champagne, and a heavy heart cannot make a bubble dance, so do what you can, Eulalie. Do what you can." That's how long ago it was; she still had a name.

"Do what you can, Hector," she told the new patron saint, and he smiled, reminding her again why it was so easy for him to melt hearts hardened by even the most awful gloom.

"You'll see, La Petite," he said. "I'm doing what you told me, just in my own way. It will work out. It always does."

Déception

That evening Clementine made her first round of the vats to taste the freshly pressed grape juice. Despite her generally uplifted spirits, she had been putting this off, her hums stacking up in her chest like airplanes in a holding pattern at a busy airport. It was the very first step in the art of blending, after all, this first tart taste of what the berries had to offer.

She poured herself a splash of the pinot noir, which grew down in the valley where she had fallen off her bike, and took a sip. It tasted peppery and raw on her tongue, but as it warmed her blood, it brought in its wake the doubt that all the near happiness in the world could not keep at bay.

Everybody knew the secret of champagne was in the blend.

It was what made sense of growing grapes in the precarious climate of the Marne, the ability to mix each year's wine from all the different plots with the precious reserve wines from previous years.

It was how the *Champenois* managed to make their house champagne tingle on the tongue in the exact same way year after year despite the fact that every vintage produced an entirely different-tasting assortment of grapes.

Some years the pinot noir lacked complexity while the chardonnay lacked delicacy, yet in others the pinot meunier was too fruity while the pinot noir was not fruity enough. When the crop yield was low because of frost or heat, it did not matter that there was less of the latest wine because there were always the stocks of reserve from earlier, more bountiful harvests.

It was a delicate balancing act performed nowhere else in the wine-making world, this mixing of the wines from the past and present. It was the point of champagne, the beauty.

It was also a skill that Clementine did not believe she possessed.

Her palate, as her father had told her years before, was as blunt as a stone. She knew in her head all the requirements of the house style *cuvée*, and she could pick their own finished product out of a label-less tasting of a million bottles. Yet when it came to *assemblage*, to sampling those raw young wines and selecting which ones should go into the blend and in what quantity, her good sense eluded her.

"You are blind," her father had roared at her the last time she had joined him in the process, before he banned her from the blending process altogether, unable to tolerate her incompetence. "Blind, blind, blind!"

In other champagne houses *assemblage* was a vital period not just for the champagne but for the *Champenois*. At Krug three generations still gathered in the same room to settle on the blend; at Tarlant in Oeuilly it was four. Each winemaker passed down his knowledge, his memory to the generation below so that it was never lost, so that the taste of the house style was imprinted in the blood like DNA, moving invisibly from one century's *vignerons* to the next.

Olivier had not been able to do this; he had lost the ability to share in such a way. In the early days he had wanted to talk to his daughter, to pass on his secrets, but his festering grief eventually robbed him of the necessary skills. Then in latter days his misery curdled completely, and his earlier truly good intentions were lost to him and, as a result, lost also to Clementine. Words that might once have expressed kindness and encouragement were replaced with grunts and, more often than not, insults.

I am blind, Clementine thought sadly, pouring the pinot down the drain. Blind, blind, blind. She could do nothing but hope that when it came time for the blend, she would be able to pull a rabbit out of a hat. Still, it was something of a magic trick for Clementine to even factor in hope. It had been in short supply for so long, yet here she was considering her blindness and the price she might have to pay for it but at the same time feeling a flutter of something that was not panic.

For once, fear was not holding her hostage. She had a new secret that had nothing to do with her deficient taste buds, that was setting her free, reddening her cheeks, and sending shivers down her spine.

"Mentine, here you are!" Sophie's voice jolted her out of her daydream, and she felt another rush of pleasure at seeing her little sister. Feeling an urge to bond behind the '99, she turned, smiling. "Sophie, what good timing." She pointed in the direction of the reserve barrels. "It's been so busy. I've been looking for you, but somehow . . . Anyway, come, I have something I want to tell you."

"Oh, goody, Mentine, because I have something I want to tell you, too."

Clementine felt the thrill of anticipation. This was the sister she

had once dreamed of. Here was the nest of confidence and cama-
raderie she had lacked her whole childhood. She whipped quickly
down to the '88 and pulled out a bottle and two glasses, and then
darted back to their spot and nestled in next to Sophie.

"So," her youngest sister prompted, "what is it?"

"You're not going to believe it. Well, I can hardly believe
it myself. I wanted to tell you sooner, but I have hardly had a
chance—the *vendange*, you know. Anyway—" The cork popped
out with a sly hiss and the bubbles poured delightedly into the
glasses. "Finally, Sophie, finally something truly wonderful has
happened to me!"

"Oh, Clementine, don't keep me in suspense. What is it? You
look so . . ." Sophie couldn't think of the word but felt better just
seeing the joy on Clementine's face.

For about a second.

"Hector!" His name tripped across Clementine's lips so effer-
vescently that for the first time in her life she felt bubbly, truly
bubbly. She fizzed and gurgled and popped with the sheer bliss of
loving and being loved by the perfect specimen that had entered
their lives so unexpectedly.

It was difficult for her to believe what had happened, but that
very first night Hector had arrived, the night Clementine herself
had so bitterly jumped to the conclusion that he would not even
notice she was breathing, let alone feel her breath on his naked
skin, he had slid silently into her room and slipped beneath the
covers of her creaky bed.

Clementine, feeling the springs bounce, the warmth of another
body so close to hers, had assumed she was dreaming and sighed
into her pillow, wriggling backward so that her smooth bottom

inside its white linen nightgown fitted neatly into the lap of the man she was imagining lay behind her.

The man's lap sprang to attention, and upon feeling this, the sleepy smile disappeared from Clementine's face and her eyes opened wide in the darkness. She felt him move even closer, heard the rhythm of his heart beating against her back, smelled his salty skin, a hint of rosemary from the duck they had had for dinner. She knew she should repel him, that he had no right, that it was a crime to sneak into a woman's bed unbidden. But she had dreamed of someone just like him doing something just like this for so long that her heart felt no fury, only the pleasure of finally having some real warmth blast into its cold lonely chambers.

She turned over and found that her body, too, was free of indignation, that it had intentions all its own, and far from shrinking away, it was calling out for whatever Hector had to offer. In the end there was nothing unbidden about it. He helped himself to the parts of her that had lain abandoned for so long, and she welcomed him as he had never been welcomed before. It was an extremely inspiring experience for both of them.

"Why?" she had whispered when they lay curled together afterward, his fingers tracing circles in the soft flesh of her white belly. "Why?"

It had been so unlike her one night with Benoît. (So flushed was she in the aftermath of having been with Hector that her hums did not come.) She remembered little but tears and anger and regret from the night Amélie had been conceived, yet this night with Hector there had been only ecstasy—sweet, delirious, hot, sweaty, salty, naked ecstasy. With a hint of rosemary.

"I should go," Hector whispered back instead of answering

Clementine's question. He was nothing if not honest and didn't particularly want to mention La Petite's role in what had just occurred. Instead, he slid out from beneath Clementine's sheets, kissed her bruised and happy lips, and disappeared into the darkness.

She floated through the next week of riddling and preparing for the *vendange,* working her fingers to the bone and focusing on her grapes, her vines, as always. But still an uncustomary smile was never far from her lips. At night, exhausted but exhilarated, she bathed and then crawled into bed and waited for Hector.

She had been so busy reveling in this happiness, this long-awaited delivery from misery and, of course, the wonderful bountiful harvest, that she had quite failed to notice the same symptoms in Sophie.

"Me, too" was all Sophie said in a small voice as Clementine finished telling her about the secret trysts she had been sharing with their extraordinary visitor. "Me, too."

It took a while for Clementine to register this. She was concentrating on the '88, feeling the finish linger on her tongue, the faint trace of apples catching at the back of her throat.

A sourness crept into her saliva. "What do you mean, 'me, too'?"

"I mean *me, too,*" Sophie repeated, her face white, her eyes huge and disbelieving. "With Hector. He wasn't disappearing into the darkness, Clementine. He was coming to me."

"You?"

Sophie nodded miserably. He had been a busy boy the first night he arrived, sliding into her bed, too, the difference being that it was later and she was there waiting for him with open arms. They hadn't spoken at all; they just loved each other, three or four times in a row, the way she knew they would, the way she expected. And he had been back for more, and she was willing to give it, every night since then. It hadn't even occurred to her to wonder what he was doing before he came to her. She assumed he was spending time with La Petite.

Sophie watched the happiness leech out of Clementine before her very eyes; the sourness spread around her sister's body like morphine.

Of course, Clementine snickered cynically to herself, happiness like that didn't belong to her. She had been a fool to relax for even a moment and think that it could. Happiness never belonged to fat, plain, almost virgins who couldn't even bear to think of their lost babies. Happiness belonged to skinny little strumpets like Sophie. Sweet Sophie. Kind Sophie. *Her* Sophie! How that betrayal hurt. And she had been hurt so many times before that she thought she couldn't feel another pain, and yet there it was, that feeling of being left in an ice storm without her skin.

She stood up and, with a grunt that could have belonged to her miserable father, disappeared up the spiral stairs.

Sophie was about to chase after her but found her heart just a bit too broken to manage it right then, so she just sat behind the pinot and wept until the moment passed. She had seen this all coming, after all, and had long acknowledged her expertise at happy beginnings, not endings. But she just hadn't counted on Clementine being a factor. She would stand back and let her sister have Hector, of course: she would have been standing back to let him have someone anyway. But in the meantime she was allowed her little bit of heartache.

Partager

"What have you been sniveling about?" Mathilde accosted Sophie as she snuck back into the house some time later. "Don't tell me the little mouse and the big ox have fallen out! I heard Clementine blubbering her way up the stairs just before. What's going on?"

"Sophie!" La Petite's voice was not strong, but it had a strange way of carrying itself, sort of in a waft, like smoke. Sophie and Mathilde both looked up the stairs as if they could see it snaking its way toward them. "Sophie!" the old woman called again. Mathilde physically recoiled.

"Now you've gone and woken Yoda," she hissed. "So get up there and see what she wants before she starts making a nuisance of herself."

Actually, La Petite had hardly made a nuisance of herself at all since the *vendange* began although it was true that before that she had appeared a little on the demanding side, sending Sophie to the butcher for a particular slice of charcuterie and asking Clementine to mend a tear in her ancient bloomers, for example. Mathilde's sisters had been most obliging. They were women starved of their mothers after all, so they were enticed by La Petite's matriarchal leanings. Mathilde, however, avoided her like the plague. So desperate was she to avoid detection by the old woman that she even slipped her heels off and tiptoed past her room. She never did hear that scratchy old voice call her name, but she could feel her pull nonetheless. Instead of letting it reel her in the way her sisters did, though, she pulled against it, leaned further and further away, still furious that La Petite had exposed her one real weakness: Edie.

The subject of her ten-year-old daughter had been robbing Mathilde of sleep ever since the child's existence had been revealed in that smelly little room. She had her reasons for leaving Edie behind. She just didn't want to have to justify them to anyone, especially her two dim-witted sisters and some half-deranged, wizened-up old raisin. She knew how it looked to them, how it would look to everybody—she was in PR after all—but it was nobody's business but her own, her own and George's and perhaps that of the highly strung little madam they had brought into the world all those years ago and who had spent every minute of her life ever since screwing up Mathilde's.

She had been cursing La Petite for exhuming her buried family, so invasive was she finding her thoughts of them. In fact, her entire body had revolted, breaking out in an unsightly rash that she had kept hidden for the first few days but which was now spreading up her neck toward her face.

She could read the questions in her sisters' eyes every time they looked at her; she felt her skin crawl with every obvious thought. "You've been here all this time, and you have a ten-year-old daughter at home?" She kept hearing that sow Clementine's disbelieving voice ringing in her ears. So strong were the images of Edie, her impossible child, crowding her head, she had barely given a thought to that other daughter La Petite had unveiled.

"For God's sake, Edie, will you just go!" she shouted at Sophie as La Petite called her name again. Sophie looked more bewildered than usual, and, realizing her slipup, Mathilde felt her cheeks burning but hid her embarrassment by slapping at her sister to get her moving.

"All right, all right, I'm going," Sophie said, and it truly could have been Edie. So that is why I find you so annoying, Mathilde thought, watching Sophie walk heavily up the stairs. They were so alike. Not to look at, not at all. But that neediness, that pathetic vulnerability. How could she not have noticed it before?

"Come in," croaked La Petite, and Sophie dragged her forlorn little body into the room and perched on the end of the bed.

"So you know about Hector then, heh?" the old woman asked. "The cat is out of the bag."

"Yes, well, the problem is that there are two bags," Sophie said, "but only one cat."

La Petite laughed so hard she started to choke, clutching at her scrawny chest and hooting hilariously.

"It's not funny," Sophie insisted. "It's awful."

"Maybe a little bit of both, heh?" La Petite suggested. "And anyway it's nothing you can't handle."

Sophie opened her mouth to protest but stopped to think about this a moment and found it to be true. She could handle it; she could handle just about anything. And while she couldn't quite see the humor in it just yet, she admitted that maybe one day in the not too distant future she would. She looked at La Petite and managed a halfhearted smile.

"Oh, Sophie, my little one," La Petite said in a voice so gentle it seemed to belong to a much less phlegmy person. "You must look after these sisters of yours. They need you. Desperately. Both of them. You fill all the gaps."

"The gaps?" Sophie was flabbergasted. "But I am nothing but a gap myself. I'm the biggest gap of them all. I'm useless. I can't even read."

"What does reading have to do with it?" La Petite asked dismissively. "You need to realize that no one has everything. We all have bits and pieces that on their own might make us feel like there is nothing to us, but in the right combination they have their perfect place. Just look at pinot meunier: too fruity by itself to make a drinkable wine but combined with chardonnay and pinot noir, voilà! It *makes* champagne."

Sophie had her doubts. "That may well be, but what if the chardonnay is combining with the pinot noir on the side without mentioning it to the pinot meunier? Does that still make champagne? Or does that make something you would spit up rather than drink?"

"That's entirely up to you," La Petite said.

"You're right, I can handle it," Sophie sighed. "The Hectors of this world are nothing new for me, but poor Clementine, La Petite. He has broken her heart! Combining with the two of us like that. What is he up to?"

There was the sound of someone being extremely furious outside the door, about which La Petite did not look at all surprised.

"You filthy little tramp!" Mathilde burst in, her face screwed up into an angry twist. "Sleeping with the help? A gypsy? Well, I can see why he would 'combine' with you, but that great fat heap down the hallway? It's disgusting, that's what it is. We should throw him in the loony bin along with Old Nut or Little Nut or whatever the hell she is called before his pecker falls off or his brain turns to mush, although clearly if he's screwing Clementine, we are already too late for that."

La Petite laughed, knowing full well that a bitter, angry person hates nothing more than being mocked. "Such concern, Mathilde. I'm touched."

"Touched is right!" snapped Mathilde. "They don't come more touched than you."

Clementine appeared in the room then, her face blotchy from crying. "What's going on?" she asked. "What's all the yelling about?"

Mathilde turned on her. "Just because you managed to trick some poor, blind, stupid man into impregnating you a hundred years ago, Clementine, does not mean you have to offer your repulsive self up to—"

"Don't you *dare* talk to her like that!" shouted Sophie, entering the fray, her own golden cheeks now rosy with anger. "She's your sister!"

"I don't need you," Clementine hissed at her. "I can speak for myself. Don't you *dare* talk to me like that, Mathilde. This has nothing to do with you." She stopped, a look of horror spreading across her face. "Unless? Oh, no, not you, too? I couldn't bear it!"

"Couldn't bear what?" Hector asked, appearing with a tray of bread and honey for La Petite. "Or have I come at a bad time?"

"Oh, I love it when this happens," cried his great-grandmother, clapping her little curled hands in front of her. "Encore! Encore!"

"Please tell me you didn't sleep with Mathilde," Clementine pleaded.

"Okay," Hector shrugged as he put the tray down. "I didn't sleep with her."

"But did you?" asked Sophie.

"Clementine asked me to say I didn't," Hector said, sitting on the bed.

"You are good," La Petite cackled. "You are very good."

"But did you?" Clementine shouted. "You can say you did if you did, just not if you didn't. That's not what I meant by telling you not to tell me."

"I'm a bit confused now," Hector said cheerfully. "But the truth of the matter is that I did sleep with you and Sophie, which was very nice, thank you very much, but not with Mathilde. She wanted me to, but she's really not my type."

"Why, you slimy little shit," spat Mathilde. "I wouldn't sleep with you if you were the last man on earth."

"That's not what you said when you sneaked into my room and whispered in my ear about blow jobs," Hector rebutted, at which La Petite laughed fit to die.

In fact, she made such a long-drawn-out gagging noise that ended suddenly in dead silence that everyone in the room stopped their arguing and stared at her in horror.

"Not yet," she said eventually, eyes still closed. "Don't worry, I'll give you plenty of warning."

Clementine and Sophie breathed a sigh of relief. Hector just smiled. Mathilde further shriveled with rage.

"You'll be sorry," she said, pointing a slightly scabby finger at Hector before turning her disdainful gaze on her sisters. "And so will you two pathetic creatures." And out the door she stalked.

"I already am sorry," Sophie said, looking at Clementine. "Really sorry."

"I trusted you," Clementine replied. "I thought you were my friend." She whispered the last word, so precious and unfamiliar was it to her.

"But Mentine, I am your friend," Sophie protested hotly. "I didn't know! Hector, you have to tell her. I had no idea. I would never, ever, ever do anything to hurt you. You're all I have. Please don't be angry with me, Mentine. I'll do anything as long as you're not angry with me. And, anyway, when you think about it, if you are going to be angry with anyone, shouldn't it be Hector? And shouldn't I be, too?"

They looked at him spreading honey on a slice of *pain au levain* for his great-grandmother, and even for Clementine it was extremely difficult to feel anger.

"I'm not Mathilde," Sophie said softly into the lull that followed. "I did not take Hector to hurt you, Mentine. It's not the way it was with Benoît. I would never do that to anyone, but I would especially never do that to you."

Clementine realized with a jolt that Sophie was right: it was not the way it had been with Benoît. Her feelings for him were quite different from what she felt for Hector, which was really mostly about the touch of his skin, the smell of his hair, and the angle of his collarbones. Truthfully, she did not mind so much about Hector as she did about Sophie betraying her. But if there had been no betrayal?

"It's just what we do," Hector assured them with his charming smile. "We share."

"Well, I don't know if we're a sharing sort of family," Clementine said bluntly.

"Not that sort of sharing anyway," Sophie agreed.

"Okay, then, if I have to choose one of you, I choose you,

Clementine," Hector said, taking a bite out of the bread himself. "If that's all right."

Clementine opened her mouth to say that it certainly was not all right, that she was not some piece of meat to be haggled over like a ham hock in a common *boucherie*, but then she thought of snuggling up against all that taut brown muscle and found her tongue unwilling to waggle.

Sophie took this as a yes and clapped her hands with glee. "That's settled then!" she announced delightedly and shared a special triumphant look with La Petite who had deigned to open one eye to take in the proceedings.

"Settled, my foot," grumbled Clementine, but it was without rancor. It was nice, after all, to be chosen.

Le Cochelet

The next couple of days were odd ones at the House of Peine, which is saying something because the days there were odd to begin with.

The three sisters mixed somewhat incompatibly like curdled ingredients in a kitchen bowl. Mathilde avoided everybody, and everybody avoided her, but then Clementine was avoiding Sophie, too. The bond between them had actually been strengthened by the business with Hector, yet Clementine was so grateful in a way that she felt suffocated by it. She just kept busy, delivering the *stampes* to the winery, supervising the pressing, and counting the moments until she could sneak between the sheets and be the person she had always dreamed of being with a man she had never dared imagine.

Her path barely crossed Hector's during the day, but when it did, Clementine felt as though the sun moved its beam and shone only on the two of them. It was not as though he lavished her with affection in public or anything like that. He never would, and she would die of mortification anyway, but just the way he stood so close that their arm hairs stuck out and nearly touched each other sent a thrill rippling across her skin that made her feel more alive than she had ever felt before. A few days after the business with Sophie was "settled," she came upon him at the end of a row as she was driving a tractor load of grapes to the winery. He put down the basket he was carrying, glanced casually around to see if any of his pickers were watching, and jumped up on to the tractor, sitting backward on the rusty hood so that he was facing her.

Now, watching Hector jump on a tractor was not like watching anyone else jump on a tractor. He moved with a natural grace pretty much possessed only by panthers, and it was transfixing, especially to someone like her. She could throw one supple leg over a bicycle saddle quite gracefully if no one was looking, but in company she always moved clumsily. Worse, this awkwardness of hers was often catching. Others who were normally quite fleet of foot suddenly moved stodgily in her company, tripping over things they usually would have sidestepped; catching their hips on corners they had avoided for years. But here was the thing: in Hector's presence it was different. He didn't acquire her self-conscious clumsiness; she acquired his effortless ease and found herself moving in ways that a woman totally confident in herself, her body, and her sexiness might move.

On the occasion of Hector's jumping on the tractor, before she stopped to think about it, she stood up and leaned forward, tucking a dark curl that had escaped from his bandanna behind his ear. He grinned at her, and she returned the grin, settling back lightly into the uncomfortable tractor seat—not in the way of many women who carry a few extra pounds where the relief of getting off their feet shines in every pore of their faces, but in an almost dainty fashion. Her wraparound skirt came away just then, part of one muscled thigh exposing itself to the sun, prompting a lascivious glance and a bigger grin from Hector. Clementine basked in it. *Basked.* He jumped down—it really should not have been an *aaahhhh* moment, but it was—and she watched him as he headed back to work, eyeing the easy swing of his hips and the square cut of his shoulders. She threw her head back, closed her eyes, and felt the autumn sun tickle her eyelids and massage her smile. When she opened her eyes again, Benoît was there, not a hundred meters away, sitting on his tractor, a trailer full of berries loaded up in his *stampes* behind him.

For the first time in eighteen years they looked at each other. It wasn't for long, yet it felt like a lifetime. Clementine could see the space between them packed with words, all jumbled up, separated, spelled out, and stretching in different fonts and sizes so that any meaning was lost, confused, and pointless. How can you think so much in such a short time and say none of it, she asked herself? How can we have done what we did all those years ago and never speak of it? How can there be a person out there whom we brought into the world that we have never even seen? That I can't even think about? That you don't even know about?

How did this happen to us?

If Benoît got any of this, if he saw those words and put them in order, she couldn't tell, but there was a twitch in his cheek and perhaps the beginning of a timid smile. It could have been going to say hello, that smile, or congratulations or how *did* this happen to us?

There is something between us, I know there is, Clementine thought to herself. After all this time she could still feel it, recognized it even more clearly than ever before in a way. But what was the use? She held his gaze a second longer, then put the tractor into gear and in a cloud of fumes drove away.

She passed Sophie on the road near the house and caught her eye, too. Sophie never bothered with the beginnings of a smile; hers was as big as a slice of watermelon. La Petite was spot-on when it came to the littlest Peine's heart. Sophie might not have been able to comprehend the written word with much clarity, but she sure as heck got what Clementine was feeling right down to the smallest convoluted globule of gratitude mixed with resentment and dotted with confusion. Because of this she was happy to keep her distance for a while, but she hugged closely to her narrow chest the fact that her eldest sister was still her friend.

After delivering her grapes to the winery, Clementine watched as the meunier cascaded into the press and listened to the almost imperceptible burble of the juice escaping, collecting, and pouring down to the floor below.

At the moment she was standing directly above Mathilde, who continued to grow blacker and smaller as the *vendange* progressed. The clipboard was still there, the Montblanc pen still scratching away at it. But that phone in her room taunted her now; her dreams of Edie and George had become nightmares. Her empty pastis collection was growing; the Xanax supplies were dwindling. She had picked up the cursed phone the previous night, unable to sleep, and had started to punch in the apartment phone number, but fear stopped her. Fear! Fear of what? She couldn't answer that. All she could do was despise herself for feeling it, drink more, and wait for sleep to put her out of her misery.

La Petite knew all this; she could feel it from her bed where she was cheerfully examining her slow descent toward the next phase of her life or afterlife. It wasn't an unpleasant feeling in the least, rather a cross between relief and striking just the right combination of cheeses. Anyway, she had other things to think about. Her descent was slow because she clearly still had her work cut out. Olivier had been right to feel concern for Clementine and Sophie, but those two were as transparent as water. One had been starved of love and affection and so had never known what to do with it; the other gave it away without ever expecting it back. But Mathilde, what a complicated kettle of *cabillaud* she was! She knew what love was all right and didn't want it, ran from it with all her might, which was considerable. Hers was a situation a little harder to broach, a little more challenging to reverse. Hector could not help Mathilde; he would only be more of the same. What Mathilde needed was her family—all of them.

"I think we need to write a letter, Hector," La Petite told her great-grandson later that night. He was stretched out on the bed next to her, hands behind his head. "The Americans?" he asked her.

"Of course. There's not much time, either, is there?"

"For me? We'll be finished tomorrow."

"Does the fat one know?"

"She's not really that fat, you know, Petite."

"Yes, yes, but does she know you are going?"

"I suppose. All the grapes are nearly picked, and she certainly knows all there is to know about them. And what about you, Petite? How much time before you go?"

La Petite smiled. "Truthfully, I am ready now. But these Peines are a bigger job than I expected. We need to write this letter, Hector. There's no twiddly-deeing in the world that will help Mathilde. We need the other two—the sisters—and then the other two. Do you know what I am saying?"

"About everything but the twiddly-deeing, Petite. We haven't called it that for centuries."

As usual the last day of the *vendange* was celebrated with a party, known by the pickers as *le cochelet*. After every grape had been plucked off every vine and the juice had been wrung out of each last one, La Petite's gang gathered in the courtyard between the house and the winery around makeshift tables laden with bottles of *brut*, loaves of bread, and steaming bowls of *potée champenoise*, a traditional dish of meat, cabbage, and other rich pickings from the Peine vegetable garden.

Usually, Clementine hated *le cochelet*. In previous years she had begrudgingly made the stew but had then hidden in her room while the pickers helped themselves to the Peine champagne and ignored Olivier as he drank himself slowly under the table.

This year was different. Clementine sat next to Hector at the main table, a becoming flush on her cheeks as she self-consciously urged the pickers to try the bottles of vintage champagne she had brought up from the *cave*.

Sophie sat at the next table between a dark-eyed young Hector look-alike and a grizzled old Rumpelstiltskin of a man whose eyebrows were so long they grew straight up and met with the hair on his head. This was Sophie's first harvest party, and she was loving it. The atmosphere was electric with the sound of the pickers' chatter and the clinking of glasses and plates. La Petite, not wanting to miss out, had let Hector carry her downstairs and prop her up with some of her flock. She held court at the far table, huddled inside a swathe of blankets, her claw of a hand poking out, always with a glass in it.

Only Mathilde shunned the celebrations, staying in her room with a head full of dark thoughts and a heart full of turmoil.

When the music started—there were at least three fiddlers among the pickers—La Petite smiled her toothless smile as Hector pulled Clementine to her feet and whirled her around the cobbled courtyard.

"Look at what a little bit of twiddly-dee can do for a woman!" she cackled in her native tongue to the great-great nephew sitting next to her.

"She certainly doesn't look like the bitter old prune we normally see this time of year," he chirruped back, his eyes on his shapely fifteen-year-old second cousin whose bare belly button was diverting his attention.

"The prune is gone," La Petite sighed happily. "Gone."

But the prune came back briefly later that night when Hector, having wined and dined her, made love until every bone in her body tingled, and then slipped out of her bed and told her he would see her the following year.

"Next year!" Clementine cried, sitting up, one round naked shoulder glimmering in the moonlight. "But! But! But!"

"But what did you think?" Hector asked her gently, sitting back down and tracing a line from her ear down to the spongy valley between her breasts. "I'm the head of the pack now. We're due elsewhere."

"There's more sharing to be done, I suppose?" she asked, already moved on from angry to wistful.

"It's what we do, Mentine," he said and proceeded to kiss his way up her neck and then whisper in her ear. "And doesn't it feel good? Like *sabayon*!"

He had just strolled into Clementine's life, this perfect specimen, and laughingly thrown all her dismal expectations up, up, up into the air, never to fall back to earth in quite the same spot.

And now it was over. She knew that. But she could no longer honestly reclaim her best friend, bitterness, because she also knew that she was better off being loved by Hector for a short time than for no time at all.

She had sadness and plenty of it, but she had happiness, too—the sort of happiness she didn't know she could have until Hector came along.

Given all this, there was nothing to do but pull him back for one last round of twiddly-deeing.

And then she let him go.

Encore des Invités

The warmth was moving swiftly out of the Marne, dragging with it the vibrant greens of the leafy vines and leaving behind a mottled carpet of brown and tan.

When the first frost of the season arrived, there was not so much as a burp of indigestion from the *vignerons*. A frost at this time of year could wreak little havoc. The *chaufferettes* could stay quietly rusting in the barn. The leaves were about to fall anyway, clearing the way for the arduous task of pruning in the chilly days that lay ahead.

No, the only sleepless night in the valley on that first frosty night was had by Mathilde, and it was sheer coincidence that when the temperature plummeted she plummeted with it, hitting rock bottom that very morning and not with a dramatic thud, either, but with a whisper so sly no one heard it, not even her.

She had lain awake the whole night and lay awake still as the sun rose and shone harshly through her curtainless window. It was bright enough to hurt her eyes but had nowhere near the oomph required to keep the room from freezing; her quilt offered little respite from the chill that ate away at her bones. All she could rely on for warmth were the dwindling contents of the near empty bottle that she clutched beneath the covers.

Had Mathilde been a vine, her Peine forebears would no doubt have compared her to the flourishing specimens growing on either side and seriously weighed her viability. Something had gotten under her skin and was sucking the life out of her, that was obvious. And any *vigneron* worth his salt knew that there were only two options for a vine in that condition: give up, rip it out of the ground, and throw it on the compost heap, or persevere, save it, and graft it onto new, healthy rootstock.

But Mathilde was not a vine. She was floundering alone on a rocky outcrop. Nobody had even noticed her deterioration. Her body, lying in its bed all on its own, curled around a bottle, was only just this side of being emaciated. She was as thin as a post; her skin was still scarred and crusty with the rash she could not shake. Her hair was limp and shapeless, its faded strawberry roots making the forgotten Paris blonde look exhausted in comparison. As her once stellar looks suffered, so, too, did her inner health. Too much drink and too little food had left her thoughts jumbled and confused. All she was really aware of now was the very real dread collecting in her shrunken stomach like a tumor, gathering momentum, getting bigger and fiercer the more she refused to confront it.

Her work in the winery had crashed to a halt a few days earlier when she had found herself suddenly unable to write down a single word on her clipboard. Her pen had become clumsy in her hand, seeming to grow comically beneath her touch until eventually it became too enormous to grasp. Her thoughts, too, could no longer fit in her head; her mind could not dictate what she wanted to think.

Mathilde had been frightened by this in a way she had never been frightened before, but there she was, alone on that outcrop, having so successfully alienated everyone with her rudeness that even had they noticed her decline, they may not have been moved to help her.

Her sisters had been giving her a particularly wide berth since her cruel remarks to Clementine following Hector's departure.

"He's probably somewhere in the Ardenne having the time of his life with an eighteen-year-old stripper by now," she had commented airily. "What a relief to no longer be tortured by such a flabby old spinster as you."

But this had been the beginning of Mathilde's downward slide because she had known as she said the words that they were cruel and would cause pain, and this, to her horror, had brought her no pleasure. Usually Mathilde felt the thrill of the hunter when she hit her target. And this thrill wasn't a made-up thing; it was a ping, a physical sensation, almost painful but with great triumph attached, that thwacked at her heart. Normally, it surged through her, and she gained strength from it—a little like being plugged into the national grid. But on this occasion the thrill had been missing, replaced instead by that infernal clawing at her innards that had rendered her incapable of enjoying anything but the harshest of spirits.

Mathilde had felt her sanity slithering between her scaly fingers ever since then; she had been drinking through the night to keep whatever it was that was haunting her at bay and had been unable to muster the energy to get out of bed—not that anyone cared.

Anyone other than La Petite, that was. For the first time in her long life she had stayed resolutely put when the other grape pickers moved on. Clementine had been baffled and Sophie delighted, but

Mathilde had all but picked her up and thrown her out the window. How she had ranted and raved about the old crone polluting their atmosphere and poisoning their lives! But the other two had ignored her, and as Mathilde lost the capacity to rant and rage, so La Petite settled into the strange new rhythm of the house.

Now, while Mathilde lay frozen and chasing numbness under the covers, La Petite sat up in her bed, warm as toast with Cochon cuddled next to her, craning her skinny chicken neck to see what the frost had done to the Champagne countryside. It was a shame she couldn't get down to see Saint Vincent. A decent frost would surely give him a sparkly white beret that would tickle her funny bone no end. Still, she sighed a little murmur of contentment at being so snug and close to heaven when Mother Nature had covered everything else in her icy blanket. This sigh led to a hiccup, which led to her calling out to Sophie to bring her a cup of coffee and some Turkish delight, which she knew was in the cupboard and about which she had had the enormous pleasure of dreaming.

She was missing Hector, as were they all, but she was stirred up by something else this particular morning, not just the promise of rose water and pistachio sweets. Today was going to be a big day. The big day. Mathilde's *vigneron* forebears might not be there to seal her fate, but they had left a proxy in La Petite, who was not going to die before she had done all she could to ensure that the middle Peine was grafted, not composted. She was particularly grateful to have woken up with this excitement jiggling in her belly because she was worried that she might have left her run a bit late or had been too slow with the letter or had not worded it correctly.

Just as she was revisiting this niggling doubt, there was the sound of wheels spinning in the driveway followed by car doors slamming, the crunch of gravel under heels, and, finally, after a selection of mutterings always brought on by the knobless front door, the rat-a-tat-tat of a gloved hand knocking on it.

Downstairs, Sophie nearly jumped out of her skin. Clementine was in the winery, seeking solace by tending her adolescent wine, so it was hardly going to be she who was knocking. But who then? The whole time Sophie had been there, only two people had come to the door, herself and some nervous pimply priest whom Clementine had yelled at so robustly, he had turned and fled, cassock flapping, returning from whence he had come without so much as crossing the threshold.

She put La Petite's tea tray down, and when she finally wrenched the recalcitrant door open, much to her amazement there was a half-sized version of her eldest sister standing on the doorstep. It was as though Clementine had been reduced on a photocopying machine. The proportions were the same, the crinkly ginger hair, the suspicious dark eyes, and even the wary, slightly sour placement of the lips, one on top of the other, slightly pinched and only too ready to be even more so.

Sophie was temporarily confused. "Amélie?" she asked. But how could it be? Amélie would be seventeen or eighteen by now. This was just a moppet.

"Who the frick is Amélie?" the moppet asked, her gaze frank, her freckles standing out like orange Icelandic poppies.

"Excuse me, *mademoiselle*," a distinguished-looking gentleman standing next to her said in dreadful French. "I regret too much arriving on you like this, but I think it is the better way. Is it possible to enter?"

Sophie's thinking was working in slow motion. She took in the gentleman. He wore an expensive black wool coat, lovely leather gloves, and shiny punched leather shoes that she thought someone other than he had probably polished. He had neatly clipped hair and white teeth. He seemed very American. Sophie's mouth dropped down to her chest. "George?" She looked back at the little girl. "And Edie? Are you Edie?"

"Well, at least she's heard of us," Edie told her father in a voice far too world-weary for someone young enough to be carrying a slightly grubby pink panther toy on one purple velvet hip. She shivered inside her sheepskin-lined tunic and then peered behind Sophie into the gloomy hallway.

"I'm so sorry," Sophie said, realizing they were still standing on the doorstep. The wind was whipping off the frosty ground so robustly that the tips of her ears were like ice chips. "I'm Sophie. Come in, come in."

"It smells funny in here," Edie said loudly as she made her way down the hallway. "I hope you have mold insurance."

"You speak such good French," Sophie said, ignoring what she had said as she led the pair into the kitchen. "Did your mother teach you?"

"Yeah, right," Edie answered. She plunked herself down at the kitchen table and nuzzled her pink panther. "Do you have any chocolate chip cookie dough ice cream?"

"Please excuse my daughter," George said. "It's been a long day, and I gave her licorice in the car."

Sophie wasn't quite sure what that was supposed to mean but nodded sympathetically and put the coffeepot on.

"He means where we come from kids aren't supposed to eat sugar," Edie explained. "It makes them hyper. So what about frogs? Do you have any of those? And snails? You eat them, too, huh? Is my mother here, by the way? She does not like mold. Do you even have a dehumidifier?"

"Edie," her father said tiredly. "Remember what we talked about in the car."

Edie bit her lip. "How you have to wash your hands after using the public restroom so that you don't get a baby off the toilet seat?"

"Edie!" It had clearly been a long trip. "You know that's not true! And that is not what we were talking about."

"Yeah, yeah, Dad." That same world-weary tone crept back. "I know. I'm supposed to keep very quiet and not say anything to Mom about running away and leaving me."

"Edie!"

"What?" his daughter asked, wide-eyed and innocent. "I'm talking to Sophie. You didn't tell me not to say anything to her. You didn't even mention her."

Sophie put a baguette and a dish of the Mirabella jam in front of Edie, and her face lit up.

"Cool! Look at this breadstick! Mom tells people I can't have gluten, but that's only because she says so, not because I'm allergic or anything. Hey"—her mouth was full already—"this jelly is good! Is that plum? I can taste ginger. Oh, wow."

George looked as though he was bursting with the effort of not telling her to slow down, but he dragged his eyes away from her and looked instead around the homely kitchen. "So, this is where she's been all these months," he said wistfully.

Sophie did not like to point out that Mathilde pretty much ventured into the kitchen only when she had filled up every ashtray in the house and needed to find a new one. "Mm-hm," she agreed politely, giving him a shy smile.

176

"Edie, would you like to go outside and play for a few minutes?" he said. "I'd like to talk to Sophie."

Edie looked at him blankly. "Play?" she answered, dramatically dropping her bread and jam back on the plate in front of her. "Where? Isn't this, like, a farm? What am I going to play on? A combine harvester? A haystack? Dad, please. I'm from Manhattan."

Sophie could only partly follow this, but partly was enough. "One moment," she said, and going to the foot of the stairs, she whistled vigorously up toward La Petite's room. No doubt at the old women's insistence, Cochon came bounding down the stairs, ears forward, and pranced prettily behind her into the kitchen.

Edie nearly fell off her chair at the sight of him. "What the frick is that?" she cried, abandoning the pink panther, getting down on her knees, and opening her arms to the little horse who nuzzled straight into them. "Oh, wow! His neck smells beautiful!" Her face was buried in it. "Like new shoes!"

"He's a dwarf miniature horse," Sophie said, "but he's named after a pig. A little misunderstanding at birth, you might say."

"He's adorable." Edie was entranced and Cochon similarly. "Dad? Don't you think? Look at his little tail and his tiny little feet. He's like a dog only like a million times better." Cochon licked her beaming face with his rough pink tongue, and then amid peals of her laughter, the two of them skated across the kitchen floor and out the back door into the cold.

Edie

"I got a letter," George said once Edie was gone, "from . . . I think she said she's your great-grandmother. Mrs. Petite, is it?"

Sophie laughed. Well, La Petite was *someone*'s great-grandmother, and she supposed it was a better way to introduce herself to George than as his estranged wife's estranged father's itinerant gypsy grape picker. "What did she say?" she asked pleasantly.

"She said that Mathilde was here and desperately needed us. I got the impression she was . . . I don't know, in some sort of trouble."

"You didn't think to come sooner? She's been here since May."

This just slipped out, and Sophie regretted it when she saw how stricken George looked.

"I know what you must think of me," he said, "and believe me, I think it, too. But the truth is, I'm afraid of flying. I haven't been on an airplane until today, yesterday, whenever it was, since I was Edie's age. I still . . ."

He broke off and then put his elbows on the table and rested his head in his hands. Suddenly his hair seemed thinner and grayer, his shirt collar not quite so crisp, and his nails not so expertly clipped.

"I'm so sorry," he said, seemingly to the table. "It's been a very long day. We got lost driving from the airport. Edie has been asking so many goddamned questions, and I don't know how to answer them. I don't know what the hell is going on. That is the truth. I don't know what the hell is going on, but—shit—that's not it, either. Shit!"

Sophie said nothing. She had seen people unravel before, and in fact George was doing it most politely. She just waited.

"To begin with, I didn't come earlier because I thought she'd be home soon," he said eventually. "I really did. She's done it before, you know—shot off for a while, left a couple of messages, acted like it was nothing out of the ordinary, and come back with expensive gifts but no apology. I mean, that is pure Mathilde. But she's worth it. I accept that. For a long while I accepted it. But this time it was different. This time, before I knew it, one week had turned into two, then two into four. She'd been gone a month, a whole month, and you know what?" When he looked at Sophie, his eyes were filled with the beginnings of tears. "I realized I liked it better without her." His voice broke. "And Edie, God, Edie has been like a different kid. Happy. Normal. No tantrums, no fights, no . . ." He broke off and let Sophie pour him another cup of coffee.

"I'm sorry," he said. "I've never done this before. I guess I have jet lag or something. You don't even know me, and here I am pouring my heart out all over your kitchen table."

"It's good like that, this table," said the softhearted Sophie with true sympathy. "So, do you want me to tell Mathilde you are here?"

George blew out a lungful of breath. "How is she?"

Sophie was nothing if not diplomatic. "I don't know how she was before," she pointed out.

"I know she can be a little abrasive," he conceded. "She's kind of famous for it—especially when she's tired. She works too hard."

"She's certainly been pretty abrasive since she got here," Sophie agreed. "And she hasn't been looking so good. She doesn't really eat. And she's drinking a lot and taking pills, too, I think." Actually, she had not seen Mathilde for the past few days. "Come to think of it, she may not have gotten out of bed for a while."

George was silent. So this was the trouble, the danger. "Back home," he said, "we call that—"

"You bastard!"

Sophie nearly jumped out of her skin but should have known better than to assume Mathilde was quietly tucked away somewhere while the secrets that made her human were being revealed.

"How dare you?"

George's mouth was open to answer his wife, but the state of her had rendered him speechless. Her bathrobe had slipped off to reveal one skeletal shoulder, her hair was lank and matted on one side, and her eyes were sunken deep into her skull.

"How dare you come here! How dare you talk to her!" Mathilde pointed one thin shaking finger at them. She looked like a witch.

With expert timing Cochon chose that precise moment to skitter back into the kitchen with a ruddy-cheeked, mud-splattered Edie in tow. She had some sort of foliage caught in one of her curls, and her pants had slipped down to reveal a pale slice of smooth, chubby flesh underneath her striped T-shirt.

"Mom!" she cried when she saw Mathilde standing there. She

started to move toward her but became uncertain when Cochon dug in his heels, rolled his eyes back in his head, and bared his teeth. Edie stopped then, too, and changed her tack. "Can I have a little horse like this one, Mom?"

Mathilde made no attempt to conceal her horror at the sight of her daughter. Sophie had to keep from crying out as she watched this instantly sink in with Edie; confusion, disappointment, and fear rippled across the little girl's face.

"Mom?" Her voice lost its excitement and took on a whining tone. She plucked the pink panther from the chair where she had left it and started tugging at its ear. "I'll feed it and take it for walks and clean up after it. The little horse. It won't be like the dog, Mom. Or the hamster. Or the rat. I promise. Mom?"

But with a slow-motion whirl of pastel chiffon, Mathilde turned on her kitten heels, floated down the hallway, pulled open the front door, made her way over to the *deux chevaux*, climbed in, and drove off.

"Shit," said George, watching her disappear in a cloud of dust from the doorstep. "Shit, shit, shit!"

"You have a car," Sophie urged him. "Follow her."

"What did I do?" Edie asked, starting to cry. "Daddy, what did I do? I never said a thing about her leaving. I just want a little horsey-pig thing. Dad? Dad?"

"Not now, Edie!"

"I'll take care of her," Sophie said to George, giving him a shove. "You just go."

"She hates me, she hates me, she hates me," wept Edie as her father scrabbled for his keys and jumped in his rental car to follow Mathilde. Sophie took the child by her heaving shoulders and headed her back inside, Cochon trotting along supportively at her side. But inside the door Edie shook off Sophie's hands and collapsed on the bottom stair, weeping as though her heart were breaking. At first Sophie tried to soothe her, but because she knew exactly what it felt like to be abandoned by your mother, she had trouble keeping this up and soon started to weep, too.

Cochon had limited patience for this sort of thing. He had grown up with Clementine and Olivier, after all, and did not particularly care for outbursts of any emotion other than anger. After a few minutes he remembered the comfort of La Petite's bed, and taking one slightly disgusted look at the two bawling beauties in front of him, he leaped between them and bounded up the stairs with his tiny horse hoof clatter.

"Sophie-e-e-e-e." The old woman's voice soon wafted down the stairs. "Sophie-e-e-e-e!" The two girls dried their tears and looked toward the ceiling.

"What is that?" Edie sniffed. "It sounds spooky."

Sophie laughed, her spirits already restored, and wiped her own nose. "It is, sort of." She got up and held out a hand for Edie to grab. "Come on. Let's go and meet La Petite."

The old woman was sitting up in bed twinkling with anticipation when the two of them stepped into the room. "Aha-a," she croaked. "At last I get to meet the new generation. Welcome, my sweet."

Edie went right to the bed and ran her chubby fingers over La Petite's crinkled face and then patted her greasy braid. "Wow! How old are you?" she asked. "You must be like a thousand."

"I certainly feel a thousand," La Petite agreed. "But I might actually be only five hundred. So what do you make of it all so far?"

"I love the little horse," Edie said, jumping up on the bed and helping herself to some Turkish delight. "But my mom has run away, which is pretty weird because she was run away in the first place. And my dad's all tense and crazy. I'm not sure how it's going to end up."

Sophie was astounded. It was as though Edie and La Petite had known each other forever and were merely picking up on strands of a conversation that had started over tea and *madeleines* earlier in the day.

"Have you two met?" she asked, sidling over and sitting on the end of the bed, helping herself to a sweet as well.

Edie looked at La Petite. "You do kind of look like Mrs. Milligan. She lives in our building," she said. "Only her wrinkles don't go in so many different directions."

La Petite hooted with laughter.

"Mrs. Milligan makes the best chocolate brownies," Edie told Sophie. "She says gluten-free is a crock." She popped more Turkish delight in her mouth. "This is really nice," she said. "It tastes like flowers."

"You certainly inherited the family way with words," La Petite told her kindly, although it occurred to Sophie that the family didn't really have a way with words. "Now what's with the tears I see shining on those cheeks?"

Edie looked at her, weighing what she should tell the old woman.

"We-e-e-ell," she eventually began, her chin jutting out in mild defiance, "I think everyone cries when their mother runs away from them. Twice."

La Petite passed a piece of candy to Cochon, but he was really a chocolate horse. He spat it out on Mathilde's Frette linen and licked at it halfheartedly before sighing and closing his eyes. "Why do you think your mother is so fond of running away?" La Petite asked.

Edie pulled at her sleeve. "Well, I guess I screwed up her life—you know, by being born and all."

"That's not true," Sophie said. "You mustn't say that."

"She says it herself," argued Edie, which somewhat diluted Sophie's point.

"She can be pretty mean," La Petite pointed out. "We've noticed that ourselves."

"You have?" Edie was astonished. "Usually grown-ups call it something else."

"Grown-ups can be very annoying like that," La Petite said, "but mean is mean in my opinion, especially when you're on the receiving end of it. Of course, there's usually a good reason for a person to turn mean. It's not an entirely natural condition."

"But what reason does Mathilde have to be mean?" Sophie felt moved to ask. "She has everything a person could ask for. What's missing?"

"Yes, Edie," La Petite asked, "what's missing?"

Edie screwed up her nose and took a deep breath. Just because nobody had ever asked for her opinion didn't mean she didn't have one. "It just hasn't turned out the way she expected," she said in a way that made Sophie want to cry again that she thought of such things. "I guess maybe she didn't know what it would be like having a kid, and if I was a pair of shoes, she would have taken me back and got a refund because I didn't fit right. But you're not allowed to do that with kids. There are laws."

"You look pretty good to me," La Petite said. "What makes you think you don't fit right?"

"We-e-ell," Edie said again, making a play of pulling at one thick, fuzzy ginger ringlet, "I think she prefers blondes."

"But that's just hair!" cried Sophie even more upset now.

"Yes, but I'm also not pretty like her, and I'm, you know, kind of tubby. I really like chocolate chip cookie dough ice cream even though Mom tells everyone I'm lactose intolerant, but it's just like the gluten. I'm not, you know, allergic or anything. I'm just not allowed it."

"Phut." La Petite was deeply unimpressed. "You poor girl. You got here just in time. Don't worry, my sweet, about your mother or your father or any little thing. It's going to end up just fine."

La Petite's great-grandfather had also taught her that sometimes all a poor lost soul needed was to be told that everything was going to be all right. There was nothing magical about that, either.

"So what about school?" the old woman continued.

"Oh, that." Edie's face fell, and Sophie felt a sympathetic strumming in her chest. "Um, well, the good news is that I'm not deep down stupid because I've had all the tests, but I don't read and write so good. I'm not the only one in fifth grade who gets special lessons, but it sure makes my mom pretty mad."

One chubby little hand reached into the Turkish delight box, icing sugar puffing up into the air as she scrabbled.

"Edie," La Petite said, sounding very serious, "I am going to tell you something that no one else may ever tell you, and I want you to listen very carefully to me. And when I'm gone, I want you to listen to your aunt Sophie because she will tell you the same thing. It is something you need to know."

Edie looked at her. "If it's about the man's penis and the woman's vagina, I've been told that already, and, frankly, I'm not surprised you all drink so much."

"The penis and vagina business I'll leave to someone else, I promise," the old woman said with remarkable composure.

"Well, that's a relief," Edie told her. "So, shoot."

"In my time, which as you know there has been quite a lot of," she said, settling herself importantly in her bed and laying her crinkled hands neatly on top of the covers, "I have seen many, many little girls who have something wrong with them, and I can officially tell you right here and now that you are not one of them. There is absolutely nothing wrong with you! Nothing at all! You are perfect just the way you are. Perfect. The trouble—and it's not with you at all, you see—is that your mother is mean. It's not her fault, but that does not change the fact that she is mean. She never learned how to be a good mother, and that's a shame for both of you. But the good news is, it's not too late. It's never too late. Your aunts and I are going to help her."

"We are?" Sophie had her doubts. "Does Clementine know this?"

"We are. Especially Clementine. She doesn't know it yet, but she will. And your father's going to help, too," La Petite told Edie, "although we may need to get him a new spine."

"My dad is actually pretty cool," Edie told them. "Well, maybe not cool, but I didn't ruin his life. He told me that. He says his life has been better since I was in it, which is a pretty nice thing to say to your kid, don't you think?"

"You, my sweet," La Petite said, opening her arms to Edie, "might even be better than perfect."

"And you might be better than Mrs. Milligan," Edie told her, climbing into her embrace. "Her brownies sure are good, but she does smell of mothballs."

Amitié

For two hours George combed the busy highways and narrow back lanes of the Marne from Chierry to Boursault looking for Mathilde, but to no avail. Of course, such was the state of his French that he'd had trouble asking anyone if they'd seen her, but he had done his best. They had seemed to understand even if his inquiries had met nothing but head shakes and looks of great pity. When he arrived back, his face gray with worry and fatigue, and she saw how distraught he was, Sophie offered to go out with him again, an offer he gladly accepted.

"What about Edie?" he whispered in the hallway. "I don't think she should come. I don't want her to see her mother—"

"I'll get Clementine to mind her," Sophie said with a confidence she did not entirely feel. She had heard Clementine's opinion of nearly every child in the village, and none of them were flattering. Still, she knew her sister well enough by now to suspect that her animosity just disguised her vulnerability on the subject of offspring, so while George waited in the car, she took Edie over to the winery. Cochon refused as usual to entertain the spiral stairs, so it was just the two of them weaving around the vats in the *cave*.

"Look at her hair!" cried Edie when she first spied Clementine. "It's just like mine!"

Clementine did not see or hear her because she was mid-hum, a more regular occurrence since Hector's departure.

"Please, Mentine," implored Sophie, rubbing her sister's arm with uncustomary exasperation. Her sister must have felt this because she came to straightaway, her eyes nearly popping out of her head when she focused on the pint-sized version of herself standing in front of her.

"This is Edie," Sophie said quickly, "Mathilde's daughter. Could she stay here with you while her father and I—"

"Edie?" Clementine was baffled. "Her father and you? Stay here while you what?"

"It's hard to explain, Clementine." Sophie was flustered. "But George and I need to go and find Mathilde. She's . . . taken off. She's missing."

"What's that smell?" Edie asked, going to look at what Clementine had been doing, which was filtering the wine from the vats where it had been fermenting into the oak barrels for ageing until it was time for the blend (another reason to hum).

"Clementine!" Sophie's voice was sharp. She needed to get going. "I'm leaving Edie with you, okay?"

Clementine shrugged, and once Sophie had left, she stood there eyeing her tiny doppelganger in the dim light of the *cave*. Unable to stop herself, she reached out and pulled at one of Edie's ringlets, stretching it straight out and then watching it ping back into shape.

"Same, same, see?" Edie said, shrugging her little plump shoulders and then reaching up and doing the same thing to one of

Clementine's ringlets. "What else? I'm a good swimmer, but I can't run very fast. I broke my arm the only time we went skiing. I'm no good at basketball. I never get picked for volleyball. I'm supposed to be a shepherd in the Nativity play this year, but I don't get to say anything. Oh! I can do this though!" She held up her her two thumbs and bent them backward unaided until they all but met her wrists.

Clementine, somewhat overwhelmed by the child's litany of sporting ineptitude, held up her own thumbs and bent them back almost as far.

"Cool!" cried Edie, meaning it. "Twins! Hey, I know what that smell is. It's blackberries! My favorite. Is it blackberry season in France?"

"Blackberries?" The wine Clementine had been in the process of decanting when Edie arrived was the lower valley pinot noir. It was more powerful than usual this year. She had tasted it in the grapes themselves and had remarked to Hector on the very subject of its blackberryness.

Still slightly stunned, she poured a little bit of the fresh pinot noir wine into a glass and handed it to Edie.

"You're giving me wine?" she asked, amazed. "But I'm only ten!"

"You're a Peine," Clementine told her, "there's no doubt about it. You should have been tasting since you were five. Just drink it. No, don't gulp. Sip it! That's right. Swill it around in your mouth. Feel it on your tongue and at the back of your throat. Now spit it out and tell me what you think."

Edie spat it out. "I think Diet Coke has better bubbles," she said. "Dad told me champagne had bubbles."

"They haven't been born yet," Clementine told her. "That happens later. We will blend these still wines together." She swallowed a hum. "Then we will bottle that wine, and the bubbles will come as it rests, which takes a few years unlike Diet Coke, which probably takes four seconds. And, anyway, I don't care about Diet Coke. I care about what you think of the pinot noir."

"Okay, okay, keep your hair on." Edie took another sip, swilled it around in her mouth, felt it on her tongue and the back of her throat, and then spat it out again. "I can definitely taste blackberries," she said. "Only it's not like actual blackberry juice. I've never tasted blackberry juice, but I think it would be sort of thinner. This is kind of thick, more like milk, only it catches when you swallow. You know what? It reminds me a little bit of cough syrup," she said, holding out the glass for a refill, "only it's good."

Now Clementine was truly staggered. For the child to pick blackberries in the first place showed a level of skill most adults couldn't muster, but to pinpoint the texture? To appreciate the taste? At ten?

"I like you," she told Edie. "I like you a lot."

"Good," Edie replied pragmatically, "because I need all the friends I can get."

By the time Sophie and George got back—still without Mathilde—Clementine and Edie had tasted seven more wines, and Edie had identified jasmine and nuts in the chardonnay plus apricots and mangoes in the meunier. Clementine, who had never tasted a mango in her life, had been flabbergasted, especially when Edie went on to describe the fruit as "sort of like summery bubble gum but not stretchy, more canned peaches slippery." Clementine knew exactly what she meant.

But the child's confidence slid away when her father returned minus her mother. "You didn't find her?" she asked anxiously, plucking at her sleeve, as George and Sophie sought them out in the kitchen. They were sitting on either side of the remains of the Black Forest cake for which Bernadette with her Alsatian roots was justifiably famous.

"Good grief," George said, looking at Clementine sitting beside his daughter. The two were identically covered in chocolate in a way only true Black Forest aficionados can be. "You must be the other sister."

"Oh, I'm sorry," Sophie said. "George, this is Clementine."

"The resemblance is remarkable," George said. "You could be—" He didn't actually say "Edie's mother," but everyone heard it anyway. Clementine and Edie looked at each other and licked their lips; neither found the prospect repellent. Well, one of them needed a daughter and the other a mother, so it was hardly surprising.

"We couldn't find her," Sophie said gently, "and we looked everywhere, Mentine. We've been all the way to Epernay. We searched the town and checked the station in case she caught a train somewhere, but there's no sign of the car and, anyway, she wasn't dressed for it. I went to Christophe's office, but he hadn't seen or heard from her. We went to Le Bois, too, on the way back, but she hasn't been there, either."

"Should we call the police?" George asked no one in particular. "I'm really not sure what to do."

Just then they heard the sound of a car approaching, its horn being leaned on in a forceful fashion as it spun to a halt in the courtyard. George and Sophie rushed to the front door, hauling it open just in time to see a furious Odile Geoffroy emerging from her Peugeot, Mathilde slumped precariously in the passenger seat beside her.

Sophie quickly turned and stopped Clementine and Edie from coming any farther and seeing any more. "It's okay," she said calmly. "George and I will deal with this. Clementine, maybe you'd like to take Cochon for a walk down to the river. I'm sure Edie would love to see him swim."

"He can swim?" Her little face lit up so enchantingly that Clementine, although suspicious of what was happening in the courtyard, whistled for the horse, who again obligingly abandoned La Petite and came to knicker at his new friend as they headed out through the kitchen.

In the courtyard Odile was fuming as she stalked around the car in ridiculously impractical heels to pull open Mathilde's door. "You're all the same, you pathetic Peines. Not worth a tin of fish, the lot of you. Why don't you just do yourselves a favor? Sell up and get lost! Go drink yourselves to death somewhere where the land isn't more precious than gold. The things we could do with your pinot noir."

"You shut up about our pinot noir," Sophie surprised herself by saying. "You'll be laughing on the other side of your face when you see what Clementine does with this year's Peine. It's our best ever!"

Odile spun around to eyeball her. "Who do you think you are kidding? Without Olivier, there is no Peine," she said nastily. "Even with him it was starting to taste like cat piss. He knew it, we knew it, the whole of Saint-Vincent-sur-Marne knew it. Your days here are numbered, Little Miss Fifi's Bastard. Why don't you just go back to wherever you came from?"

George pushed past Sophie until he was facing Odile, so close he could have spat right in her eye.

"Get off this property, or I will have you arrested for kidnapping," he said although it took a moment or two for Odile to work this out. When she did, her already sour visage spoiled further.

"Kidnapping? You must be joking, whoever you are. This stupid drunken slut," she leaned into the car and started slapping at Mathilde's face, "came to my house and was—"

"Lay another finger on my wife," George said, his voice chilly with an authority that had up until then been missing as he took Odile's slapping arm in a vicelike grip, "and I will have you charged with assault as well as kidnapping. You are on our property, and we have asked you to leave."

"Your *wife*?" Odile's nasty eyes narrowed even further as she shook him off. She stood back and crossed her arms over the powder blue sweater that was bursting with the effort of keeping her enormous bosom under wraps. "How about you keep your *wife* away from my *husband*, monsieur, or never mind your ridiculous charges, I will make you all sorry you were ever born."

"Did you hear that, Sophie? That's a threat. We need to document it."

Sophie felt severely out of her depth at this point. All she knew was that she did not want the subject of Mathilde and Benoît to be further plundered. Without knowing Clementine's exact coordinates, it was asking for trouble.

"She doesn't look as though she weighs much," she said to George, looking at the prone Mathilde who was oblivious to all of this in Odile's Peugeot. "Let's just carry her inside."

George agreed and managed to extract his unconscious wife

from the front seat, taking her in his arms and turning toward the house. Sophie was right; she didn't weigh much at all.

Odile wasted no time in climbing into the driver's seat as quickly as her too-tight black miniskirt would let her.

"Just make sure you keep that bitch away from my Benoît," she growled through the open car window. And off she drove, spitting gravel and covering them all in dust as she did so.

When Mathilde woke up in the middle of the night with a gasp and the raging dry horrors, a movie reel of half-remembered images flickering in her mind, George was lying beside her, looking at her with that look, that infernal look! Before she could even think of what to say or do or how to extricate herself from the horror of how she felt, she began to weep.

And as one day crept miserably into the next, she wept still.

Le Nuage

If George had thought his troubles would end with finding Mathilde and sobering her up, he was wrong.

She was back and safe, but her histrionics were more than he could handle.

For the first week he left her to it, but by the second he knew he was out of his depth and sought the advice—at Sophie's insistence—of someone much older and much wiser than himself: La Petite.

What he wanted to hear was how to get his wife to return to the United States with him. Unfortunately, this was not what she wanted to tell him.

"Edie thinks Mathilde has been disappointed by motherhood," she said as he sat on one of the rickety chairs that now dotted the old woman's boudoir. "Do you think that's true?"

George reddened. "I'm not really comfortable talking about—" he began.

"Well, get comfortable," snapped La Petite. "Do you think what Edie says is true?"

"I'm not sure how I would know that," George responded

somewhat sulkily before Sophie shot him a warning look. He tried to relax his shoulders and let go of his discomfort.

"George," La Petite said, although she pronounced it Yorg, which never failed to make him flinch just a little. "I am not judging Mathilde, and I am not judging you. I am just asking if you agree with your daughter's observation about her mother."

"Being disappointed?" George asked tiredly. "Yes, I suppose it's possible but . . ."

"But what?"

He hesitated. "I don't want to be disloyal especially when she is clearly unwell, but Mathilde can be an easy woman to disappoint. I know I certainly manage it."

"Well, you are a grown man, Yorg," La Petite said, "and you may well have done things to deserve Mathilde's disappointment, but your daughter is ten years old and she has not."

George squirmed in his chair, his neck hot and prickly under his collar.

"I agree it is uncomfortable to think about these things, heh?" La Petite suggested. "For you, for your wife, for any of us. But there's a little girl with her whole life ahead of her who needs us to think about these things. So her life can be a good one, heh?"

"She needs her mother," Sophie said sadly, staring out the window, remembering herself needing just the same thing.

"I know," George agreed, "I know. But Mathilde's just so . . . wretched. The last time this happened it was different. She was not emotional. She never cried at all. She just stayed in her room, wouldn't get up, wouldn't speak to anyone, wouldn't hold the . . ." His voice trailed off.

"Baby?" La Petite finished for him. "Wouldn't hold the baby."

George nodded but did not look up.

"You mean Mathilde had postpartum depression?" Sophie asked. She had seen enough of that in her time to know how ruinous it could be, how far-reaching its effects, but it had not occurred to her that Mathilde could suffer from such a thing.

"It was never diagnosed as such," George said, "because she refused to see anyone about it other than to get medication. And, anyway, that was a long time ago. You can hardly blame postpartum depression now."

"It might have started out as that and turned into something else," Sophie surmised. "That can happen, can't it, La Petite?"

"It most certainly can and does," the old woman answered. "Where I come from we call it *le nuage*, the cloud. It can happen to anyone at any time but often falls on young mothers, sometimes for hours, sometimes for days, sometimes for years. Of course, the difference with our way and yours is that we don't hand out pills to lift it, we encourage it."

"You encourage it?" George found this hard to swallow. "Depression?"

"We see it as part of life," La Petite said with a shrug. "For good health *le nuage* needs to be dealt with, that's all. If the grapeworm attacks the vine, you don't fix the damage by ignoring it, do you? No. You chase it, you catch it, you crush it. Well, that was the old way anyway. Of course, now it has all changed. Although you still deal with the problem, you don't pretend it's not there. That's the same. That's my point. So what if you are using the sexual confusion with the little plastic things. Oh, Sophie, what are they called?"

"Pheremones?"

"Yes, pheremones, that's them." La Petite fell silent. Sexual confusion. She had mixed views on that. All her people did.

"Um, *le nuage?*" Sophie prompted.

"We humans are not so different from vines, you know," La Petite said quickly as though she hadn't forgotten at all what she had been talking about. "One has blood, the other has sap, but all wounds need tending, heh? Do you see what I am getting at?"

"To be perfectly honest, Mrs. Petite," George could not help calling her that even though it wasn't her name, "no."

"Then let me make it plain for you, Yorg. Mathilde strikes me as a woman who is not dealing with her grapeworms. Do you understand that much?"

"Mathilde is not a vine, Mrs. Petite." George was getting impatient. "She does not have grapeworms. Jesus, I don't even know what a grapeworm is. This is ridiculous."

"Trust me, Yorg." La Petite's voice was sharp with warning. "A woman who cannot look her own daughter in the eye has grapeworms. Big ones."

He was having trouble hiding his exasperation now; one leg was jiggling involuntarily on the floorboards. "Listen, I appreciate what you're saying, but I really think the most important thing now is to somehow stop Mathilde from crying."

"Come here, Yorg," La Petite leaned back weakly in her pillows and beckoned to him. "Come. No, closer. Closer than that. Closer still. Lean in. Yes, that's right. Closer. Closer. Closer. Now, take that, you fool!"

One whippet-thin arm flew through the air and clipped him

around the side of the head. Then she let out a string of what were clearly expletives in an enthusiastic language George didn't need to understand to get the gist of.

"What did I do?" he moaned, leaping back and rubbing the ear she had belted. "What?"

"You did not appreciate what I was saying," La Petite snapped, little raisin eyes blazing, "because you didn't even hear it. Mathilde needs to cry. You shouldn't be stopping her. You should be finding out why she needs to cry so much in the first place."

"La Petite," Sophie interrupted, worried for George's sake, "don't you think you're being a little harsh? He's only trying to help."

"That heart of yours," La Petite said, looking at her fondly. "Always in the right place, just sometimes at the wrong time. No!" Like that the fondness was gone. "The wrong help is worse than no help at all. Mathilde needs rescuing for Edie's sake as well as her own, and Yorg just may not have the balls to do it because it's not going to be an easy job. She's had thirty-five years to become like this. There is a lot of damage to be undone. You think Mathilde was born bitter and hard? You think she came out of the womb like that? Do you know how many helpless little babies arrive in this world cold and unlovable like Mathilde? No? Well, I do. None. That's how many. Not a single one. We all arrive with the same capacity to bear fruit, but somebody somewhere along the line needs to tend us."

"I think it would be great if it were that simple," George said, still rubbing his throbbing ear. "But it's not. And by the way, I have done my share of tending, Mrs. Petite."

"Well, your own vines could have done with a bit more attention, monsieur, but that's another matter."

"Oh, shit!" The sight of Mathilde quivering wanly in the doorway drove the breath from Sophie's lungs. For a split second the room was silent. No one could be sure how long she had been listening to La Petite's diatribe on untended vines. But they could all be sure that it had struck a deep, dark chord.

"She never chose me," Mathilde whispered as she collapsed against the doorjamb, a torrent of fresh tears exploding. "My mother. She never once chose me."

La Petite opened her withered arms, and with an anguished cry the middle Peine plunged across the room and fell into them.

Obviously, this was progress of a momentous nature. Whoever would have thought Mathilde capable of displaying herself as weak and vulnerable? Junior psychology students the world over—even ones who were too busy smoking pot to go to class—would have said this was the moment when Mathilde accepted the wounds of her own flawed childhood and finally allowed them to heal.

Yet the reversal of Mathilde's cold and unlovable status was not to be an overnight affair. She did not become sweet and adorable right away. Far from it. In fact, for the first few days after she climbed into bed with La Petite, she refused to get out again, hissing and spitting at anyone who came into the room. Now that she had let the old woman in on her secrets, she did not want to share her and told her sisters, her husband, her daughter, and, of course, Cochon to go away and leave them alone—although not so politely.

Eventually, the long-suffering La Petite, whose health continued to fade, whispered enough sweet somethings into Mathilde's ear to get her to return to her husband in the room down the hall.

It then became clear that Yorg's balls were perhaps not quite up to it after all.

If he had thought that living with Mathilde's aggression and buttoned-up perfection was challenging, living with her self-obsessed soul searching was torture. One minute she was screaming at him to get out of her sight and never come back; the next she was sobbing and pleading with him to take her in his arms and hold her forever.

After a few days, to his secret shame, he found himself preferring the first option. The truth was, George wanted to get back to New York. The longer he spent at the House of Peine, the smaller his balls felt even to him.

Sure, he had not expected Mathilde to be the sort of woman who would abandon her family for months with little more than a message on the answering machine by way of explanation. But then neither had he expected her to be the needing-to-be-taken-in-his-arms-and-constantly-comforted type. Somewhere between these two women the real Mathilde lay, he felt sure, but until she discovered herself, his arms felt like doing nothing other than driving him to Charles de Gaulle, and throwing enough Valium down his throat to get him on the plane and back to the States.

"I need to go home," he told Edie as the month drew to a close. "But I'm not sure your mom is ready to come with me."

They were in the 2CV on their way back from Epernay, where George had assuaged his guilt by buying enough groceries to see the Peines into the next decade.

"What do you mean?" Edie asked, her bottom lip immediately wobbling and tears gathering in her eyes. "What about me?"

"If we leave tomorrow, you'll still make the rehearsals for the school Nativity play," George answered, at which that lip instantly stopped its quivering.

"I don't even get to say anything," Edie said, looking out the car window at the white chalky tracks leading over the hills like snail trails. She thought of her dear little furry friend Cochon and of La Petite, whose kindness shone through that dull crinkled skin. She thought of Sophie, the little aunt who seemed to know how to hold them all together, and Clementine, the big aunt whom Edie couldn't have dreamed up any better if she had tried. Then she thought of Mercedes McLaren, the itty-bitty blonde who was playing the Virgin Mary for the third year in a row and got to say more than the rest of the class put together.

She did not think of Mathilde, not at all, but nevertheless she said to her father, "Do I have to go, too? Can't I stay?"

George was a good man but not especially brave. He would fight a little for his family to come home with him, but if Edie really wanted to stay with her mother, he would not fight that.

Hiver

Olivier

The promise of snow hovered threateningly on the horizon the whole first week of December, the landscape pulling its grim gray outfit from its winter closet and hugging it close.

For the most part Clementine kept busy out among the vines pruning the canes, her fingers red and raw with cold but her cheeks glowing if Edie was there, bouncing along behind her. She had started at the local school and taken something of a shine to her teacher, which meant she was as happy as any little girl who had never liked lessons before could be.

Mathilde, her decorum more or less restored, was quietly reveling in what could optimistically be called her rehabilitation, although it was definitely a work in progress. She still struggled to show warmth toward her sisters and daughter but found comfort in the challenge of correcting the family finances.

Sophie, meanwhile, was busy perfecting a recipe for *pain d'épice* to La Petite's exact specifications and spent much of her time with the old woman whose breaths grew shorter with every winter day.

Such was the equilibrium reached in the household that by the second Thursday in the month, the Peine sisters were able to tolerate each other long enough to sit around the kitchen drinking coffee together.

It was more an uneasy cease-fire than out-and-out peace, but still it was a start.

Sophie, however, was fretting because La Petite had not eaten her breakfast.

The old woman had never stopped reminding them that she was on her last legs, that the end was nigh, that a distant voice was calling her toward a bright light, but never once, until today, had she let a tray of food go untouched.

Sophie was contemplating the uneaten *croque monsieur* as it sat cold and congealing next to the sink when the back door burst open and in clattered Edie and Cochon, both looking as though they had just been lightly iced like lemon cake.

"It's snowing!" Edie cried delightedly, pulling out the chair next to Clementine and flopping into it, Cochon's little head resting on her lap, his mane spotted with snowflakes. "And it's better than New York snow, too. It's all French!"

She spotted the *croque monsieur*, her eyes lighting up further. "Want to split that with me, Mentine?"

"Really, Edie, must you?" Mathilde asked. Clementine was just about to launch into a robust defense when there was a loud knock at the front door, still a rare enough occurrence to surprise them all.

"Oh, I forgot!" said Edie. "There was a man coming up the drive."

"A man?" The sisters' ears all pricked up.

"What sort of a man?" asked Mathilde.

"Um, tall," answered Edie. "Older than me but younger than Dad. From a long way away he looked a bit like Johnny Depp."

Who is Johnny Depp, wondered Clementine?

Hector, wondered Sophie? And just as she was thinking his name and remembering the exact salt quotient in his sweat, he appeared in the kitchen. He had only knocked to be polite, and, besides, no one had even moved to answer the door.

"Ladies," he said to the Peines, "and young lady. A pleasure to make your acquaintance." Up close, he had also been lightly iced like lemon cake and didn't look quite so much like Johnny Depp, but even at ten Edie recognized his deliciousness.

The sisters said nothing. Mathilde because she was still smarting over what hadn't transpired between them, Clementine because she found herself feeling a sudden unexpected pang for Benoît, and Sophie because the look on Hector's face made her think she was right to worry about the uneaten *croque monsieur.* Why else would he have come back?

"No, no, no," she moaned, getting to her feet. "Please, not yet."

"No, not yet," Hector agreed gently, coming to give her a little squeeze, "but not much longer. We should go up. I know she will want to talk to us. All of us. Yes, you, too," he added to Edie.

"Oh, please," grumbled Mathilde, but still she joined the somber procession up the stairs, Edie and Cochon bringing up the rear. They trailed quietly into La Petite's room, and at first Sophie thought that perhaps Hector had been wrong, that he was too late. La Petite lay as still as a stone, her eyes closed, her face gray and half disappeared already.

But Hector was not at all perturbed. He went to sit quietly on the bed as the others sat in their favorite chairs, the ones their bottoms had started to automatically lead them to in the weeks since La Petite had infiltrated their lives and they had sought her company.

Cochon trotted around the far side of the bed and rested his chin on the pillow next to the old woman's crinkled face. It was not the first time he had done so, because there was a hodgepodge of drool stains on Mathilde's Frette. Mathilde hissed at him and flapped her hand uselessly in his direction.

"Leave him alone," Clementine whispered furiously.

"Mind your own business," Mathilde hissed back. "Edie, get that thing away from there."

"No, she's right, leave him alone," Edie whispered back fiercely, moving her chair closer to Clementine.

"You do as I say!" Mathilde demanded, barely containing herself.

"You say something different!" Edie replied.

"How dare you!" The whispering was gone now.

"How dare *you*!" Clementine was back in the fray. "Let the poor child be."

"What's it to do with you?" Mathilde was furious. "She's not your daughter. Although where that poor creature is—"

"Stop it!" Sophie cried. "All of you. Just stop it!"

"For the love of Saint Vincent," La Petite announced tiredly from her bed. "Thank you, Sophie." She opened her eyes and smiled at Hector. "Oh, it's you. I thought it might be today," she said. "I've never turned my nose up at Emmenthal before."

"La Petite," her great-grandson (or something like it) said fondly, leaning in to give her a gentle kiss.

The sisters fell silent.

La Petite coughed dramatically, rising out of the bed with each hack perhaps a little more than was strictly necessary. "I'm not well, you know," she reminded them, adding a tremble for good measure. "And this time I mean it. I'm going. I am definitely going. But before I go, I need to lend you poor Peines a helping hand."

"Poor Peines? A helping hand? Oh, please," Mathilde started.

"That will be all from you, *madame*." La Petite shut her down with a voice that showed no particular sign of pending deceasedness. "I'm lending you a helping hand, and you will do me the honor of accepting it. Quietly. Because I'm doing it as a favor to your father, who loved you."

Sophie clasped her hands to her chest, her eyes shining, while Clementine shifted uncomfortably in her chair. Mathilde, however, could not hide her derision. "You mean our father who has been dead for nine months and spent the forty years before that not giving a shit?"

"Oh, he most certainly did give a shit," La Petite disagreed. "And he didn't come back from the grave to ask me for the favor if that's what you're thinking. I don't deal with the hereafters despite what you might have heard. No, he asked me before he died—well before, when he first realized he wasn't going to be a very good father."

"He realized it in advance?" Mathilde was incredulous.

"That's better than not realizing it at all, don't you think? You especially, Mathilde?"

Edie's eyes nearly popped out of her head, but she didn't say a word in case she was asked to leave. It seemed to her that the conversation was not the sort to which children were usually privy, and although she didn't completely understand what was going on, she felt a desperate need to be privy to it.

"But what made him think he wasn't going to be a good father?" asked Sophie.

"That's a good question, and I have just the answer," La Petite said, although she could feel herself starting to drift toward a faraway place where *chocolat chaud* was served every hour of the day and the air smelled only of daphne. "We're all born with the same ability to love and nurture, I've told you that, but sometimes life can deliver such a knock that if you're inclined that way, poof, you lose it. It doesn't happen so much in my world, of course. My third cousin Tomasina, now there was a—"

"La Petite," Hector gently interrupted. He was stretched out on the bed next to her now, dwarfing her, his legs crossed at the ankle, his boots further dirtying Mathilde's precious linen. "We're all born with the same ability . . ."

"And Olivier was no exception," she picked up seamlessly. "He had everything he needed to be the most devoted of fathers, but his heart was broken when you had only just arrived, Clementine, well before you were born Mathilde, let alone you, Sophie. Sadly, he chose the numbness of the bottle over the pain of mending his heartbreak. I can't imagine what that must feel like. Can anyone else in the room? Anyone?"

They all looked at Mathilde, who gazed out the window, her jaw set firmly.

"But Olivier was a farmer. First and foremost he was a farmer. And like all good *vignerons* he knew that starving you would stunt your growth. Yet, still, he starved you. Unfortunate, yes; irreversible, no. He was not so callous a man as to ignore the consequences of his actions. *Vignerons* rarely do. And so he took steps to make sure you wouldn't be shriveled up forever. He asked me to tell you one day when the time was right, when you were all together, what he had never been able to tell you himself."

"Oh, this is just plain ridiculous!" complained Mathilde.

"No, it's not. It's lovely," cried Sophie.

"What are you talking about?" Clementine was in the dark.

La Petite coughed up a huge gob of phlegm from her lungs and spit it with perfect precision out through the small open gap in the bedroom window. This certainly got their attention. Edie nearly exploded. No one had ever spit out the window in Manhattan.

"Listen to me carefully," La Petite said, pulling herself up more and employing as official a look as a very old, nearly passed-on person could manage. "I know you think your father was a mean old misery guts, and I have to say in recent years he certainly did himself few favors and those around him even fewer, but . . ." She coughed another long and phlegmy cough whose sole purpose was to remind them that the bright light was still beckoning. "But he wasn't always that way. You need to know that. As a young boy your father had so much heart, so much hope. I can see him as though it were yesterday, that lovely head of copper-colored hair, those twinkling blue eyes, that smile!"

Sophie was alone in being entranced. She could see it like it was yesterday herself, this handsome fairy-tale version of her unknown father. Clementine merely sneaked a skeptical peek at Mathilde, whose eyebrow had shot up to a record level. Neither of them could remember his copper-colored hair, his twinkling blue eyes, nor certainly his smile.

"You know, when your father was born, the *vignerons* of Champagne were not having the good time they're having today," La Petite pointed out.

"When he was *born*?" Mathilde was aghast. "How long is this going to take? I have calls to make you know."

"These are my last few breaths," La Petite said witheringly, "and I do not intend wasting them on any self-centered struggling anorexics, so if you answer that description, please remove yourself."

To think that La Petite knew what an anorexic was! To think that this actually shut Mathilde up! Sophie was astonished, Clementine confused, and Edie in absolute awe.

"Now where was I?" La Petite tried once again to regain her thread, during which time Mathilde cleared her throat and checked her watch.

This was not lost on the old woman. She turned one beady eye toward the middle Peine, raised one tiny hand from the bed covers, and pointed dramatically in her direction.

"You!" she whispered. Then, after one long terrifying intake of wheezy breath, her eyes closed and she receded back into the pillows.

"Oh, please, no!" cried Sophie, jumping to her feet and rushing to the old lady's side. She placed her small hand on La Petite's still warm forehead as Clementine hovered behind her. "Oh, Clementine, you don't think she's . . ."

La Petite opened one eye and winked at the worried faces hovering above her. Hector, who had not moved a muscle, just shook his head and sighed.

"I think we've lost her," Clementine said woodenly, attempting to play along, "and on Mathilde's fancy thread count. It will never be the same."

"Mentine?" Edie's face had crumpled, and she was getting ready to cry.

"Oh, for Christ's sake," snapped Mathilde, getting to her feet and going over to the bed. "Have you nitwits never seen *ER*?" She tugged on La Petite's big toe beneath the quilt. "She's acting."

The old woman opened both eyes and smiled her toothless smile.

"You have a lot of spirit for a mean person," she told Mathilde. "I almost like you."

"Whatever." Mathilde rolled her eyes in exasperation but returned to her seat, crossing one long thin leg over the other. "Just get on with it, will you?"

Les Barriques

"The *vignerons* of Champagne were not having the good time they are today, remember?" Sophie prompted La Petite when they had all settled back into their chairs.

"Ah, my little one, so like your grandmother," sighed the old woman, causing a tug of envy in Clementine's breast, "although, of course, she looked more like Clementine. Such a fine woman. And so strong! Elegant, though, in her own way and clever, too, of course, like you, Mathilde, although not nasty, not ever that I know of. The things that woman lived through: hunger, poverty, widowhood, Hitler."

The room grew cold, and Clementine pulled her moth-eaten cardigan closer to her body.

"Your grandfather died at the beginning of the second war," La Petite continued, "and we arrived for the *vendange* not long after he had passed. Tsk, tsk. Poor Micheline, newly widowed with a young son. And I tell you I've seen some terrible vintages in my time, but I barely remember a single ripe grape in '39, and once again no men to do the picking or pressing. Just women and children. Your father, Olivier, was only ten years old—your age, Edie—and working a full day alongside his mother."

Edie grimaced at such a prospect.

"Those were terrible times," recalled La Petite with a faint shake of her head. "It must have been Hitler himself who worked out that if you want to ruin a Frenchman's day, there's no better way to do it than drink his wine. A sword through the heart would hurt less. I remember being over at Le-Mesnil-sur-Oger the day the Germans came in on their shiny motorbikes and cleared out all Salon's '28. The '28! The shame of it! They didn't go for the poisonous pig swill old Rimochin across the road made. Oh, no. Only the best for Hitler's mob."

Sophie's eyes were as big as saucers. "Did they clear out our champagne?"

"They tried. Peine had a good name back then, remember, and the soldiers heard about it from someone down the road who no doubt was trying to save his own hide. Anyway, they arrived one morning, and your father, who was eleven or twelve by then, held them at bay long enough for your grandmother to do some quick restocking in the winery. They didn't take anything she didn't want them to have, that I can tell you. You'd be surprised just what that grandmother of yours managed to hang on to. A magnificent woman. She taught Olivier a lot."

"A lot of what?" Mathilde asked. "Do tell. The suspense is killing me."

"Well, I am the one dying, so mind your manners," snapped La Petite. "Besides, there are some things you need to find out for yourself, smarty-pants. The Peines have always been good at hiding things and just as good at revealing them when the time is right, brick by brick, if need be. You should try it, Mathilde. You'd be a better person for doing so, let me tell you."

"I'm better enough as it is," answered Mathilde.

"Well, that's a matter of opinion," La Petite retorted. "I wouldn't go asking for a show of hands if I were you."

Edie giggled, Clementine looked at her shoes, and Sophie squirmed some more but broke the awkward silence by asking, "What else? About the war? About Papa?"

"He met Clementine's mother," La Petite said proudly, "his finest hour."

Clementine felt an unfamiliar shudder and looked up to find La Petite staring straight at her through crinkled lids. "It's a great shame he could never talk to you about her," she said, "because she was a wonderful woman, and they were a wonderful pair. She was kind and honest and clever, and to him she looked just like the Mona Lisa."

"That's what people used to say about my mother, too," Sophie said wondrously. "The Mona Lisa bit, that is."

"Mine, too," Mathilde said with a yawn. "Big deal."

"I suppose you could say that Juliette Binoche has a touch of the Mona Lisa about her, do you think?" Sophie was suddenly excited. "That secretive smile of hers. That night at the video store perhaps . . ."

"Never mind Juliette Binoche," Clementine interrupted. "What about . . ." She couldn't bring herself to say *maman*. "What about Marie-France?"

"She arrived here during the *vendange* of '43, a better year than '39 but still hardly worth picking. Anyway, your grandmother had never forgiven France for rolling over for the Germans the way they did, so every now and then she helped a little with the Resistance, hiding people mostly, in the *cave*. And she wasn't the only one. Cellars all over France were hiding Resistance fighters by then. At Moët in Epernay they had a whole city just about in the underground *crayères*. A hospital even! You can still see the markings on some of the walls in the cellars if you visit—a red cross for the nursing station, a blue cross for the soup line, a white cross for a hideaway. Oh, indeed, such terrible times—"

"Marie-France," murmured Hector who was still lying back, hands behind his head, eyes closed.

"Yes, yes, Marie-France," La Petite said, snapping back to attention. "She was just fourteen when she arrived here. Her parents had been taken in Paris, I think, and the Resistance was trying to get her to England. I was here when she came to the door, and you could see it straightaway, with her and your father, I mean, Clementine. There was something in the air, something everyone could feel. It reminded us all that there was still room for joy in the world, room for the future."

"Oh, Clementine," Sophie cried, looking at her sister with tears in her eyes. "Can you believe it?"

With all her heart Clementine wanted to.

"I can see them now," La Petite continued dreamily, "huddled down behind the reserve wines whispering to each other. Young love! There's nothing like it. But after a week she had to be moved—it was risky to stay too long in any one place—but there was some problem with the usual transport. The rail line, I think, was no longer safe. Anyway, it was your father who had the idea for how best to smuggle her to safety. He saved her life—saved many lives, in fact."

"He was a hero," breathed Sophie.

"I think so," agreed La Petite, "although he would say he was just doing what needed to be done. He was the son of *vignerons*, after all, plus he was in love, so what do you think he did? He worked out that a girl the size of his wife-to-be would fit in a wine barrel, so that's just where he put her and then her drove her across the demarcation line in a horse-drawn cart, right through the German checkpoints, to where she was picked up and taken across the Channel."

"In a wine barrel?" Mathilde said scathingly. "Are you kidding me?"

"How did they get her in the barrel?" Sophie asked. "There's just a tiny hole."

"Yes, how *did* they get her into a wine barrel?" Clementine had been wondering the same thing.

"It wasn't so much that she went into the barrel," explained La Petite, "as the barrel went around her, stave by stave. It took two hours to build the cask around her and another two to get her out at the other end. Oh, I remember your father's pinched face the day he drove off with his future wife rattling in the back of the old wooden cart. If he was scared, you would never have known it. He was willing to do whatever it took to save her. At fourteen, heh?"

"But why did they send him?" Sophie wanted to know. "He was only a boy."

"You wouldn't have done the same at fourteen, Sophie? I think you would have. Your grandmother wanted to go, but Olivier insisted. And it probably did make more sense for a young boy to be delivering barrels of wine than for the woman of the house. It was a journey he made many times after that. He saved a lot of lives, Olivier Peine. Without him the world would be a much emptier place."

Clementine could not help but feel a little doubt since the world had been a pretty empty place with him in her opinion. "So then what happened?" she asked.

"He waited," La Petite said, "and waited and waited. And

many, many years later, well after the war was over, Marie-France came back, just as she said she would."

"Oh, that's so romantic," Sophie cried. "Don't you think? He waited for her, and she came back."

"Well, what took her so long?" Mathilde demanded.

"That I can't say for sure," La Petite said. "She lost both her parents to the camps, as it turned out, and was sent to live in Canada or somewhere cold. I don't know the details, just that she came back. And he was waiting for her. And if he'd become a little icy since the war, he thawed the instant he clapped eyes on her." La Petite allowed a tear to spring from an already watery eye. "And that was that. They got married, lived here as happy as the angels, and tried and tried and tried for a baby, which was you, Clementine, you."

Clementine could feel some foreign emotion vibrating inside her. It was such a romantic story even for someone who only just believed in romance. Yet how could it have gone so wrong?

"It was the usual disease, of course," La Petite said, answering her silent question, "the one that's killing everybody these days. She'd probably had it for some time. It was a miracle that you were even born, Mentine. Everyone said so."

"Everyone except Olivier," Clementine barked more harshly than she intended.

"Oh, no, he said it first," La Petite assured her. "I know you think he didn't love you, but I am telling you now I have never seen a father look at his child with such adoration. He felt blessed, Clementine, truly blessed. You were the twinkle in his eye, the spring in his step. He was utterly devoted to you. But when Marie-France went, well, your grandmother was in poor health by then herself—a little forgetful, shall we say. She tried to cook her shoes and wear the bread. Truly, when she passed, Olivier was bereft, that was all. He was not up to it."

"Well, what a weak link he turned out to be for all his supposed bravery," Mathilde said, her frostiness hiding any emotion she might otherwise be feeling.

"I wouldn't expect you to know what it feels like to lose the love of your life, Mathilde, because you've never had one," La Petite said sharply. "Clementine here, she knows. It was a long time ago and she didn't trust it at the time and might no longer believe in it, but still she knows. She's stronger than your father, too, because she's survived. The little one, yes, Sophie, my little one, she's had more loves of her life than all of us put together. Just look at her. And not only has she lived to tell the tale, but she has loved living to tell the tale. But you, Mathilde, you! You wouldn't recognize the love of your life if he slapped you in the face. You'd be too busy driving in the opposite direction in a fancy car drinking white spirits and smoking tobacco."

"La Petite," said Hector, his eyes open now, "calm down. It's all right."

Mathilde was speechless.

"It's not just about you, Mathilde," La Petite addressed her directly. "It's about your daughter. It's about all your daughters." She looked from Mathilde to Sophie to Clementine. "The House of Peine is theirs, too, remember. You need to know how much you were loved so that you in turn can love. That's how it works, how we all keep going. And you all were loved," she said. "So you all can."

Sophie started to sob. Clementine, too, wept quietly. Even Edie had tears in her eyes even though she was only ten and didn't have a daughter. Only Mathilde remained stone-faced as she resisted believing what La Petite was telling her. She wanted proof that she had been loved, and it was too late for that.

"That's it?" she asked coldly. "That's your helping hand?"

La Petite coughed undramatically and closed her eyes.

"Next time, perhaps, I'll try a helping foot," she murmured tiredly. "And I know just where to put it." She breathed a long, deep sigh and sank farther into her pillows. "Brick by brick," she muttered. "Don't forget that."

In the early hours of the following morning La Petite slipped away to her hot chocolate and daphne paradise. Cochon was nestled on one side of her, Hector on the other, and Sophie across the bottom of the bed. The old gypsy grape picker left without a fight. In fact, the vaguest of smiles was still playing across her lips long after the last breath had left her lungs. And although Sophie cried when she was truly gone, she didn't feel sad for the old woman, just sorry that she herself could no longer have her.

Hector held his great-grandmother for a long while, singing some foreign lullaby and weeping gracefully. When his tears had dried, he laid her back on her pillow, kissed his own fingers, and placed them on her leftover smile. Then he took Sophie by the hand and led her down the hallway to her bedroom where he made love to her with a delicacy she could not recall from any previous encounter.

Clementine was woken by the soft strains of Hector's lullaby and by Sophie's quiet sobs, and she heard the two of them shuffle eventually past her door. She lay there wondering why she didn't feel more aggrieved. Then she realized that what Hector did best was provide comfort, and Sophie on this occasion needed it the most. She pulled her bedclothes closer and returned to her dreams.

As dawn broke, Hector slipped out of Sophie's bed and started to dress.

"I have to take her with me," he said, "to our people. She wouldn't want to be in the ground near a church."

Sophie just nodded, her eyes filling with tears.

"It's not a sad day for us," he said, although she wasn't sure which "us" he meant. "It's a joyful one. Explain to the others, will you?" He came back to the bed and kissed her on each cheek. "I'll be back next year, little one," he said. "I'll see you then."

And just like that the gypsies were gone.

Bonne Année

The New Year brought snow by the bucketload, transform-
ing the acres and acres of bleak brown vines into a far more
glamorous landscape—the snow doing for them what a mink coat
can do for a plain woman of a certain vintage.

Its dull stumps thus disguised, the valley sparkled.

Inside the House of Peine, however, the feeling was one of
gloom. La Petite's departure had left something of a hole in their
Christmas spirit, which lingered still. Sophie and Clementine felt
it especially, but even Mathilde had been subdued since the old
woman's death. For days those wheezy words about being loved
and in turn able to love had rung in her ears, ears that were usually
deaf to such harsh criticism. Without the numbing effects of alcohol and tranquilizers, Mathilde was confronting more than she
had in a while, and some of what La Petite had said had slipped in
through the cracks in her veneer. Mathilde was selfish and proud,
there was no doubt about that, but she was not stupid. At some
previously untapped level she truly did not want Edie to feel about
her the way she felt about her own mother. With no true example
of her own to follow, though, Mathilde found little more than an
empty well when she reached for ways to show her daughter that

she was not unloved. She tried being affectionate but sometimes chickened out halfway so that what she had planned to be a hug became a straightening of the hair or an intended kiss on the cheek became a close inspection of a freckle. What was love anyway? Just because she had come to the realization she hadn't had enough of it didn't mean she understood it any better. Edie, with the intuition of any watchful child, sensed the effort, however, and was in extremely good humor, being the only one among them to show much enthusiasm at all for Christmas.

She had insisted they all go to midnight Mass, for example, which was somewhat horrifying for Father Philippe because Cochon accompanied them. The little horse was on his best behavior, though, and very kindly refrained from defecating inappropriately, as was sometimes his wont. Instead, he just trotted over to snort at the baby Jesus in the sacristy and then lay down next to a chipped plaster donkey twice his size and went to sleep.

Sophie had suggested rather halfheartedly that they stick with tradition and go home for *réveillon*, the customary post-midnight Mass supper, never having celebrated *Noël* this way herself, but Clementine could not be convinced. Christmas Eve to her was the very proud full stop at the end of the long rambling sentence of pruning. She had been working fourteen-hour days throughout December trying to get the job done while the snow was playing with the land, not lying on it. Her vines were all safely nipped and tucked now and could come to no harm as they slept through the winter. But it was all Clementine could do to pull on her church clothes with hands that were callused and swollen with chilblains. She, too, wanted to sleep though the winter and made quite a good start by snoring gently through Father Philippe's rather insipid sermon on goodwill to all men.

Once home again, she perked up enough to manage a couple of slices of the outsized *bûche de Noël* chocolate log that Sophie had made. Then, almost too tired to lick the cream from the corners of her mouth, she dragged herself up to her room, bidding a weary good night to her sisters and promising Edie that there would be gifts for her in the morning.

She slept deeply, dreaming of a dark-haired man on a gently purring tractor, and woke up feeling strangely content, especially when she remembered there was still a good deal of the *bûche de Noël* left. By the time she got down to the kitchen, her sisters and niece were already feeding on it, and Edie was jiggling with excitement at the prospect of presents.

Her father had sent her a cell phone about which she showed very little interest, and Mathilde presented her with clothes that she'd had George send over from Barneys. They were one size too small, causing Clementine and Sophie to swap a worried look. But Edie herself was quite delighted because the previous Christmas her presents had been three sizes too small and were still lying in the bottom of her closet in Manhattan, never worn. One size too small she could manage.

Nevertheless, the colorful pile of clothing was tossed aside when Sophie surprised everybody by presenting her with a watercolor she had painted of the view from Edie's attic room at the top of the house. Even Mathilde's jaw dropped to her chest as the picture was unfurled. Sophie may have struggled with reading and writing, but her raw talent shone when it came to painting. The view she had captured showed the vines rolling down from the house with the curlicue gates in the distance and a ray of winter sunshine pointing like a silver beam at an abandoned jardiniere overgrown with red geraniums, which sat halfway down the drive.

"I didn't know you were artistic," Mathilde said, her trademark sarcasm absent.

"You whip Andy fricking Warhol's butt!" exclaimed Edie excitedly. "I could sell this for a million bucks on eBay, but I'm not going to."

"The colors are so real," added Clementine, who had never heard of Andy Warhol or eBay. "I've never seen those colors in a paintbox."

"Oh, I've always been good at colors," Sophie said shyly, but she was clearly delighted.

No amount of ever-so-tight hipster flares or dreamy watercolors, however, could compare with Clementine's gift to Edie.

It was Cochon.

Clementine had thought long and hard about what she could give the child that would really mean something to her, and from the very first instant she had known it was probably her little horse. But Cochon meant a lot to Clementine, too. She would have died of loneliness the past few years had it not been for him. He had been her only friend for such a long time. Yet in the end it was because of this, not in spite of it (self-discovery was catching on among the Peines), that she wrapped a ribbon around his furry little neck and presented him to her niece once the chocolate log breakfast was nothing but a pile of creamy twigs. The look on Edie's face was worth it—and a thousand more dwarf miniature horses for that matter. Her eyes filled with tears, and she fell on Cochon, throwing her arms around him and hugging him as hard as she could. Cochon rested his chin on her shoulder and looked for all the world as though he, too, was crying with happiness—although it could have been conjunctivitis, to which he was prone.

Seeing this, Clementine felt even more certain that she had done the right thing by giving him away. He had not been himself since La Petite's demise, as had none of them. But only he had gone missing for two days after her departure, returning to the house looking dreadfully woebegone, the distinctive smell of burned heather wafting about him. This made Clementine wonder if he had followed Hector and even attended the old woman's passing ceremony, however that was managed where she came from. They would never know, of course, and wherever it had been, it had not cheered him up in the slightest. Upon his return he had spent much of his time slumped dejectedly at the foot of the stairs, yet upon being wrapped up and gifted to his freckle-faced ten-year-old friend, he quite literally got the spring back in his step. Even Mathilde, despite originally being quite pinched about the lips, did not confiscate the horse or poison him or Clementine.

They had rolled over into January without much hoopla and had spent the first week of the month doing very little, which was quite common for the *Champenois*. Like the vines, they traditionally spent much of January being dormant, in most cases the blend having already been chosen.

The blend in the Peine's case was still causing round-the-clock humming down in the winery, and by the middle of the month it was driving Mathilde to distraction.

"It's like living with a jackhammer!" she roared at Clementine in the winery one afternoon, her nerves well frayed. "Do you mind?"

Part of the problem was that Mathilde had taken up daytime residence in the winery herself now; she was working out of Olivier's old broom closet of an office where she was trying to set up a spreadsheet on a new laptop. She was computerizing the contents of the *cave*, the accounts, and the slowly increasing orders, and it was a complicated business especially without a secretary or an accountant or a chair that didn't catch on all her skirts. She had initially worked in the relative peace and quiet of the house, but it was Peine blood that ran through Mathilde's veins. If she was honest with herself, she liked the yeasty, fruity smell in the winery almost as much as Clementine did, and she enjoyed looking out at the barrels of what would become her product as she sweet-talked people into buying it over the phone. She would not admit this, though. She told her sisters she chose the winery to work in because it was the one place where the stupid little horse-pig that goddamn Clementine had goddamn given her goddamn daughter could not goddamn irritate her. (Her rehabilitation was still a work in progress.)

On this particularly icy cold January day, Clementine's rising panic at the impending torture of the blend rendered her incapable of ignoring Mathilde's jackhammer jibe the way she knew it was best to do.

"Yes, I mind! I mind! I mind!" she bellowed back at Mathilde after tasting the same pinot meunier a dozen times and getting twelve different impressions. "I mind that I'm not certain we can declare a vintage this year. I mind that I don't know if the pinot noir is too powerful. I mind that we have so much beautiful chardonnay but no history of making *blanc de blancs*. I mind that I might have all the makings of the best champagne ever but no idea if I can put it together the right way. I mind that I am doing this all on my own, you stupid, thin, heartless, horrible woman. I mind! Yes, I mind!"

Mathilde walked out of her broom closet office and across to where Clementine was crumpled against the barrels of offending meunier, sobbing.

She took off her Gucci spectacles and tapped them thoughtfully against her chin as she regarded her older sister.

"If you can postpone the hysterics for just a minute," she said coolly, "you might consider that you are not, in fact, on your own."

Clementine, quite beside herself, looked up. "Oh, is that right? And who is going to help me—you?" Her voice was gluey with tears. "You will taste the reserve wines and tell me what proportions to add to which amounts of the latest harvest? You will decide how much meunier, how much pinot noir, how much chardonnay I should put in the *brut*? How much reserve wine I should use? How much I should keep? You will help me with all this?"

"Don't be stupid," Mathilde answered witheringly. "Wine gives me a headache. How many times do I have to tell you? I'm in charge of selling the stuff, Clementine. You are in charge of making it. And you've already grown the grapes, which I understand you know personally by name. You've handpicked them, you've pressed them, you've babied them into barrels, and now you have all this precious still wine just sitting here patiently waiting for you to do something with it. So here's an idea: why don't you just pull your finger out and get on with putting the stuff in bottles so we can get the bubbles going and sell it? Our overdraft is not going to last forever, Clementine. We can't afford delays. It's already going to be three years before we see a cent out of this wine, and, trust me, we need cents."

"But the blend!" Clementine cried. "You don't understand. It's all about the blend, and I've never done it on my own."

"On your own? Are you drunk?" Mathilde snapped impatiently, putting her glasses back on. "Take a look around this place: there are more Peines here now than there have been for centuries. We're like grapes—we come in a bunch, for God's sake. So why not make the most of it? Stop whining about being on your own and get Sophie or Edie to help you. And stop wearing that corduroy skirt. It makes me feel ill just looking at it."

She turned on her heels and click-clacked across the floor back to her office.

Clementine sat there, feeling the spilled meunier on the floor beneath her soaking through the corduroy skirt. She hated Mathilde all over again then; she wished those thin ankles would snap so she would tumble to the ground where she could be poked at with a pitchfork.

She knew where there was a pitchfork, too.

Saveur!

As it happened, the pitchfork stayed where it was. In fact, Clementine woke up the next morning and burned the corduroy skirt. What is more, the day after that, suppressing a panic attack that threatened to leave her once more weeping and shaking uncontrollably over the reserve chardonnay, she sought out Sophie and Edie.

She came upon them lying upside down on a lumpy sofa by the window in the hardly ever used sitting room. Cochon was nestled on a musty cushion on the floor, his legs tucked underneath him looking more like a pig than ever.

"So, look up at the sky," Sophie was saying to Edie. "Now start with the clouds. See the one that looks like a giant panda bear? With the gray spots like eyes and a dark patch on the side, above the leg? Well, come down from that, and there's a big stretch of blue sky—not bright blue and not pale blue but special winter Marne Valley blue, like milky cornflowers. See that? Okay, now move your eye very slowly farther toward the ground. See how the sky changes color? How it switches without you even noticing from milky cornflower to cornflowery milk and then to just milk, and all of a sudden you're not looking at the sky at all—you're looking at the snow? It's the same if you're the right way up, but you just see it more clearly this way. That's how you learn to blend."

"What are you talking about?" Clementine's voice made the two of them jump. They turned over so they were sitting the right way up, both faces red and puffy with the effort of having been so recently inverted.

"I was just telling Edie how I did my eyes at Guerlain," Sophie explained, but because Clementine did not know she had worked there or what Guerlain was, this sounded like gibberish.

"Never mind that," she said. "What do you mean when you say that's how you learn to blend?"

"The colors, Mentine, on the eyes, with eye shadow. That was my specialty when I worked at the Guerlain makeup counter at Le Bon Marché. Even my boss, the one who . . . Well, anyway, even my boss had to agree that I'm very good with color." She turned to Edie. "Lots of people who can't spell or read very well are," she explained.

Clementine opened her mouth to say something, but, suddenly overwhelmed by her struggle with her own hideous limitations, she instead burst into the very wet and loud tears she had been trying to avoid.

Sophie and Edie were off the sofa in a flash, drawing her back down between them and doing their best to cuddle her awkward body from either side.

"I can't do it without Olivier," Clementine sobbed. "I can do all the rest, but the blend is different. It was his. The champagne was his. He chose how to make it taste like that. He knew what to do. He just knew it. He had it in his blood, and whatever he passed on to me, that wasn't included. I can't do it, Sophie, I can't. I'm all at sea, on my own, bobbing around, and I'm frightened because if we don't get it right this year, it will be the end of us. And the Peine ancestors will haunt me into an early grave, which I probably won't even mind because I'll be in hell up here anyway. I can't make poisonous pig swill like Rimochin. I can't. But I'm not sure I can make anything better."

"What's she talking about?" Edie asked, distressed at the sight of her aunt in such a state.

Sophie shushed Clementine, pulled her as close as she could, and then said over her head: "*Assemblage*. It's when all the different wines are mixed together to make the perfect recipe for champagne before we start the bubbles. It's a special art, and our father used to do it on his own—but now . . ."

"Now he's gone, and I'm blind, blind, blind!" Clementine wailed.

"You're not blind, Mentine," Sophie said soothingly. "You just think you are. It's not the same."

"And anyway," Edie said hesitantly, "Sophie can see, and I can taste, Mentine, you told me I could. And you know the other stuff about the bubbles and all of that . . . so couldn't we do it together?"

This was exactly what Mathilde had suggested. It was a little bit ridiculous, of course it was. Sophie had spent much of her life eating out of rubbish cans and so had the most unsophisticated of tastebuds. And Edie, well, she was only ten years old and half American. But the chardonnay grape on its own made only chardonnay wine, the pinot grapes only pinot. It was putting them all together that was the secret to champagne.

Duly encouraged, the following day the three of them assembled in the kitchen where Clementine had prepared the accoutrements for the family's first joint attempt at *assemblage*.

There were nineteen samples from the different Peine plots, plus another twelve from the past six years of reserve pinot noir and chardonnay. This made thirty-one bottles all clearly marked and lined up along the weathered oak table. Olivier's notebook sat open on a blank page with their three names written across the top in big bold letters. There were buckets on the floor for spitting, there was bread for cleansing the palate, and on the sideboard stood a warm prune tart that served no practical use whatsoever but would help get them through to lunchtime.

They started with the oldest of the reserve chardonnays. Clementine poured them each a couple of inches, and they held it up to the same light, comparing the color.

"What color would you call this?" Clementine asked.

"I call it wine color," Edie answered doubtfully.

"I call it sort of an old-fashioned gold," Sophie said with far greater confidence, "with a touch of straw."

Clementine swirled the wine around, the winter light catching it as it hit the side of her glass. Old-fashioned gold is what Olivier would have called it, too, she was sure, with a touch of straw.

"A more yellow gold," Sophie said of the next wine, "with perhaps still a hint of old-fashioned gold.

"Pure straw," she said of the next. "Well, pure pale straw.

"Green-gold with silver-gray," she announced of the 2002.

Any doubts Clementine might have had about what assistance Sophie could offer immediately disappeared. She agreed with every one of her sister's calls, noting each comment dutifully in the notebook. ("Look at her writing," marveled Edie wistfully as she did so. "It's all going the same way.") Olivier himself had always said that color could tell a person almost as much about the personality of the wine as the taste. Clementine mulled this thought over in her mind as she watched Sophie examining a glass of the 2003. She saw, just for a moment, a glimmer of that crusty old man in her sweet young sister as her eyes scrunched up for a different perspective just as Olivier's had once done.

Better still, it turned out that despite her time spent delving through the trash cans of Paris—or perhaps because of it—Sophie had a good nose as well as a good eye.

"I can smell creamy honey!" she exclaimed at one point. "And fresh figs," at another. "This one actually smells green. Is that possible? There's Granny Smith apple in here," she said assuredly. "And there's orange in this meunier or citrus of some sort. Actually, maybe it's mandarin."

"Okay, Edie," Clementine said once she had completed her smelling notes. "Time for tasting. This is where we need your help. Now, I want to know your first impression and then your second impression. Do you know what I mean by that?"

Edie shook her head.

"The first impression is what it feels like on the tongue, and the teeth, and the roof of the mouth. It's a close inspection of the real taste. But the second impression is what it reminds you of, how it makes you feel. If it sounds a little airy-fairy, I used to think so, too, but I know that's how Olivier did it and it's how the Geoffroys do it, too, and the Tarlants. How much easier it would be if it was all about science, hm? But no such luck."

"No such bad luck," Edie said cheerfully. "I suck at science."

"Let's start on the 1999," Clementine instructed, slowly swirling the golden wine around in the glass, breathing in its aroma, and then taking a mouthful. Sophie did the same, as did Edie.

They sucked it through their teeth, let it roll around on their tongues, and felt it splash against their palates. Then they spat.

"Well, it tastes like bananas, but it reminds me of honey," Edie said definitely.

"I agree," Sophie said, taking another taste. "Although I'm not sure if I thought that until you said it."

"It is fruity," agreed Clementine. "Tropical fruity. I think there is some of your mango there, Edie, would you say?"

"Uh-huh." Edie nodded. "And something else. It sort of reminds me of the coconut cream pie my grandma used to bake when I went to visit."

They all took another taste.

"Coconut," Clementine agreed. "It really is coconut." The other two nodded enthusiastically, sharing a look of great delight. Then Clementine couldn't stop herself: she tipped back her head and released a clear, sweet laugh—the absolute opposite sound of a misty hum.

That first day she got detailed notes of all the reserve wines. The following day they tasted the latest meunier, the day after that the pinot noir, and the fourth day the chardonnay. All the chardonnay from the recent harvest was better than usual, but the grapes that grew behind the château, closest to the woods—the ones Clementine worried had not ripened enough—had grown into the most intense wine she had ever tasted.

"It tastes like Philly cream cheese and apricots to me," Edie said with great certainty. She truly was an expert by now. "But it reminds me of Bernadette's *pain au chocolat amande.*"

Bernadette's *pain au chocolat amande* was a treat she made

every other Saturday. It was her ordinary croissant dough spread with almond custard and infused with Valrhona chocolate before being rolled, baked, and then sprinkled liberally with slivered almonds and icing sugar. Clementine and Edie could spend hours just talking about them, and even Mathilde had been known to wake up with a quiver of extra excitement on the days when she knew there was such a pastry downstairs waiting for her.

"You're so good!" cried Sophie. "It reminds me of Bernadette's *pain au chocolat amande,* too, but I just couldn't pinpoint it until you said it. You're a genius, Edie."

"She is," agreed her other aunt. "It is *pain au chocolat amande* all over. It's the buttery quality, I think, from the oak and the sharpness of the Valrhona. But the almond I missed. You are right, though, Edie. It's there, as plain as the nose on your face. I got the apricots, too, and perhaps there's a hint of mint there as well."

The *pain au chocolat* chardonnay, as it came to be known, stood head and shoulders above the rest. With its creamy stone fruit notes they all agreed it had almost as much going for it as the earlier reserve chardonnay, which had the benefit of four or five years ageing in barrels. That a new wine showed such character was a rare and thoroughly heartening sign at a blending.

Once they had characterized all the recent wines, they separated them, regardless of their variety, into those that were straightforward, unusual, robust, acidic, sweet, those that danced on the tongue, those that sank, those with a lingering finish, and those with little.

Then they divided all of those into three groups: harsh, smooth, and special.

Finally, after deciding among themselves that this new blend needed to be perhaps a tiny fraction softer, Clementine took a glass measuring flask from the center of the table and poured in equal measures of the wines from the smooth category until the flask was just over a third full.

"And we want the blackberries, don't we?" Edie wanted to know.

"Not in the *brut* but in our vintage," Clementine decided, knowing with all her missing certainty in that single moment that there would be one and that it would be special. "The vintage will also have the *pain au chocolat* chardonnay. It will be a truly stunning blend."

"So we'll save those two then?" Edie asked. "We won't go using them up in the regular nonvintage stuff?"

Edie was a Peine, all right.

La Fête de
Saint Vincent

With the two Peine sisters and their niece working at it for the best part of two weeks, the exact blend for the *brut* was finalized on the twenty-first of the month, the eve of Saint Vincent's Day. It was heavier on the chardonnay than it had been in previous years, but then their chardonnay harvest had been so good. It drew generously, too, from the reserve pinot, the '99, in fact, to which there was a certain resonance—that wine having played such a role in combining Sophie with Clementine all those months ago. After much tinkering, they all felt that they had managed to balance the sharp with the smooth, adding just enough of the special so that it was reminiscent of what Peine had always been, but with a touch of something extra, something new.

"With bubbles," Edie announced happily after a final taste, "it will be perfect."

"And now," Clementine added solemnly, "for the vintage."

As it turned out, this brew needed hardly any consideration at all. They simply mixed the blackberry pinot noir with the *pain au chocolat* chardonnay in almost equal measures and then added just a suggestion of the sprightliest pinot meunier that grew at the feet of Saint Vincent.

"It's all fluffy like clouds but sweet, too, like candy," Edie cried.

"You'd expect the mintyness to be too tart with the blackberry, but it's not," Sophie added. "The chardonnay somehow irons out the wrinkles. It's quite amazing."

It was indeed a wine of uncompromising power and complexity, and although she could feel in her bones that it was the right blend, Clementine was nonetheless worried. This vintage wine would be like no other champagne Peine had ever produced, nor any other house for that matter.

"But isn't that good?" wondered Edie. "We don't want to make the same as everyone else anyway."

"The problem is that if we make it too different," Clementine told her, "it might look as though we don't know what we're doing."

"But you do know what you're doing, Mentine," Sophie insisted. "It's just all there, inside you, as it was with Papa."

Half of Clementine (the old half) wanted to snap back that what exactly would Sophie know about "Papa," but the other half (the new one) wanted to believe her. How good could Olivier's choices have been in recent years with his dependency on pastis to make it past breakfast time? Who was to say she didn't know as much as he? More, even?

"I'm just not sure," said the old and new halves together. Clementine had come along in leaps and bounds recently, yet some doubts still lingered. "I just don't know."

"Is there someone who does know?" Edie asked suddenly. "You know, someone we could ask?"

Sophie looked expectantly at Clementine. It really wasn't such a stupid idea.

"Who?" the eldest Peine countered. Who else was in a similar situation to them and might be happy to share? A shadow fell across her face. Benoît, of course, was in the same situation, and in an ideal world she would have asked him. But in an ideal world they would be standing there together now anyway, with Amélie and an assortment of other little Geoffroy-Peines buzzing around them. This impossible image pulled at her insides; any chance of living in an ideal world had been shattered eighteen years before. She tried to curse Mathilde the way she had done ever since, the way that usually gurgled up unbidden through her spleen. But to her own surprise there was nothing there, not a trace of venom where once there had been nothing else. Amélie, she thought again to herself, staying on that picture in her head, seeing the young woman her daughter might have become standing there in the space between her sister and her niece.

"What's the matter?" Sophie asked. "Are you all right? You look as if you've seen a ghost."

A ghost? Clementine thought. In her mind Amélie had dark curly hair and was on the plump side but so pretty, with Benoît's cupid lips and a breezy smile that came from neither of them.

"Mentine." Edie tugged at her. "Are you all right?"

Clementine blinked. Her daughter might not really be there, but she was somewhere: she was not a ghost.

"I have never been better," she said calmly.

It was true. Her life was so much more worth living now than it had ever been before. It had been changed immeasurably by these people who had come into it. It could change still with more people perhaps.

"Well, since you're in such a good mood," Sophie tentatively suggested, "do you think we could go to the Saint Vincent's Day

Parade tomorrow? Edie is dying to go, and you must admit we've hardly left the house since Christmas."

"Does she realize it means going to church again?" Clementine said gruffly, but she was not really thinking about church. She was thinking about another Saint Vincent's Day Parade many years before.

"Yes, but there's a party afterward, isn't there?" Edie was jiggling with excitement. "Laurent Laborde told me."

"A party?" harrumphed Clementine. "Well, I'd hardly call it a party. More like a bunch of old gasbags sitting around moaning about the harvest."

"Oh, come on, Mentine," Sophie coaxed with a twinkle in her eye. "We'll go together, all of us. It will be a family outing. It might even be fun."

Again, the concoction of bitterness and regret on which Clementine had come to depend did not rise up and stick in her throat with its usual conviction. Even if she had wanted to attend the parade any January in the past eighteen years, Olivier had long since been excluded thanks to a rousing bout of fisticuffs with a dozen or so other *vignerons*. In previous years she had sat in her cold house with her silent father cursing the wretched saint for not taking better care of them. It wasn't as though he warded off the frosts or warmed the temperatures when the berries were ripening, after all.

This year, though, she found herself begrudgingly joining her sisters and niece for Mass and the procession afterward to leave gifts at the foot of the statue. Clementine personally thought the notion of dressing up like olden-day grape pickers was at best misguided, but it was something of a thrill to see Edie, who herself drew the line at dressing up in a cloth hat and apron, skipping through the crowds with Cochon in tow, other children her own age dancing around her. She looked so normal, so happy, so part of it all, and this gave Clementine great pleasure because she knew that for Edie, as it had been for her, this was rarely the case.

It was the most beautiful of crisp, clear days, the snow still thick and crunchy white on the ground. The Marne looked so clean, Clementine could not help but notice. And the villagers were all smiling, sometimes even at her. Mathilde was deep in conversation with the mayor, Sophie was chatting with a good-looking young man wearing clogs, and Edie was laughing and showing the children how she had trained Cochon to stand on his back legs and beg like a dog.

So busy was Clementine marveling at this unfamiliar new family of hers as she trudged away from the statue that she failed to notice old Madame Monet, the hunchback who lived in the town's narrowest house, stop suddenly in front of her, causing Clementine to bump into her and lose her balance. She reeled backward to keep from falling on the old crone and then felt the crunch of someone else's toes beneath her heels. Spinning awkwardly around she found herself in the arms of Benoît Geoffroy.

He held her by both elbows, steadying her, looking straight into her eyes, his weathered brown ones clouded with their own dark secrets.

The village, the crowd, the gifts, the noise, the cold, it all seemed to gather up in some silent tornado and start spinning around the two of them as they stood there frozen still.

How did this happen to us, Clementine yowled silently yet again? How can all these years have passed by with nothing between us but a few stolen glances? She held her breath, expecting at any moment to feel the release of his pressure on her arms as he let go, but he didn't. He held on. Tightly, he held on.

Amélie, Clementine imagined saying. The effort of not telling him about their daughter was like a physical pain in her chest, a terrible clawing at her heart. I don't know for sure what she looks like—she could picture herself mouthing the words—but I think she has your lips.

"Clementine," Benoît said, as awkward as she, but still he held on.

"I need to know," she whispered, trying to bite back the words as they escaped her. "I need to know."

"You need to know what?"

She was making the most terrible fool of herself. She knew that. She could rescue her dignity by asking him about the blend, the *vendange*, his father, anything, yet her heart would not allow it.

"If you wanted me to come to the parade with you back then, before . . ." Tears were streaming down her face. How easy it was to speak to him! What a waste of all these years worrying that it was impossible!

Up close his hair was flecked with gray, and the skin around his eyes was etched with wrinkles. Like her he looked gnawed at by the wind, grizzled by life among the vines. And even though she had seen him this close on only a handful of occasions, every inch of him looked utterly familiar to her, the way a famous painting does when you finally see the real thing after years of looking only at a postcard.

"Of course," he answered, gripping her elbows even tighter. "Yes."

"I shouldn't have . . . if only . . ."

"No, it's my fault," Benoît said hoarsely. "I'm so—"

"Don't say sorry." Clementine simply could not bear it. "Please, please, don't say sorry."

"But I am," Benoît told her. But just as he was about to go on, he dropped his hands from her arms so smartly, it was as though she had scalded him. A hardness that had not been there before crept into his eyes as he looked behind her, and with that she felt the sharp claws of a well-manicured woman digging into her shoulder. "What is the matter with you Peine women?" Odile Geoffroy growled, spinning Clementine around to face her. "Get your hands off my husband, do you hear me? I've already told your stupid slut of a sister, and now I'm telling you. Get your own husbands. Leave mine alone!"

"Calm down, Odile." Benoît tried to reason with her although he was clearly flustered. "There's no need to speak like that."

"My sister?" Clementine stuttered. "I don't understand. We were just talking. I was just asking."

"I know exactly what you were asking for, too, you trollop," Odile hissed. "The same thing your trashy sister was asking for when she turned up on my doorstep wearing next to nothing: a piece of my husband. Well, he's not up for grabs, so take some advice: back off and leave us alone, or you'll be sorry. You'll all be sorry!"

"Odile, you're being ridiculous," Benoît said. "We are neighbors. We should be able to—"

"Ridiculous, am I? How dare you embarrass me like this. It's an outrage." Odile's voice was indeed outraged; her double chin was quivering furiously. "And as for you," she turned on Clementine again, "you lumpy slattern, you keep your hands to yourself and tell that drunken American sister of yours to do the same. He's my husband, do you hear? *Mine.*"

At this Benoît, suffused by embarrassment, took his wife roughly by the elbow and with some force turned her away, pushing her through the crowd and leaving Clementine standing there, humiliated.

"Come on, Mentine," Sophie said with a laugh as she came up behind her, oblivious to what had just occurred. "The banquet's in the town hall. Goose, I believe. Your favorite. And I hear Bernadette has excelled herself with kirsch soufflé and Chantilly meringues. Mathilde says the mayor—"

"Leave me alone," Clementine cried, and turning on her heels, she ran home, the trampled snow now dirty and slushy beneath her feet, the villagers no longer smiling at her.

She had thought it would change her life knowing that Benoît had meant it all those years ago about the parade, that she hadn't imagined the sparkle of promise between them. But it hadn't changed her life at all. No jewel of a word, no matter how precious on its own, could change the fact that he had married Odile.

Once back at the château, Clementine crawled into her bed with a box of nougat and wept into her pillow for what had been lost and could never be regained.

She wept for Benoît and Amélie.

And herself.

It was a long, sleepless night.

Amour

In the morning, sick from too much sugar and too little sleep, Clementine appeared at the breakfast table red-eyed and trembling.

The other three were already there, enjoying what looked like the remains of the soufflé.

"Mentine, look what we—" Sophie started, but Clementine cut her off.

"Just when I was beginning to get used to having you here," she said to Mathilde, "and to think you really cared for us. You had me thinking it could all work out. You really did. But how stupid could I be? It wasn't enough the first time, was it? You just had to come back and take him from me all over again."

Mathilde was bewildered. "What on earth are you talking about? I haven't taken anyone anywhere."

"Benoît," Clementine said bluntly. "Yes, Benoît. I know you've been over there again, wearing next to nothing and trying to seduce him in front of his own wife. Yes, Odile told me all about it yesterday at the parade! She thought I was trying to do the same thing. She called me a slattern, a trollop! What have I done to deserve this, Mathilde? Tell me, will you? What?"

Mathilde coughed politely and wiped at the corner of her mouth with a napkin. "Edie, darling, why don't you run outside and play with your little mule," she suggested in an almost motherly voice.

Edie looked from her to Clementine, eyes wide with understanding that trouble was afoot. Then she dropped her baguette and skedaddled out the door.

"Clementine, I think you should sit down," Sophie suggested nervously. This was not the warm, friendly Clementine that had been emerging in recent months but the bitter, unhinged one of days gone by.

Clementine ignored her. "Why do you get such pleasure out of torturing me?" she asked Mathilde.

"You've got it all wrong, as usual," Mathilde answered impatiently. "I may have gone over there to talk to him a few times, but it was in a casual neighborly fashion. Can I help it if that hatchet-faced wife of his jumped straight to the wrong conclusion?"

"Yes, Mathilde, you can! Why don't you just leave him alone? He doesn't mean a thing to you. You can have whomever you want, whenever you want, but I have wanted Benoît all my life. All my life! And I will never have him. Never."

"So that's what's got you all upset," Mathilde said. "Well, for a start, that's nonsense. And for a finish, you could snatch him away from that old witch at the drop of a hat if you put your mind into it."

"I couldn't!" Clementine cried. "I couldn't. You see? You just don't understand. You can't see that others don't have what you have. That it's not as easy for everybody as it is for you. That some of us live in agony, full of doubt and regret. Regret! Do you know what that feels like, Mathilde, sitting there with your skinny little legs and that . . . that cleavage and all your vile revolting sex appeal?"

"Frankly, no, I don't," Mathilde said coolly, "but then I don't spend all day wallowing in the mud like a hippopotamus and feeling sorry for myself, either. Don't blame me if you let Benoît slip through your fingers or your hoofs or whatever they are, Clementine. You're big enough and certainly ugly enough to take that one on the chin yourself."

Clementine lunged across the room and would have had Mathilde's throat between her hands and strangled the very life out of her had Sophie not jumped in between them.

"Stop it, Mentine," she begged, ducking and weaving.

"Yes, pick on someone your own size if you can find anyone barn-shaped," Mathilde retorted rudely, holding Sophie's hips from behind and using her like a shield. But at this, Sophie pulled away, furious.

"Why do you always have to make it worse?" she demanded. "Can't you see that this is a sensitive subject? Don't you care how much you've upset her?"

"By doing what?" Mathilde asked. "By having a bit of slap and tickle with the boy next door a hundred years ago? By taking him a bottle of single malt when I was desperate for a bit of stimulating company? It's hardly a crime. I really don't see why you're making such a big deal out of it."

Sophie stepped away, placed a wiry little arm around Clementine's middle, and guided her back to a chair. She forced her to sit and then knelt next to her on the floor, smoothing those angry ginger curls.

"She actually doesn't know what it feels like, Mentine," she said soothingly. "That's why she can keep doing it. It's not her fault, but that's why she can hurt you, why she can hurt Edie. She doesn't know what it feels like."

"Oh, for God's sake, stop talking such nonsense," Mathilde snapped. "Hurting Clementine? Hurting Edie? I'm not hurting anybody. I'm just minding my own business, our business. I don't know what the hell you are going on about."

Sophie stopped smoothing Clementine's curls. "You have hurt Clementine, and you have hurt Edie, Mathilde." The power in her voice was unmistakable. "Trust me. My mother left me, too, and it hurt."

"Well, boo hoo," Mathilde replied. "Time to get over it."

"Just like you got over how your mother treated you?" Slowly Sophie got to her feet and looked her sister straight in the eyes. "And how have you done that exactly, Mathilde? Because you may not be the same unhappy runaway you were when you first got here, but it seems to me you're still a runaway."

"How dare you, you little pipsqueak," seethed Mathilde. "When you've lived my life, then you can have an opinion on how well I've managed it, but until then keep your half-baked psychobabble to yourself. My mother dumped me on whoever was nearest every time she sniffed out a new husband, once for a whole year, which means I know exactly what it feels like. I'm just not so weak and pathetic that I have to show it."

"But it's not weak and pathetic to show it!" Sophie thrust her hands defiantly on her hips which made her look a little like a ruffled Peter Pan. "It's human. It's brave. In fact, the bravest thing you could do for Edie is show her how you feel about her, Mathilde, instead of ignoring her or avoiding her the way your own mother ignored or avoided you. Can't you see that? It's what La Petite was trying to tell us."

"That old witch!" cried Mathilde, but her voice showed none of Sophie's power or control. "It's all such drivel. I do not avoid . . ." She was starting to lose her composure. "She doesn't know. I have been trying. It's just that I . . ." Each breath was more shallow than the last. Her face was crumpling, her body folding. She was coming undone right in front of them. "When I think about Edie, what I feel . . . oh, I don't even . . . but I know that it's just . . . You two idiots wouldn't understand, but for me it's different. I just find the whole thing totally . . ." Suddenly she was crying fat heavy tears. "Unbearable. Sometimes when I look at her, I just feel physically sick I'm so, so, so . . ." Her words dissolved into wretched sobs.

"So what?" Sophie asked softly, dropping her hands from her hips.

"Scared!" roared Mathilde. "I'm so scared!"

"Scared of what?"

"I don't know. Just scared. Scared down to the marrow of my bones."

"But Mathilde," Sophie said in the gentlest of voices, "that's love."

"That's *bullshit*!" bellowed Mathilde. "Love doesn't make you want to hide and never be found or pull your heart out of your chest and stomp on it. It's not frightening. It's not uncontrollable. It's not bitterly fucking disappointing."

"It does," Clementine said almost to herself, thinking of Benoît, of Amélie. "It is."

"It's painful, Mathilde, because the moment you care that much about someone, you have a lot to lose, and that is what hurts," added Sophie.

"But why?" Mathilde wept. "How does it? Who would?" She was hiccuping great gulps of air, her body shaking with the pressure of trying to regain control. "What the hell's the matter with me?" she sobbed. "What's wrong?"

Watching such misery, Clementine found herself surprisingly overwhelmed with pity. She knew exactly what it felt like to be a prisoner of that confused jumble of feelings. Whoever would have thought she shared this, of all things, with Mathilde? She turned to Sophie and held up her hands in a gesture of helplessness.

Sophie went to Mathilde's side and then indicated that Clementine should come, too. "There's nothing the matter with you," she said, laying an arm around her shoulders. "You just have to realize that you are better off feeling what you're feeling than not feeling anything at all."

In her patient embrace, Mathilde soon calmed down.

"How do you know all this?" she asked Sophie. "You're nobody."

"She's not nobody," Clementine rebuked gruffly, approaching Mathilde from the other side and laying a weathered hand on top of Sophie's where it sat on their sister's shoulder. "She's one of us."

Sophie's smile said it all, and she nestled in closer to her sister. "And you are, too, you stupid woman," Clementine added to Mathilde. "So stop your sniveling."

Mathilde lifted her own trembling hands and laid them on top of her sisters', and the three of them stayed just like that for a while, soaking up one another amid a strangely comfortable silence.

Anybody who knew anything about the Peines would have fainted with disbelief had they peered through the kitchen window and witnessed this scene. Nobody did, though. Edie and Cochon were happily playing outside and missed the whole thing, yet, strangely, Cochon never flattened his ears and bared his teeth at Mathilde ever again.

The following morning she came down late to breakfast, receiving an exuberant "Good morning" from Sophie and a sheepish smile from Clementine.

"Coffee, anyone?" Mathilde asked. It was not a question she had ever asked before and was not in itself important, but it gave rise to one of those moments when everybody realized that something significant had changed. A layer had been peeled away that could not be replaced again. It was slightly embarrassing because the two older Peines were simply not used to such exposure and felt a little naked. But it was also rather wonderful.

Mathilde poured herself some coffee and on her way to the table gave Clementine's shoulder a squeeze.

Clementine looked up at her in surprise but said nothing.

"I've been thinking," Mathilde said quietly as she sat, "about what you said yesterday about regret and everything." She was uncharacteristically awkward but determined to proceed. "I've been thinking about Benoît and what he means to you, Clementine. And it occurs to me that perhaps he was more than the boy next door."

Sophie reached across and clutched Clementine's arm, which had frozen on the table. "Don't be afraid, Mentine. Maybe you should tell her why he means so much to you. Maybe it's a secret you've kept too long already."

"Your daughter," Mathilde said. "I should have asked you about her before."

"Amélie," Clementine said, staring straight ahead and nodding. "Her name is Amélie."

"And Benoît is the father?"

Clementine kept nodding.

"But he doesn't know?"

The nodding stopped.

"Why haven't you told him?"

"I hadn't even spoken to him since that day you and he—"

"There is no he and I, Clementine."

"But there was. Back then. I went over there. Just the once. After you and he . . . You knew I wanted him, Mathilde, and yet you went over there and took him from me."

"You haven't spoken to him since then?" Mathilde was aghast. "But that's ludicrous, Clementine. That was so long ago, and I was just a horny seventeen-year-old doing what horny seventeen-year-olds do. I didn't know what he meant to you, or if I did, I probably didn't care. But I do now. I know, that is, and I care. And I'm sorry. I'm truly sorry."

For a single heartbeat Clementine saw that this could be true, that the whole miserable tragedy could have been caused by nothing more than raging adolescent hormones and that Mathilde could be truly sorry.

She had to decide then whether to cling to her bitterness or let it go, and for a moment, she chose to treasure it. It had been part of her life for so long she was almost afraid to be without it. But the weightlessness of compassion, such a rare commodity in her life until recently, was for once so easily within her reach that it was a temptation she simply couldn't resist. Like chocolate éclairs.

"Apology accepted?" Mathilde asked gingerly.

"Apology accepted," Clementine begrudgingly replied, and her misery floated off like a hot air balloon.

Entre Soeurs

The harsh cold weather continued into the next month, the vines staying safe and sleeping beneath their freezing blanket. Inside the House of Peine, on the other hand, the thaw was well under way. Certainly the walls remained cold to the touch and the windows a little icy, but the atmosphere itself was anything but frosty. In fact, had that imaginary passerby who'd looked in and fainted the previous month peered once more through the kitchen window on a chilly evening, he or she might even have dreamed wistfully of belonging to such a group.

Who ever would have guessed that the poisonous Peines might one day conjure up such envy?

Edie was enjoying the winter holidays, further impressed with the exuberance with which the French embraced the notion of the vacation. She talked excitedly to her father during his weekly phone calls of roasting chestnuts and building snowmen before passing the phone over to her mother. School forgotten for the time being, Sophie had been teaching her to paint and bake, two skills at which she showed some aptitude, adding to her growing confidence.

Her daughter thus soaked up by the extended family, Mathilde was relatively content working on her campaign to get the next release of Peine champagne into as many restaurants and wine shops as possible. As she worked the phone scaring up orders, Clementine beavered beside her in the winery, and, working in her usual slow and steady way, she completed the blend.

The new wine was all now safely mixed in its barrels where it would stay until it was bottled.

Nothing ever stayed still for long in a Champagne winery, however, and the next big job at hand was disgorging the champagne that Mathilde was doing such a good job of selling. Clementine had been dragging the chain on the disgorging because it was a mammoth task requiring all hands on deck, and some of those hands, she feared, were a little too likely to drop and waste her precious bubbles. In the end, a couple of weeks into February, it was Mathilde who tugged the chain.

"Our bank manager has a little problem," she announced one afternoon following a visit to Epernay. She didn't mention that the little problem he had was that he had finally worked out that his stubby fingers were never going to tickle her slender thighs, and this had catapulted him into a most unpleasant frame of mind. "He is becoming slightly disagreeable," she said instead, "over the matter of our overdraft, and we need to address our cash flow. Clementine, how soon do you think we can start selling the new release?"

"Well, it's all riddled, but it will take a week to disgorge—if we all work very carefully, paying particular attention to what we are doing and keeping any tragic slipups to a minimum."

"Yes, yes, and then?"

"And then we need to let it rest for about another six weeks."

"Another six weeks!" Mathilde rolled her eyes in exasperation. "Are you joking? The infernal stuff has been resting for four years already!"

"It's for exactly that reason we need to let it rest some more." Clementine stood firm. "Remember, Mathilde, our bottles lie quietly in the *cave* for all that time, giving birth to their bubbles, and then we turn them upside down, freeze the neck, whip off the lid, pop out the sediment, top them up, and then wedge in a cork. Imagine if all that happened to you in one day? Trust me, it needs more rest. Anything else would be downright cruel."

Mathilde momentarily pondered the possibility of having someone whip off her lid and top her up, so to speak. It had been a while, a long while; her cork was firmly wedged, and imagining anything otherwise was something of a distraction. She banned such thoughts. "So we disgorge now and can release it at the end of March?" she asked Clementine.

"The beginning of April, perhaps. And then we can bottle the new wine because there'll be room in the *cave*." Winemaking was a constant juggling act. Every minute could be used some way or other, and ever centimeter of space, too.

"Okay," Mathilde said authoritatively. "We need to start disgorging as soon as possible so we can get the champagne out into the market. Leave the bank manager to me. I think I can keep him at bay a while longer." At least she had the phone number for his superior in Paris and had threatened to ring it should the manager not accommodate her for another month or so. "But it's imperative we have some dates firmly in place, and we need to meet all the deadlines. If we are delivering in early April, we can expect payment in early May. I'll have to make sure that happens, but

I've done that before. Prompt payment is essential if we have any chance of . . ." She petered out, not meaning to alarm her sisters, but she was too late. High finance was well above Sophie's head, but she could sense pending penury when she sniffed it.

"Are we in trouble?" she asked.

"We are sailing close to the wind," Mathilde admitted. "But people have sailed closer. Generally, it is just a matter of keeping everyone informed and knowing when they can expect product and when we can expect payment."

"At least it's the 2002 we are releasing," Clementine told her. It had been a good year, and there was plenty of it. The House of Peine aged its champagne longer than other houses—Olivier had insisted on it—and some were about to release their 2003. Thanks to the frost and heat that dreadful year, they would be lucky to have half their normal stock heading for the stores and restaurants. "Although I suppose that means we'll have cash flow problems again next year," she added miserably.

"Never mind next year," Mathilde said crisply. "We'll cross that bridge when we come to it. We need to get through this year first."

That very evening Clementine got the rusty forklift out of the barn and drove it around the side of the winery. One of the good things about the *cave* her ancestors had dug into the chalky earth was that because it was underground, it remained at a constant cool temperature. One of the bad things was getting anything in or out of it. During the *vendange,* the wine traveled from the top floor to the *cave* via hoses, and the winemaker went down that narrow spiral staircase. But to get the barrels, bottles, vats, and anything of a decent size in or out of the underground level, there was a steep driveway dug into the earth down which bigger machines could make deliveries to a set of heavy steel doors, close relations to the Peine château gates, it would seem, if their reluctance to open when you needed them to was anything to go by.

For the next couple of days Clementine negotiated the steep driveway and sticky doors time and time again. With much grinding of gears, burping of fumes, and unleashing of ripe expletives, she picked up the pallets of riddled bottles and delivered them around the outside of the winery to the top floor for disgorging. Once all the bottles were there, she enlisted the help of her family.

They were reminded on a half-hourly basis to pay particular heed to what they were doing and so managed to keep tragic slipups to a minimum. For a week the four of them worked on the production line, freezing the bottle necks, removing the plugs of sediment, adding the final *dosage*, putting in the corks, fitting the muzzles, adding the foils, and packing the bottles right side up back onto the pallets. It was exhausting work—and noisy—and they were dog-tired by the end of each day.

But it was with great satisfaction that Clementine stood back the afternoon they finished and admired those fifty thousand bottles, now one step closer to improving the day of perfect strangers by providing their delightful effervescence for some future special occasion.

She hitched up her skirt (not exactly Chanel but a vast improvement on corduroy) and was about to jump on the forklift again when Sophie stopped her.

"What are you doing, Mentine?"

"I may as well start delivering the pallets back downstairs," Clementine said, albeit wearily. "What I don't do now I'll only have to do tomorrow."

"Oh, come on," Mathilde interrupted. "We've worked our fingers to the bone here. Surely this calls for a celebration."

"Yes, Mentine, what about a bottle of the '88? You deserve it." Sophie had tasted it only a couple of times, but it was a taste that needed as much revisiting as possible.

Clementine paused, thinking about Olivier and his unwillingness to share his best work, his difficulty in appreciating the very thing he once worked so hard to produce. She decided the forklift could wait until tomorrow.

"You're right," she said. "I'll go and get the '88 if you go in and light the fire."

Some time later they sprawled, relaxed, around the now oft-used sitting room. The burning coals in the fireplace threw out a gentle amber glow, illuminating Clementine who sat on the floor, her back against the lumpy sofa, with a sleeping Edie in her arms.

The child had enjoyed a whole glass of champagne, picking up some of the most subtle herbaceous notes, before falling into a weary slumber from which her aunt was reluctant to wake her. School started again in the morning, and although she found lessons easier in Saint-Vincent-sur-Marne than she had in Manhattan, it was still enough of an ordeal for sleep to provide a welcome refuge.

"You'd make a good mother, Clementine," Mathilde said thoughtfully.

The fire popped and a floorboard creaked upstairs.

"Have you ever thought about finding her? Finding Amélie?"

Sophie's stomach gurgled. She had been having trouble with indigestion, and fear at how Clementine would take this intrusion further curdled the contents of her stomach. She watched carefully to see how her eldest sister would respond.

Clementine stared into the coals, seeing tiny flickering images of her dark-haired daughter dancing and weaving between the throbbing oranges and yellows pulsating in the fireplace. "Not really," she eventually said in a surprisingly relaxed voice. She had barely dared think of her daughter at all until recently.

"Would you think about it now?" Sophie asked.

Clementine bent forward and smelled Edie's hair. It had the yeasty fruit of the winery in it still, but also the undertones of some lollipop-flavored little-girl shampoo.

"What would I do if I found her?" she wondered. "Just say that I did, and just say she wanted to meet me. I could hardly bring her here, with her father next door not even knowing she exists. What if she looks just like him? What if he sees her?"

"What if you tell him?" Mathilde suggested carefully. "What could happen?"

"Odile could throttle me," Clementine pointed out. "Look what happened when I just tried to speak to him at the parade. Can you imagine what she would do if I turned up with our daughter?"

"They don't have children of their own," Mathilde said. "You may well surprise Benoît, but then he may surprise you."

"I surprised him once before, and it wasn't a beautiful experience," Clementine said shortly. "I doubt very much he would want to relive it. I know I don't."

"Yes, but keep in mind that he shares his bed with odious Odile," Mathilde said with a glimmer of her old vicious wit. "The poor man must be desperate for something halfway appealing to wake up to. I'd rather have you any day."

Sophie laughed, and a smile even occurred to Clementine. It was a compliment, after all. Her mind turned then to the subject of bed-sharing. If she could use what she had learned from Hector with Benoît . . .

"You're blushing, Clementine," Mathilde said.

"It's too hot in here." Clementine extricated herself from Edie. "Help me get her up to bed, will you? I'm going to have an early night. Sophie, you should, too. You look exhausted."

The three of them carried the slumbering ten-year-old up the stairs and put her to bed where the moon threw a slice of light over her face as she lay there, illuminating a corrugated skein of Clementine-like hair.

They all stood there looking at her for a few moments, thinking their different thoughts. Then they bid each other good night and headed to their rooms and to deep dreamless sleep. Apart from Mathilde, that is. She had a change of heart at her bedroom door, and after waiting until she heard that her sisters had turned in, she slipped back down the stairs.

Catastrophe

It was two in the morning when Cochon jumped on top of Edie. He was small and unshod, but, still, he was a horse, and having his hooves on her chest woke her up in an instant. He was snorting and shaking his mane in a most frenzied fashion, plus he smelled strongly to her sharp young nose of smoke.

Edie sat bolt upright, feeling a jolt of fright, then noticed a faint glow through the curtains in her room. She jumped out of bed and flung them open. Across the courtyard an orange flame shot out the door of the winery and licked the wall like an illuminated tongue.

"Mommy!" she screamed, running into the chilly hall. "Mentine! The winery's on fire! Wake up!"

For a split second there was no sound at all. Then there was the thud of heels on floorboards, an anguished cry from Sophie, and a strangled moan of panic from Clementine, who burst into the hallway in her nightgown, her hair wild, her eyes terrified.

Mathilde alone was calm yet white-faced. "Call the fire brigade," she told Clementine. "Don't panic, Mentine. Just do it."

Then she and Sophie, who clutched an old wool jacket around

her, grasped the whimpering Edie and ran down the stairs and out into the courtyard.

At first Mathilde thought that perhaps they could contain the fire themselves. Flames no longer shot out the door or any of the small windows on the courtyard side. There was just a lot of thick black smoke. The winery was made of stone, after all, she reasoned. But what she could not see was that the flames inside the building did not need to exit the doors and windows now. They had found their escape upward and were jumping to lick the heavy exposed wooden beams that ran the length of the ceiling.

Just as Clementine emerged from the house, the roof with its tantalizing wooden shingles caught alight with a single "poof." It was all the more frightening because the noise was barely more than a whisper, yet the ensuing flames lit up the surrounding countryside in a violent glow that illuminated every grapevine from the snaking Marne River below them to the church spire peaking on a distant horizon.

Sophie had clumsily hauled the hose from the vegetable patch around to the courtyard and was calling for Edie to find the faucet and turn it on, but it was useless. They could all see then that it was useless.

The sound of the first bottle exploding was like a splinter in Clementine's heart. She fell to her knees on the gravel, both hands stuffed in her mouth, the heat from the flames burning her face, that crinkly hair crackling and shrinking in sympathy. Through the hiss and roar of the blaze she heard another bottle explode, then another and another and another until the cold night air rang with the almost musical notes of some terrible twisted symphony.

Imagine how this cacophony would sound to a woman who battled tears when a single bottle of Peine was dropped and wasted? Each note was like the clash of giant cymbals crushing the breath from her lungs and the hope from her heart. This was not only her past but her future going up in smoke—and all in front of her very eyes.

The fire brigade arrived quickly considering that Gaston, the lazy grave-digger, was in charge of coordinating the volunteers. Yet despite his relative speed and efficiency, fifty thousand freshly disgorged bottles of champagne were history by the time the fire-fighters got there. Clementine was in some sort of a stupor then from which neither her sisters nor her niece could release her. She was collapsed on the gravel, her eyes wide open and black with the horror of what she had seen, and her skin was raw from the cruel combination of intense heat and nighttime winter chill.

Sophie and Mathilde tried to drag her farther back from the burning winery, closer to the house, but she would not be moved. She could not keep her eyes off the flames that were gobbling up four years' hard labor and who knew what else. In the end the four of them, five including the shuddering Cochon, sat huddled helplessly together in the courtyard, clutching one another beneath a blanket, strangely transfixed by the terrible sight.

"It's the noise," Edie said wondrously at one point as though she were watching a documentary on the Discovery channel. "I never knew fires were so loud."

It took little more than half an hour for Gaston and his crew to battle for control of the flames. It almost seemed an insult that their lives could be ruined quite so quickly. There was not that much to burn, Gaston told them, once the wine had gone and taken the roof with it.

His boss, the fire chief Xavier Martinot, a big man with a walrus mustache, ordered most of the firefighters home an hour or so later and then gruffly explained to Mathilde that the fire seemed suspicious. It had started, he said, among the stack of new oak barrels that Patric Didier had delivered earlier in the week. The oak was dense, he explained, and needed quite some provocation to burn, but once it got going, "kaboom!"

"But who would do that to us?" Sophie asked quietly.

"Who indeed," Martinot agreed. "Usually it's a family member." He passed a black eye across the startled group in front of him. "Or it could be an enemy. Or a totally unrelated random arsonist. They're the worst."

"Oh, well, that gives us something to be getting on with then, doesn't it?" Mathilde said although her sarcasm was lost on him.

"Indeed," he said again. "I'll be checking the surrounding area in the morning. Don't worry, I'll find your firebug. They always leave a clue."

After he left, Mathilde attempted to get closer to have a look at the damage but was hustled by Gaston back to her sisters. Even from where they sat they could see what little had survived. The champagne was no more, the press was no more, and only the bones of the rusty forklift smoldered darkly where Clementine had left it.

They were all devastated, of course, but none more so than she. She could not speak. Not even Edie could break her trance or Cochon, climbing into her lap, quite wretched. When the departing ambulance officer suggested she be given a sedative, Sophie assumed she would object, but Clementine wordlessly took the pill and eventually let herself be led up to her bed where she slept the sleep of a woman who might as well be dead.

When she awoke, Edie was in bed next to her, clinging to her, and Cochon was nestled on the floor as close to the bed as he could possibly get. Clementine wondered for a glorious innocent moment if it had all been a horrible nightmare, but the insides of her nostrils were burned and sooty, and the room stank of smoke: an instant bitter reminder that she had not been dreaming, that they had truly lost everything in a fire.

She freed herself from Edie, stepped over Cochon, and pulled back the curtain. The stone walls of the winery were blackened with soot, and wafts of smoke curled almost cheerfully out through the open top of the building. Gaston, to his credit, was still there—admittedly asleep in a portable chair in the courtyard, but there nonetheless beside the fire truck, hoses at the ready should any hot spots appear. Although how he'd know she wasn't sure.

She pulled on her robe and, too sickened to open the window and shout at him for his incompetence, headed for the kitchen. Sophie sat at the table as pale as a ghost while Mathilde smoked by the kitchen counter, her eyes focused out the window on the burned remains.

"I always thought it would be the cold that ruined us," Clementine said, her chair scraping harshly across the stone floor as she sat. "The frost. Not the heat."

"Are we ruined?" Sophie asked, looking at Mathilde.

Her question went unanswered.

"Is there insurance?"

Once more, no reply. Insurance was a swindle in which Olivier did not believe, a view that Mathilde did not necessarily share, but, nonetheless, the financial state he had left them in had not allowed for it.

"I can ask George to help," Mathilde said, "to tide us over for a month or so but . . ."

The silence that ensued fostered a trickle of dismal possibilities in each of them but was followed by a pert knocking on the front door. The sisters looked at each other, and then Clementine got up, shuffled down the hall, and pulled it open.

It was Bernadette herself, bearing two *patisserie* boxes and a delectable smelling bag.

"You're answering the door!" she exclaimed.

"You're knocking on it," Clementine replied.

They stood there staring at each other.

"Do you want to come in?" Clementine finally asked.

"No, I don't," Bernadette replied. "But I'm impressed you asked. These are for Sophie," she added, thrusting the goodies forward, "and the little one, Edie, and for her mother—you know, the thin one—and for you, too, Clementine. Yes, for you."

A belch of something black and sooty escaped through the open roof of the smoldering winery, and they both looked around and surveyed the wreckage.

"I'm sorry," Bernadette said, wiping at her eyes. "I truly am. We've never been—well, you know what I mean. Friends. You've been a reliable customer, though, one of my best. And you've worked hard all your life. I know that much. And it can't have been easy." She gave a clipped little nod and then turned around and climbed (with less grace than Clementine, it must be said) onto the bike. Then with a shake of her head at Gaston, snoring rudely in his chair, she departed.

Clementine carried her bounty into the kitchen and opened the first box.

It was full of *pain au chocolat amande*. She should have been repulsed, she knew that; she should not have been able to stomach the thought. Yet her mouth watered, and she licked her lips and then looked hopefully at Sophie, who promptly dashed to the back door and vomited delicately into a lavender bush.

"But it's not even Saturday," said Clementine sadly, contemplating the unscheduled *pain au chocolat amande*, and to her surprise, Mathilde laughed—a pretty, feminine sound that she wasn't sure she had heard before.

Sophie, appalled, wiped at her mouth, her huge violet eyes saucers in that little white face. Then she gurgled, which turned into a giggle, which then developed into a laugh of her own, and before they knew it, the three of them were sitting there around that faithful oak table roaring as though they had not a care in the world. They were unhinged, all three of them, completely.

Edie came in then, with a subdued Cochon close at her heels. "What's so funny?" she asked blearily. "Didn't the winery burn down? It smells so smoky."

Her childish gloom halted their laughter. Like Mary Poppins and her charges, glum thoughts brought them back down to earth with a bump. Clementine swept into action, insisting that Sophie sit down with her head between her legs. The smoke inhalation, they decided, had been too much for lungs used only to the smog of Paris. Settling down again as Mathilde made more coffee, the smell of the fire infiltrated their thinking. Edie was right: the kitchen stank of smoke, and the disaster filled up every nook and cranny in the house. They had been mad to laugh. This was no laughing matter.

"There's no point asking George for money," Clementine said flatly. "Tiding us over is not going to be enough." There was no quick fix for this crisis. After everything she had been through these past few months, these last few years, after all the worry and fear and anguish, it was something quite out of the blue that had taken her down for good. "It's finished," she said in that old flat tone. "We are finished."

"But there are the vines," Sophie insisted. "We still have those. They're not even touched, Mentine. Please don't give up hope now. We can get through somehow."

Clementine looked at her and then at Mathilde.

"How?"

Mathilde wished she had a better answer, but there was none. "I don't know, Mentine. Sophie is right. We still have the vines, but it will be four years before we see a cent out of those if we continue to make our own champagne, and we don't have four months, let alone four years."

"If we continue?" Sophie asked. "What do you mean?"

Clementine closed her eyes. "We can sell our grapes to Moët or Veuve Clicquot," she said, "for cash flow. For the next *vendange*. But we wouldn't be able to afford to make any wine ourselves. And we still have to find a way to live between now and then."

"And don't forget old man Joliet," Mathilde reminded her. "He'll be sniffing around in no time at all, the old *mec*, but I'd kill the vines with my own bare hands rather than sell our land to him."

Clementine looked at her sister in amazement. "You would?"

"Of course I would," Mathilde said. "I might be mean and insensitive, but I am not brainless. If we sell the land, we really do have nothing."

"But you could get the money and go home," Clementine replied.

Mathilde lit another cigarette and looked out the window, chewing her lip.

"She is home," Sophie said softly. "We all are."

And so at the very time in her life when Clementine thought that all was lost, she instead discovered that all was found. That her future did not depend on the champagne she had nurtured until it was ready for its journey out into the world. That a bubbly tipple really had nothing to do with it. Her future lay with these women, with this family.

It wasn't quite the family she had dreamed of as a little girl, perhaps, but then who in their right mind would dream that a stroppy businesswoman, a shrewd urchin, and a lonely *vigneron* would one day combine to form a balanced household—along with a troubled red-haired ten-year-old and a dwarfed piglike horse?

The three sisters looked at one another around the table and felt Peine blood coursing through their veins as sure as if it were butter on freshly baked bread. Then they had a *pain au chocolat amande*—even Mathilde. "No point starving to death just yet," Clementine said, nibbling the almonds off her pastry. "Well done, Edie. You've gotten Cochon to eat a croissant. And here I was thinking he'd switched entirely to chocolates."

Espoir

Once they had polished off their pastries, Mathilde created something of a stir by washing the dishes, which no one had ever seen her do before. After putting the last plate away she turned, her jaw firmly set, and suggested they go and have a closer look at the damage to the winery.

"Come on," she urged them. "We have to face it sometime. Maybe there's something we can salvage."

"Or maybe we can find a clue as to who would do this to us," added Sophie. "Do you really think it was deliberate?"

"I don't see how the fire could have started itself," Clementine said, "but I don't know who would want to hurt us this badly."

"You don't think old man Joliet . . ." Sophie suggested.

"For centuries those Joliets have been after Peine land," Clementine told her, "and never before have they resorted to arson."

"Yes, well, there's a first time for everything," Mathilde interjected as they approached Gaston, who was still snoozing in the courtyard, a waterfall of drool pooling on the shoulder of his tatty volunteer uniform. "Is it safe to go in?" Mathilde asked him after kicking his chair all but out from underneath him to wake him up.

"Why would you want to?" he replied grumpily, blinking in the watery winter sunshine. "Even if every last bottle hadn't exploded, it wouldn't taste very good. Clementine should know that."

Mathilde kicked his chair again, harder this time, even though he was clearly already awake.

"What was that for?" he asked.

"Show some respect," snapped Mathilde. "We've just lost everything we have in a suspicious fire, and the last thing we need are smart-ass comments from a bum like you."

"Your father would be so proud," grumbled Gaston as they walked away from him. "Just what Saint-Vincent-sur-Marne needs, another chip off the old block! Although I'll say one thing for Olivier Peine: you never found him exaggerating. He was a crusty old goat but he never painted a picture blacker than it already was."

Clementine and Mathilde kept heading toward the winery door, but Gaston's comment stopped Sophie in her tracks.

"What do you mean," she asked, turning back, "exaggerating? Who is exaggerating?"

"The skinny one," he said, spitting on the ground. "You haven't lost everything, have you? There's the *cave*."

They all stopped at that, even Cochon, and turned to look at him.

"The *cave*?" Clementine repeated stupidly.

"Of course," Gaston answered. "The hatch was down. The drains were plugged. The floor is two feet thick. Fire goes up. They knew what they were doing, your Peine ancestors. I'll bet you a week's worth of pastis at Le Bois that the temperature in the *cave* is still ten degrees and that there's not a drop of water down there."

Clementine broke into a trot, swerving away from the gaping hole that was once the entrance to the burned winery and running instead around the outside and down the difficult driveway to the heavy steel doors built into the ground. Mathilde and Sophie flew to opposite sides, and together they pulled and jiggled and pushed and cajoled. As soon as the doors finally agreed to shudder apart, the sweetest air spiraled out of the opening between them. Clementine smelled it straightaway. She didn't even need to step inside to know that Gaston was right: the contents of the *cave* were unharmed.

Heart pounding, head reeling, she slipped inside and went straight to the reserve barrels, pouring herself a glass of the '99 pinot. It was perfect, absolutely perfect.

"Thank God!" she breathed. "Oh, thank God." She ran next to a barrel of the newly blended vintage and poured herself a splash of that as well. Blackberries as strong as ever, and buttery croissant, too. This was not the Peine bad luck she was used to.

"I can't believe it." Sophie was ecstatic. "That upstairs should be gone, poof, and down here it's as though nothing ever happened. We're going to be all right, then, aren't we? We're saved! Doesn't this mean we are saved?"

The smile slid off Clementine's lips and the bloom of relief faded from her cheeks as she looked at Mathilde. "Oh," she said as her thoughts fell into place. "Oh."

"I don't understand." Sophie looked from one sister to the other. "Isn't this the best thing that could happen?"

"Next to not having a fire burn up any chance of pulling us out of the shit?" Mathilde asked her. "Yes. But we are still in the shit."

Sophie's mind was whirring. Cash flow. She looked down the

arched alcove that housed the resting 2003 that had yet to be riddled or disgorged. "What about that?" she pointed. "Couldn't we
sell that?"

In theory it wasn't a bad idea. In practice there were fatal
flaws.

"Well, correct me if I am wrong," Mathilde said, looking at
Clementine for assurance, "but even if we did not leave it on the
lees as long as we usually would, we would need to riddle it, yes?
That's eight weeks, which would take us to April. Then we would
need to disgorge, fine. But to disgorge we would have to rebuild
upstairs. Now that would probably take about eight weeks, too, so
theoretically that could work out all right. There's just one problem. To get the money we need to pay for the rebuilding, we need
the profit from selling the very wine that needs to be disgorged."

Clementine groaned. Of all the years to be relying on! The very
wine they couldn't afford to release was the 2003, of which there
was so little in the first place.

"But still we are more saved than we were before," Sophie said
with her trademark optimism. "We must be!"

"Just not saved enough," Clementine told her.

"We are still looking at Moët or old man Joliet," Mathilde
agreed glumly, "or a miracle."

Clementine slumped to the floor. "If only I had started bringing
the bottles down yesterday afternoon," she said, her head falling
into her hands. "We might have been all right. We might have
been able to sell enough to get us the cash flow while we sorted
everything out."

"Then it's my fault," Sophie said with a heartbroken gasp.
"You wanted to keep working, but I wanted to celebrate. I'm so
sorry, Mentine. I should have let you be. It's my fault!"

"It wouldn't have made enough of a difference," Mathilde told them. "How many bottles could you have moved in two or three hours? This disaster is bigger than that, I'm afraid."

Gaston appeared then with Cochon prancing around him in circles and Edie bringing up the rear. In one hand he held up an empty gasoline container, and then he turned to Edie, who produced the charred remains of a high-heeled pump.

Gaston rattled the can at the three grim-faced women. "Xavier found this on his way back here this morning," he said. "It was in the grass at the bottom of the drive. And your dog found this shoe in the remains near the forklift. It would seem that he was right, that the fire was not an accident and most likely was lit by the wearer of this shoe."

"He's not a dog," Clementine and Edie said at the same time, but Sophie was looking at Mathilde. She was the only one among them who wore high-heeled shoes, after all.

"Oh, my God," Mathilde whispered, also looking at the shoe, the color leaving her face. "I don't believe it."

"Don't believe what?" Clementine wanted to know.

"The shoe, Mentine," Sophie whispered, pointing at Mathilde. "The shoe."

"What about it?" Clementine looked at the burned heel again and then at Mathilde, finally registering with a stomach-churning thunk what it all meant.

Of course, she thought, her heart shriveling instantly in her chest. There was no hope for someone like her. She had been a fool to think she would ever be part of a family that cared enough about her not to burn her livelihood to a crisp, leaving her penniless, homeless, and alone in the world without even her little horse for company.

"Oh, Mathilde," she whispered as all dreams of happiness started to dissolve. "We were so close to being . . . How could you do this? Burn down our wine, ruin us like this. Ruin me and Sophie?"

"And me," piped up Edie.

"Oh, ye of little faith!" the resilient Mathilde complained without a shred of worry. "Can you imagine the size of the hoof that would fit into that shoe?"

They all turned again to the charred pump and then back to Mathilde's slender ankles. The burned shoe was at least three sizes too big for her.

"Then whose is it?" Sophie asked.

"Yes," agreed Gaston. "Whose?

"I would bet money, if we had any, that the person who lit the fire was Odile Geoffroy," Mathilde said. "Nobody else around here has bad enough taste to be teetering around the countryside in those things, and that's saying something. Get over there right now, Gaston. Put the shoe on her and then arrest her, put her in jail, throw away the key, and give her a good kick in her fat despicable rump while you're at it."

Gaston had a soft spot for Odile's rump and was momentarily enthused by the idea of making contact with it.

"Odile?" Sophie was confused. "What are you talking about?"

"Clementine, you are going to hate me all over again." Mathilde took a deep breath and looked at her as pleadingly as she ever had at anyone. "But you must believe me when I say I never thought for an instant I was doing anything other than trying to help you."

"What are you talking about?"

"Last night after you all went to bed," Mathilde said quickly as if getting it over as soon as possible would somehow lessen the blow, "I went over to talk to Benoît. Odile must have seen me."

Both sisters paled and gasped. "You did what?" Clementine cried. "Again? After everything?" This was really too much for that overworked organ in her chest. There really was no such thing as good luck or happy families or . . .

"No! Not like that." Mathilde interrupted her hysteria. "Listen to me. I didn't go over for anything like that, Mentine. I went for you. I went to help you. I went to tell him about Amélie."

Clementine and Sophie gasped again, twin shoulders rising toward twin ears in horror.

"Amélie?" Gaston repeated. They had forgotten he was still there. "Who's Amélie?"

"She's Clementine's baby that she had with Benoît next door," Edie informed him.

This time the gasp was tripled.

"Jesus!" cried Clementine. They had forgotten Edie was still there. "How much worse is this day going to get?"

"Benoît?" Gaston leaned against a barrel. "A baby?" He looked at Clementine as though for the first time ever. "You?"

"What, you've never seen a woman who's had sex before?" Clementine snapped. "Not up this close, no, I can well imagine that."

Gaston's eyes, too close together as it was, were swiveling in his head with these new revelations. What a treat he would have for his pals at Le Bois tonight!

"Mentine, perhaps Gaston would like a drink," Mathilde cleverly suggested as she watched him. Unless they wanted their private business to be broadcast around the neighborhood by lunchtime, they needed to get the grave-digging firefighter drunk enough to rattle his brains. She was a quick thinker, Mathilde. And on this occasion the shell-shocked Clementine, usually so slow on the uptake, was only one step behind her.

"Yes, yes," she agreed, albeit slightly dazed. "I know Olivier kept some of his famous Cuvée Supérieur down here somewhere for special occasions just like this one." There was indeed a case or two of Supérieur in the *cave,* but it was only special in the same way as the bottles Olivier's mother had fobbed off on the Germans all those years earlier. Some time ago Olivier had caught a disgruntled worker drinking out of each bottle before disgorging and topping them up with the contents of his bladder. The normal thing, of course, would have been to empty those bottles down the drain, but instead Olivier had corked them and kept them especially for the likes of greedy Gaston, who licked his lips and rubbed his blackened hands together at the prospect of tasting it.

"Give me a hand to find it, will you?" Clementine commanded her sisters, and then she led them down to the recesses of the far alcove. It was an unpopular vein of the underground winery, that particular one, being darker and smaller at the far end than the others as though the Peine ancestors excavating it had grown shorter as they dug. Clementine fetched a lamp off the wall and held it up as they moved farther into the darkness.

Pétiller

"How could you do that, Mathilde?" Clementine hissed furiously as they hunched over, away from Gaston's prying ears, the lamp throwing an uninterested light across a collection of lumpy stacks with an old oilcloth thrown over them at the dead end of the tunnel. "How could you tell Benoît? And now on top of our livelihood being snatched away from us by his wife—oh my Lord, Odile!—that idiot Gaston knows my secret, so by the end of the day everybody else will know it, too. After nearly twenty years! I can't bear it, Mathilde. I thought my life was bad before, but it's only going to get worse. Who would have believed that was possible? Nobody, that's who. I can't breathe. Sophie, I can't breathe. I think I'm going to faint."

"Calm down, Mentine," urged Sophie. "Take a deep breath."

"I know you won't be able to forgive me," Mathilde whispered. "Forgiveness does not seem to come naturally to the Peines, but you have to believe me when I tell you I thought I was doing a good thing, a kind thing."

"Well, next time you want to do a kind thing," Clementine's voice was rising, "just disembowel me with a blunt knife or shoot me and leave me to bleed slowly to death and be eaten by rats."

"Oh, for God's sake, stick a sock in the melodramatics, Clementine. Yes, I've made a mistake, a big one, and it's led to a few more, but let's not forget the bottom line: we are all in this together."

"You can shove your bottom line where the sun doesn't shine," Clementine hissed. "We never even had a bottom line until you turned up."

"Please, it's so musty and cold back here," broke in Sophie, trying as usual to appease her sisters. "Let's find what we are looking for and get on with it. Are we going to give Gaston some of this wine here, Clementine?"

"No, we're not going to give that layabout real Peine champagne. What a waste! Olivier kept some champagne down here specially for the likes of him. We'll have to force-feed that blabbermouth every last drop of it if I'm to survive this day with even a shred of dignity. Oh, Mathilde, why would you do this to me? Why has this happened? I curse that randy old father of ours, lumping me with you like this. How he must have despised me!"

"Oh, please, don't be like this, Mentine," begged Sophie. She hated to see her sister seek refuge in her old angry armor. "It's not Olivier's fault."

"Yes, it is!" insisted Clementine. "He fathered us and abandoned us, each one of us, whichever way you look at it. I might have lived with him, but he wasn't here, not for me, anyway. I felt his absence more than either of you, I bet I did, because I sat across the table from it. But he never saw me, Sophie. He never once saw me, who I was or what I might have become. He gave me nothing! And he gave you nothing, either. Not any of us. Nothing!"

"You think you had it so bad, you selfish cow! He ignored me for the first seventeen years of my life, then brought me here to ignore me again, and then sent me away only to ignore me some more. And in the meantime I've been ignored by four other so-called fathers."

"At least you know the meaning of the word!" cried Sophie in an uncustomarily raised voice. "I don't even know what he looked like, what he sounded like, what made him the way he was."

"That's pathetic," said Mathilde. "You should count yourself lucky."

"Don't you call her pathetic," shouted Clementine. She was hunched over in the tight space, comical in her anger in such a position. "You've no right, absolutely no right!" She was pointing at Mathilde, waggling an accusing finger that forced her sister to step back farther, at which she banged her head on the low curved ceiling, then lost her footing and fell on the oilskin-covered pile. An old chair cracked and fell apart beneath her, a rotten wooden box spewed old *pétanque* balls onto the ground, and a collection of bottles clinked and fell noisily to the ground, breaking and leaking on the cold stone floor.

"You vile wretch," Mathilde cawed, trying to stand up and turning to see what mess she had landed on. But as soon as she faced the wall, her hand dropped away from the bump that was forming on her crown. "A white cross," she said in quiet amazement. "Look, you two, look! It's a white cross."

"In the middle of my darkest hour she talks crosses," cried Clementine. "Oh, it's just like you to find religion at a time like this. How convenient! You will be the end of me, Mathilde. The very end."

"No, you don't understand," answered Mathilde, the anger gone now from her voice and her fingers scrabbling at the wall behind the deconstructed pile. "It's a white cross! Like the red cross and the blue. Remember?"

Sophie moved to her side, holding up the lamp to illuminate the cross. "'A red cross for the nursing station, a blue cross for the soup line, a white cross for a hideaway.'" She turned to Clementine. "That's what La Petite said about *les crayères* at Moët, Mentine. Remember? That a white cross marked a hiding place. This is definitely a white cross. What on earth can it mean? Do you think she was trying to tell us something?"

"Yes, she was our fairy godmother, and she has left us a trunk full of pirate's gold," scoffed Clementine, but she shuffled closer nonetheless.

"Look! I don't think this wall is chalk, Mentine. Can you see?" Sophie was rubbing furiously at the cross with her sleeve. "It's a different color. And these ridges, they could be bricks."

"Don't be so ridiculous," Clementine harrumphed, but she peered closer to the wall. Sophie was right. The wall on which the white cross had been painted was a different color, and as her sisters rubbed, the outline of stacked bricks was indeed emerging. Clementine shuffled back and got another lamp and then joined Sophie and Mathilde in clearing a wider arc around the cross until they came to the places where the brickwork met the chalk. After five minutes of somewhat frenzied attack, their movements sweeping across a bigger and bigger area, they stood back. They had exposed an archway that was clearly the closed-up opening to another smaller finger of the *cave*.

"'Brick by brick,'" Sophie breathed. "That's what La Petite said. They were her last words. Mathilde, do you remember? She said some secrets need to be uncovered brick by brick."

Mathilde shuddered. "I'm with Clementine on the fairy god-mother front," she said. "I don't think those things happen in real life. In my experience secrets usually mean bad news, not good news."

"Mine, too," Clementine said, adding somewhat spitefully: "Knowing Olivier, he probably has a dozen other wives buried in there."

"Oh, don't be so grumpy," cried Sophie. "Please, let's just find out. Clementine, how do we take down the bricks?"

"How would I know? This is the first bricked-up miraculous hiding place full of pirates' gold that I've ever come across, if you must know. I'm a little at a loss as to how best to plunder it."

Mathilde, her curiosity piqued and her pragmatism in full working order, took the lead. "We need to find the Cuvée Supérieur," she said, "and start feeding it to Gaston. He already knows too much, and we don't want him knowing this as well. Then we need to get a pickax and a sledgehammer from his fire truck and start smashing down these bricks."

"Obviously not the first bricked-up miraculous hiding place she has ever come across," Clementine grumbled as she finally located a box of the dusty pissed-in bubbly and dragged it out from behind a broken wine barrel. "I should have known."

Within the hour Gaston had polished off his first bottle ("A delicate drop, quite *piquant*. I can see why Olivier kept it to himself.") and was starting on his second. Edie had been employed to lure him into a game of *pétanque* in the courtyard while the three sisters plundered his truck for tools and scurried back to the *cave*.

Sophie attempted the first swing of the pickax but just about fell over backward with the weight of it. Her sisters watched skeptically as she had a second go and a third, and then Clementine snatched the heavy tool away from her and took out the best part of a whole brick with one single swipe. Mathilde then instructed Sophie to find a wheelbarrow and a shovel, and while Clementine hacked at the bricked-up entrance, the other two cleared away the debris. After an hour a small hole had formed in the middle of the archway, enough to make it clear that there was an empty space behind the bricks, that a secret was indeed being uncovered. They fought over the right to peer through the small gap but could see nothing but darkness, so Clementine kept going until it was big enough for Sophie to stick her head through. Still, she could see very little. It smelled musty, she said, and sad, whatever that meant, but was still too dark. Again Clementine, tired now, smashed at the wall until the hole was bigger still, and then Mathilde was dispatched to Gaston's truck to filch a flashlight because the lamps were not shining any light on the contents of the secret *cave*.

When she returned, their three heads gathered to shine the beam through into the hiding place. It was another alcove, similar in shape to the tunnel in which they were standing, but on an even smaller scale. And on each side lay row upon row of champagne.

"What the . . ." Clementine could barely believe her eyes. She knew that many *Champenois* had bricked up secret supplies of champagne during the Occupation, but those hiding places had been pretty smartly revealed the moment the German threat was gone. Why would Olivier still have champagne hidden? It didn't make sense.

With renewed vigor she attacked the bricks again until the hole was big enough for Sophie to squeeze through.

"Get in," Clementine insisted, giving the littlest Peine a push.

"Yes, hop to it," added Mathilde. She was intrigued by the mystery, as anyone in their right mind would be, but also by the possibility that a secret stash of champagne could indeed turn out to be their miracle.

And it was—but in more ways than any of them could ever have imagined.

"Well, come on," Clementine urged through the hole as Sophie, crouched in the darkness, gingerly pulled out a dusty bottle from the rack nearest her. "What is it?"

"Oh, my," Sophie cried, shining the flashlight on the label and promptly bursting into tears. "Oh, my, Clementine. I'm not sure, but I think . . . Oh, my!"

"Pull yourself together, girl," Mathilde barked. "What is it? Hand it here."

Sophie, tears streaming spookily down her face with just the flashlight beam shining on her, passed the bottle through the hole to Mathilde, who blew the dust off the label, her jaw dropping as she saw what it read.

"Oh, my," she echoed and looked up at Clementine. "It's for you."

Clementine took the bottle from her and turned it up to the light so she, too, could see it.

It was a bottle of 1961 vintage, and it was called Cuvée Clementine.

Stunned, she turned the bottle around.

"A magnificent, sensual wine of uncompromising strength" read the tasting note on the back label. "Dominated by the pinot noir grape, this is a plump, generous champagne that may prove too powerful for some but will reward those who persevere through the sharp notes with the warmth of what lies beneath. Made with love by Olivier Peine."

"There are hundreds of bottles of it," Sophie said from the hole. "Hundreds. And—oh, my!"

She handed a bottle of Cuvée Mathilde, 1970, out through the hole.

"A wine with the utmost finesse," Mathilde read, her bottom lip wobbling, "and a lingering elegance. Mostly chardonnay, this champagne will age with grace and beauty, revealing a rare softness and maturity that will pave the way for future vintages. Made with love by Olivier Peine."

She looked at Clementine, her eyes glistening, unable to speak.

"Is there one there for you, Sophie?" Clementine asked, her voice distorted with emotion, through the hole. "Is there a '79?"

All they heard was a wail and a sniffle. Then another bottle was handed through.

"Read it to me, will you?" the littlest Peine asked in a tiny voice.

"A clever champagne of hidden depth," Mathilde read out in a shaky voice. "Pinot meunier is often underrated, but in this blend the fresh, fruity spirit of this delightful grape emerges strong and triumphant for all to adore. A truly rare gem. Made with love by Oliver Peine."

Sophie stuck her face through the hole in the bricks. She had cobwebs in her hair and dust on her face, but she had never looked more beautiful.

"Don't you see?" she wept, looking from one sister to the other.

"He did see you, Clementine, what you were and what you would become. And he saw Mathilde and me as well. He did give us something. He really did."

There was no other sound then but the weeping of three children, all grown up now but desperate just the same for proof that the father they never knew had in his own peculiar way truly, madly cared for them.

Printemps

Joie

Spring came early to the Marne, softening the ground and adding a light coat of cheerful green to the landscape. The sap was rising in the canes, another generation of berries on their way.

And on the subject of generations, Olivier Peine's secret cache meant his children and their children, to whom he had bequeathed his kingdom, after all, would get to keep it. The discovery of his hidden champagne made headlines all over the country. Well, how could it not with a PR genius at the very epicenter? It turned out there were some two thousand cases of the precious vintage wines behind that white cross, and after all the media uproar, connoisseurs the world over snapped them up as quickly and expensively as they could, save a few dozen cases the sisters kept for themselves.

Peine champagne was thus propelled back to the top of the list of favored champagnes at home and abroad. Rémi Krug himself even came to the château at Saint-Vincent-sur-Marne and purchased a dozen of each of the three sisters' cuvées and stayed for some of Bernadette's kugelhopf. The bank manager got what he wanted (money, that is, not Mathilde), and the future of Saint-Vincent-sur-Marne's best house was secured once and for all, or at least until the next natural disaster. They were farmers, remember.

In April, George came for a visit, and to her own amazement, Mathilde was truly pleased to see him and let him top her up and plug her cork in ways she had previously not allowed. He truly loved her—she saw that properly for the first time—but she was still new to the idea of true love and not yet rehabilitated enough to know if that was what she felt for him. She did know, however, that she would not be returning to the States any time soon, that her home was in Champagne now, and that she would like George to join her but would understand if he didn't. George said he would think about it.

Edie loved having her father around but needed him less than she ever had in her life, which saddened and delighted him at the same time. She spoke almost entirely in French, had a horde of local friends, and was more comfortable in the dilapidated Peine château than he had seen her anywhere else. Champagne was her home, too: he could see that. And he would not disrupt it but made plans for Edie to travel home in the summer and spend time with him in New York.

Before he left, on the anniversary of Olivier's death, the whole family went to the *vigneron*'s grave site, and Edie laid a bouquet of purple hyacinth and scarlet geraniums on his grave. She also suggested that her mother and aunts fork out for a headstone, which Clementine had previously not contemplated but which she agreed they should now obtain, as long as the epitaph did not read: "He was a complicated man."

"He was a complicated man," Father Philippe began when it came time for his little speech, and the Peines dissolved into muffled laughter. Less nervous than he had been the year before, however, the priest flashed them a shy smile and continued. "And although he may often have struggled to express his emotions in a, shall we say, optimistic or constructive way, I am sure it is of some comfort to his three daughters that such emotion was not entirely beyond him nonetheless. While regrettably he could not bequeath his love and pride in person but kept it tucked away and hidden from them, the miracle is that he felt that love and pride in the first place and made sure it was discovered in the end—one way or the other. As it says in the Bible, better late than never. Amen."

Afterward, the sisters invited him, Gaston, Bernadette, and Christophe Paillard back to the house for a special celebration in which they cracked open a bottle of each of the hidden vintages to toast Olivier's life and wish him a peaceful rest.

Christophe watched in quiet amazement as Clementine, Mathilde, and Sophie clinked glasses. They were transformed, utterly transformed. Clementine, that once miserable face now wreathed in smiles, was almost unrecognizable. She stood straighter, was slimmer, he was certain, and her copper-colored curls had lost their frightening frizz and fell in great loose coils down her back. Mathilde had gained weight, which added a missing softness to her previously harsh lines, and she seemed positively coy in the company of her husband and daughter. As for Sophie: she had come a long, long way from the fragile little chick he had entertained in his office the previous year. Yes, Sophie looked to him like a woman who had suddenly found herself in possession of everything she had ever dreamed of having.

He licked a bead of Cuvée Clementine off his lip as it suddenly occurred to him that Olivier had not been monstrous in uniting this unlikely trio. Quite the opposite. He had given them to each other knowing that what one lacked another had in plentiful supply, and looking at them now it was clear what a priceless gift that was. This was no longer a house of *peine*, he thought with a smile, but a house of *joie*. And although he really had nothing to do with this miraculous transformation himself, he glowed with a pride that was often missing in his work.

"What are you smiling at?" Gaston demanded grumpily as he sidled up to him. "If it's something special you want to drink, you should get them to open the Supérieur. Miserable with it, just like their father."

The following week it became clear that Sophie, who had been feeling tearful and poorly for some time, did not have indigestion or, as Edie had suggested, an enormous fricking tumor, but was pregnant with Hector's baby.

For once the man in her life had left her with more than a tender embrace, and when the doctor confirmed her condition, she was delirious with happiness, as were her sisters and niece.

Her little belly stretched and grew and brought them good luck throughout the crucial month of May when the *saints de glace* frosts skipped right over Saint-Vincent-sur-Marne, never once stopping to visit their viciousness upon them.

Throughout flowering and fruit set, Sophie helped Clementine in the vineyard as much as she could, letting Edie pick up her slack in the afternoons after school. The valley was lush with the season's new growth, and the excitement that buzzed in the air between the rows as they trimmed and tied the shoots was as much about the new life that bloomed inside her as it was the pending harvest.

One hot sunny day in late August the sisters decided to take a bottle of special cuvée and a Black Forest cake down to the river for an afternoon picnic. They stretched out on a tartan blanket on the banks of the Marne, laughing first at Clementine's pale

skin, then at Sophie's domed belly, and then at the tiny suggestion of something other than skin and bone on Mathilde's thighs.
"Well, I wouldn't call it fleshy, but it's a start," Clementine said
approvingly.

As they lay there gossiping, the warmth of the sun, the burble of the flowing river, and the peace in the valley made them
drowsy.

"So, Clementine, what's happening with Benoît?" Mathilde asked,
eyes closed and soaking up the sun. "Are you or aren't you?"

Ah, yes, Benoît.

Odile had not been charged with arson. Xavier, although convinced she had started the fire, could not find enough evidence
against her, not even the other high heel. The day after she had
been questioned, however, she left Benoît and went back to her
father's vineyard—for good.

The day after that, Benoît had come to see Clementine. Finally,
a rendezvous! It was not the happiest of meetings, however, because he had been quite distraught and initially unforgiving on the
subject of Amélie.

"But why didn't you tell me?" he repeated desperately over and
over again. "Why?"

There was little she could say that would make him feel better.
There was no good answer to such a big question. In the end she
simply told him the timing had been wrong and she hadn't known
how to tell him, for which she was sorry. It was an awkward dis-
cussion, yet inside Clementine rejoiced that he cared.

"What shall we do next?" he asked her, and although his face
was crumpled with worry, the "we" made her heart swell when it
jumped from his lips.

They met regularly after that, and while the conversation was sometimes stilted, Clementine was certain the magnetism that had pulled at her all those years before and that had survived nearly two decades of separation hummed between them still.

Eventually, trying to contain their hope, they tracked down the whereabouts of Amélie's adoptive parents and spent an entire week of nighttime get-togethers drafting a letter asking for permission to make contact if their daughter desired it.

During that week the conversation had strayed on occasion from Amélie to other things, including their grapes, their wines, and their hopes for the future.

It was not going to be easy, Clementine knew. Much water had passed beneath both their bridges, and neither of them was young or flexible but entrenched in separate ways and shy of change. She no longer took the blame entirely on her own shoulders, either. Benoît was not perfect. He had let himself be bullied into a loveless marriage and had done nothing to get himself out of it.

Still, she liked his imperfections.

"We might," Clementine said, grinning into the sun that afternoon as she lay with her sisters on the banks of the slow-moving Marne.

"One day you will paint the kitchen, Mentine?" teased Sophie.

"One day I will replant those woody geraniums," answered Clementine.

Mathilde turned over on her side. "I think it will happen," she said.

"So do I," Clementine answered, rolling over to face her, and across the naked hump of Sophie's growing belly they shared the sort of smile that only sisters can share.

"Boy or girl?" Mathilde then asked, glancing at Sophie's middle.

"Girl, of course," Clementine announced without hesitation. "All the best *Champenois* start off as girls. Oh, sure, that old fart Dom Pérignon gets all the credit for discovering corks, but his champagne was cloudy—and ours would be, too, if it hadn't been for the widow Clicquot. She invented *remuage*. Plus, before the widow Pommery dropped the dosage and made a *brut*, champagne was sickly sweet. Imagine that! The widow Olry-Roederer was the first to insist on growing her own grapes instead of buying them, and then there are the widows of Laurent-Perrier. That house has had more than its fair share of troubles over the years, just like the House of Peine, but those widows kept it going. By hook or by crook they kept it going."

"So the best *Champenois* start off as girls but finish as widows," Mathilde said drily.

"They're survivors then, aren't they?" Sophie pointed out dreamily. "I can't think of anything better to hope for my daughter than that she's a survivor."

"I'll drink to that," nodded Mathilde.

"Me, too," agreed Clementine.

She sat up, and taking a bottle from the ice box, ripped off the foil, untwisted the muzzle, gently coaxed the cork out, and then poured three glasses of those lively golden bubbles.

"*A votre santé*," they saluted together, and lifting their glasses to the heavens, they drank to one another's health and to survival.

Sophie had just half a glass and Mathilde not much more: champagne really did give her a headache although she had certainly grown to appreciate the taste. Clementine, on the other hand, savored every last drop of two crystal flutes, which left her hot and stripped of inhibition. Throwing all caution to the wind, she stood up, unbuttoned her shirt, and announced that she was going for a swim in the river.

Her sisters needed little encouragement, and within seconds they had dropped their clothes and were running naked toward the water. Clementine plunged in first, shrieking with the cold, followed by Sophie who was helpless with laughter, and Mathilde, who looked less like a Manhattan businesswoman than anyone else on the planet.

They laughed, they splashed, they swam, they screamed. The Peine sisters bubbled, all three of them. Anyone could see that. And when they picked their way up the riverbank back to their mounds of discarded clothes, it was Mathilde who suddenly became helpless with laughter. She stood there, doubled over, helpless with hilarity.

"What?" her sisters asked. "What?"

"Our surname isn't the only thing we have in common," she finally managed, pointing at the tops of their thighs. "Look."

Three matching curly ginger triangles glistened with droplets of Marne River water. Three laughs rang out above the valley.

It was a sound the vines were to hear a lot more of.

But no sound was more beautiful, perhaps, than the surprised cry of Olivie Josephine Ann Marie-France Peine, who entered the world on the eve of the *vendange*, her eyes wide open and the beginnings of a smile already curling her little rosebud mouth.

Her father was there to catch her, her mother to hold her, and her aunts to cry and forget to take photos.

In the vineyard the grapes prepared themselves for the *ven-*

dange. In the rebuilt winery the presses sat waiting for them. In the *cave* the bubbles gossiped excitedly in their bottles.

And at the bottom of the drive, the postman stood on the outside of the grand repainted gates, rummaging around in his mail sack as he admired the powder blue baby's bonnet Edie had affixed to Cochon's head and which did look strangely fetching.

"Ah, here we go," he finally said, pulling out a scented envelope bearing a handwritten address, the *i*'s dotted with tiny vine leaves, and passing it through to Edie. "For Clementine. From Bordeaux. You know someone there?"

"We certainly fricking hope to," Edie said with a grin. "Another Peine. The '88."

fin

Glossaire

A

amies, amis	friends
amitié	friendship
amour	love
arrondissement	district of Paris
assemblage	champagne blending process
au revoir	good-bye
automne	autumn
a votre santé	French salutation meaning "To your health"

B

barriques, les	barrels
blanc de blancs	champagne made from chardonnay grapes
blanc de noirs	champagne made from pinot noir and/or pinot meunier grapes
bonjour	hello
Bonne Année	Happy New Year

boucherie	butcher's shop
brut	dry; also dry-style champagne
bûche de Noël	traditional creamy chocolate log

C

cabillaud	cod
ça va	How's it going?
cave	cellar
Champenois	people of Champagne
champenoise	champagne-style
chaufferette	smoking chimney stack lit to ward off frost
chocolat chaud	hot chocolate
citron	lemon
cochelet, le	end of harvest party
cochon	pig
compôte	stew (usually of fruit)
crayères	underground cellars connected by tunnels
croque monsieur	toasted cheese sandwich
cru	official Champagne village
cuvée	vat of wine or blend of wine

D

dauphinoise	style of cooking potatoes
débourrement	bud burst
déception	disappointment
dédicace	dedication
dégorgement	process to remove sediment from bottles

désespoir	despair
deux chevaux	model of car also known as 2CV
dosage	added sugar

E

entre soeurs	among sisters
espoir	hope
eté	summer

F

fête de Saint Vincent, la	Saint Vincent's Day
fin	the end
floraison	flowering
fraternité	sisterhood

G

gendarme/s	police
glossaire	glossary
grandes marques	major champagne houses
grosses bises	big kisses
gyropalette	mechanical riddling machine

H

hiver	winter

I

invité/invités	guest (male/female)

J

joie	joy

K

kugelhopf	nutty cake from Alsace

M

madame	title for married woman
madeleines	little sponge cakes
mademoiselle	title for young woman
magret	cut of duck meat
mairie	town hall
maman	mother, mom
mec	bugger
merde	shit
mille-feuille	yummy custardy pastry
monsieur	mister
mousse	bubbles
must	fermenting grape juice

N

Noél	Christmas
nuage, le	cloud

O

oh-là-là	oh-là-là

P

pain au chocolat amande	chocolate and almond pastry
pain au levain	sourdough bread
pain d'épice	gingerbread cake
partager	sharing

patisserie	cake and pastry shop
pâtissier	pastry chef or baker
peine	sorrow
pétanque	French bowling game
pétiller	sparkling
petite noix, la	little walnut
piquant	refreshingly interesting
pommes	apples
potée champenoise	Champagne-style stew
printemps	spring
pupitres	inverted-V-shaped riddling racks

Q

quatre quarts	four quarters

R

racine, la	the root
remerciements	acknowledgments
remeurs	riddlers
remuage	riddling or twisting of bottles to move sediment
réveillon	Christmas Eve feast

S

sabayon	egg-based sauce
saints de glace	three particular days in May where frost can do terrible damage
saveur	taste
sommelier	wine waiter
stampes	crates for carrying grapes

T

tabac	bar or café
truite ardennaise	French trout dish

V

vendange	harvest
veraison	changing color of grapevines
veuve	widow
vignerons	winemaker
voilà	lo and behold
volonté	willpower

Remerciements

When you're writing a book about champagne, you do not skimp on the research. Trust me. As one friend said when I explained I was off to France for a second investigative trip, "Something tells me you'll never be setting a book in the slums of New Delhi, Sarah-Kate."

Well, how could I when the person I always rely on first and foremost for my research is Master of Wine Bob Campbell? What does he know about New Delhi? And what doesn't he know about wine?

Thanks to Bob's contacts I was much feted at Moët and Chandon and trod in the footsteps of Dom Pérignon himself at the famed Abbey of Hautvillers. Also, I had the pleasure of lunching with Arnaud de Mareuil at Trianon (the hotel built for Napoleon to stay in on his way to war). It was Monsieur de Mareuil who first pointed out that my three sisters needed to blend just like the three grapes of Champagne. Of course, I knew that already. He just said it with a French accent. And he also served champagne with dessert. Sigh.

My friends at Cloudy Bay (try the Te Koko sauvignon blanc if you're sick of bubbles) got me in the door at Veuve Clicquot where for the first time I experienced the chill and splendor of the amazing underground cellars and also learned about one of the world's first businesswomen, the widow *(veuve)* Clicquot. My host, Isabelle Pierre, is also an art historian, so I had the added pleasure of a guided tour of the beautiful Reims cathedral. Later that evening I had another more unscheduled tour of the backstreets of the city as my dining companion, the enthusiastic and funny Emmanuel Frossard, insisted there was no way my hotel could not be up this lane or the next one or the one after that or perhaps the one before. "I hope the spirit of Mme Clicquot and the bubbles of her champagne will help you in the year to come!" Emmanuel wrote to me after our wonderful meal together. "And thanks for teaching me where the Hotel Templiers is." Charm, charm, charm. Where do they get it?

More charm was poured on me not long afterward by the exquisite Pascale Rousseau at Krug. Frankly, it's just not fair that someone can be that beautiful and funny and smart and able to wear three different shades of caramel and two scarves. Pascale is the epitome of the sophisticated Frenchwoman and a source of great inspiration herself, but she also ensured that I was wined and dined by Rémi Krug himself, a highlight to say the least. Champagne changes with every mouthful, says Rémi. "But then, so do you!" Despite the prestige of this "king" of champagnes, Rémi believes Krug is to be drunk, not revered. (Psst: and he thinks beer goes better with oysters.)

The *Champenois* Tarlant family I managed to find all by myself, although "find" is perhaps the wrong word. The Tarlants live in Oeuilly, about ninety miles from Charles de Gaulle Airport, but for reasons involving getting stuck on the right motorway going in the wrong direction, it took me five and a half hours to get there. Somehow, Micheline Tarlant knew when I arrived that I desperately needed a small bottle of champagne, some cheese, and a slice of homemade pear tart to calm my frazzled nerves. Four generations of Tarlants still gather for *assemblage,* and their boutique style of champagne making and grape growing is very much the inspiration for the House of Peine.

Philippe Wibrotte at the CIVC in Epernay was a brilliant source of information, as was Delphine in the CIVC's extraordinary tasting room.

If anybody is interested in reading more about what happened in Champagne during the German occupation, I devoured the book *Wine and War* by Don and Petie Kladstrup (Broadway Books). It opens with a young *Champenois* soldier, Bernard de Nonancourt, finding Hitler's secret stash of stolen wine in Eagle's Nest. When I had lunch with Philippe Wibrotte in Epernay, Monsieur de Nonancourt was sitting at the next table! After the war he returned to Champagne and took over Laurent-Perrier, elevating it from the bottom of the barrel (ranked ninety-eight out of a hundred) to one of the top ten houses and cementing himself as one of the area's priceless characters.

Champagne is full of many such treasures bubbling with passion and vigor, and I thank each and every one for showing me such enormous kindness, often accompanied by a drop of vintage. (The Krug '88 for elevenses sure beats a cup of Earl Grey.)

At Penguin it is another big thank-you to Allison Dickens, who I wish lived around the corner, and a big smooch to my agent and friend Stephanie Cabot for believing in me so wholeheartedly.

Also, my devoted husband Mark Robins has proved himself to be, as always, a tireless supporter and cook and cleaner and just this morning put a pink tulip in a champagne glass on my desk to cheer up my office. Really, every home should have one.

Grosses bises.

—Sarah-Kate